CHRISTMAS PROMISES AT THE GARLAND STREET MARKETS

BOOK 5 IN THE NEW YORK EVER AFTER SERIES

HELEN ROLFE

B
Boldwood

First published in 2019. This edition first published in Great Britain in 2022 by Boldwood Books Ltd.

Cover Design by CC Book Design

Cover Photography: Shutterstock

Every effort has been made to obtain the necessary permissions with reference to copyright material, both illustrative and quoted. We apologise for any omissions in this respect and will be pleased to make the appropriate acknowledgements in any future edition.

A CIP catalogue record for this book is available from the British Library.

Paperback ISBN 978-1-80415-647-6

Large Print ISBN 978-1-80415-646-9

Hardback ISBN 978-1-80415-645-2

Ebook ISBN 978-1-80415-648-3

Kindle ISBN 978-1-80415-649-0

Audio CD ISBN 978-1-80415-640-7

MP3 CD ISBN 978-1-80415-641-4

Digital audio download ISBN 978-1-80415-644-5

Boldwood Books Ltd
23 Bowerdean Street
London SW6 3TN

For my writing family, The Write Romantics.

1

CLEO

Cleo was back in New York City, in the depths of Manhattan where it had all begun after she moved here from England all those years ago.

At the end of Garland Street, not far from Greenwich Village, she stood in front of a row of run-down stores, breathing in the crisp wintry air, the smog, the atmosphere bathed in the sounds of the city and lights that dazzled even at this early hour of the morning. She looked along the broad sidewalk and took in the thirty Swiss-style wooden chalets all at various stages of getting ready for business on the first official day of trading.

The Garland Street winter markets were new to Manhattan and Cleo hadn't hesitated to sign up for a stall when she heard about them. She thrived on doing anything to take her business to the next level, whether it was sourcing new and amazing yarns for her store, the Little Knitting Box, running workshops, or reaching a new clientele like she could do here for the next few weeks. Dylan had been hesitant about her taking on this particular project; he thought time might be better spent planning their wedding, which they still hadn't managed to set a date for. Sometimes Cleo didn't really see why they had to change anything. They made a good team with four kids between them – Ruby and Jacob from Dylan's first marriage, their daughter Tabitha who was almost three, and baby Emily who'd just turned sixteen months – did they really need a piece of paper to prove their commitment? And just because Grandpa Joe kept telling her he wasn't getting any younger and her dad was desperate to walk her down the aisle, it didn't stop Cleo worrying about ten-year-old Ruby. She was misbehaving and pitching Cleo against Dylan whenever someone mentioned the word wedding and Cleo wondered why the little girl had suddenly gone from being a friend to acting like the enemy.

'You'd better get organised.' Mitch leaned another Christmas tree against the chalet he'd reserved after hearing Cleo's plans for this market and wanting in. They'd come into the city together today. 'I'll send Jude down with more of your boxes.'

She snapped into the present and out of her New York daydream – the feeling of being back here, taking it all in for a moment before she got busy. 'I was soaking up the city atmosphere but you're right, I need to be ready for those customers.' She hoped despite the markets being new, the footfall wouldn't be much different to other venues, although maybe on the first day it might be quite nice if it started off slow.

While Cleo and Dylan had been sitting in Marlo's, the neighbourhood café in Inglenook Falls, a few months ago they'd been debating the merits of branching out to a city market as well as the local winter markets and Mitch had overheard them. He'd recently opened up his Christmas tree farm to the public and with a lot of encouragement from his girlfriend Holly, who was sitting with him in the café at the time, Mitch ended up agreeing with the idea and signing up at the same time as Cleo for the Garland Street winter markets. He'd paid for a prime spot at the end of the row on Garland Street, the only one big enough to take all the trees, and already each stallholder had been told by the organisers that next year wouldn't be so easy; they'd have to sign up at the end of this season if they wanted a hope of getting a chalet again.

Mitch carried on hauling trees from his truck parked on the corner, the scent of pine filling the air and bringing Christmas to Garland Street before anyone else got a chance. Cleo, armed with a big box of woollen products and the key to unlock her very own chalet, made her way past stallholders clutching their cups of coffee, others buzzing with the excitement of it all. One couple was already hanging jewellery on hooks on the folded back doors of their chalet and the atmosphere had a similar feel to that of Christmas morning, everyone waiting for the off.

The kids would be at home with Dylan now, in that crazy rush that happened before school, and Cleo was glad to be out of it for the time being. She reached number twenty-two, balanced the box between her knee and the door, undid the padlock ,and crept inside the generous, wooden cube. The smell of freshly cut timber that came with these sorts of chalets hung around and she couldn't wait to get her display ready and fill the place with garments she'd made from the yarns at her store. She wouldn't be allowed to trade for another hour so she moved the tables around inside, pushed them all together to create a big central table instead. A smaller table sat in the corner with a couple of fold-up chairs and she had knitting with her in case the day had slow pockets, something she couldn't really predict. She put a money belt on around her waist beneath her coat and tipped in a bit of change she'd brought from home as well as the whizzy credit card machine. She'd decided against a till – far too vulnerable for light fingers.

She folded back both doors and hooked them in place. It was freezing today but she'd layered up with a thermal long-sleeved top, a chunky woollen sweater, her coat, scarf, and gloves that would only come off for the fiddliest of jobs.

'Where do you want these?' Jude, recognised only by voice given Cleo couldn't see him behind the two big boxes in his arms, was Mitch's helper for the day. And hers, right now.

Cleo took the box that enabled her to see the boy, a good friend of Mitch's and almost like a second son to him. 'You're a star, thank you. Let me lock up and I'll come back for the rest.'

'Albie's mom just dropped him off so Mitch has enough hands to line up the trees; I don't mind getting the boxes for you.'

'You're a good lad.' As was Albie, Mitch's son.

Jude blushed slightly as boys of his age did when they were given compliments and returned down the street, back to the Christmas tree stall and the truck. Cleo appreciated the help since she was on her own for now. Her assistant Kaisha would be manning the stall at the Inglenook Falls markets today, Dylan had the kids and the school run to contend with, and her friend Amelia who she'd roped in to help as a last-minute favour, enticed with free accommodation courtesy of friends Darcy and Myles, wouldn't be arriving from England until today. This was how most things worked in Cleo's life these days. Like a military operation with all bases covered, but she and Dylan were well practised. And they had good solid friendships without which Cleo wasn't sure she'd be as calm as she was. She still saw her good friend Violet who'd thrown the party where she met Dylan, but nowadays she was closer to Darcy and Myles, Holly and Mitch since their lives had become so intertwined.

When Cleo had talked with her friend Amelia on the phone yesterday to wish her a safe trip, she'd tried to explain to Amelia how she knew all these people. She'd told Amelia how Darcy had once come to Cleo's knitting workshops when she still had the store in the West Village and they'd struck up a friendship from there. Darcy went on to run the Inglenook Inn in Greenwich Village where Myles had been a guest and they'd got together despite a rocky history. Holly was the journalist who covered a Christmas story at the inn and she and Darcy had hit it off. Holly had had a career crisis – her words, nobody else's – and gone freelance rather than facing gruelling office hours in the city and when she'd gone to Inglenook Falls to cover a grand hotel opening, she'd literally fallen into Mitch's life.

Everyone seemed to lead complicated lives, they all had their share of ups and downs, and Cleo's friend Amelia was no exception. Amelia had something complicated going on at work, a nephew, Kyle, who she was incredibly close to but who kept getting into trouble, and a boyfriend everyone had assumed she would marry but who'd dumped her without warning six months ago. Amelia also had a sister, Connie, who in Cleo's opinion had always relied a little too heavily on Amelia and Cleo wouldn't mind betting that was adding to the troubles given Kyle was Connie's son. When Cleo had suggested Amelia take a holiday and asked whether she'd be interested in helping her out at the markets on a very casual basis, Amelia had leapt at the chance and asked if she could bring Kyle too.

Cleo had related much of Amelia's situation to her own friends on Halloween as she stitched up a bloodthirsty vampire costume for Jacob and wrestled an almost-sixteen-month-old Emily into a pumpkin outfit. And her friends, being the sort of great people they really were, had come up with a plan. Mitch needed some brawn on the Christmas tree stall to help net the trees and serve customers, so that would keep Kyle occupied and perhaps give Amelia a break from the worrying she shouldn't have to do when she wasn't the mother. Myles and Darcy owned a rental property they wanted to spruce up and sell and so they'd leapt in to suggest Amelia and Kyle could stay there rent-free in exchange for keeping an eye on the place for them given their own hectic work schedules.

Inside the wooden chalet now, protected somewhat from the

winter chill, Cleo took out a bottle of surface spray and a cloth and gave the tables a once-over. They were pretty clean already but she wanted to be doubly sure no dust had crept its way through the wood since she'd last been here to bring the tables and chairs. When boxes appeared at the chalet door again she took them from Jude's arms before he went back for the rest and she began to organise the table. She arranged pebble-coloured, V-neck sweaters in a variety of sizes, the deep-teal round-neck sweaters next to those, and then the dark charcoal. Next it was on to a box of ladies' knitwear: cardigans and sweaters in a multitude of colours and knitting styles. Cleo had been working flat out to get ready for the Garland Street winter markets. She was focusing here on finished products rather than the haberdashery or the yarns themselves, so next it was on to unpacking the box of scarves, hats, and socks that she'd been knitting over the last few weeks. She had plum-shaded hats with pom-poms on top, winter-leaf-patterned and cable-knit hats, gloves large and small, for men and for women, multi-patterned beanies, and the table in the centre of the hut was fast becoming a riot of colour.

'Last two.' This time it was Mitch who'd come to the hut with the remaining boxes.

When he placed them down she asked, 'Are you all set up and ready?'

'As ready as I'm ever going to be.'

'Can you believe we're doing this? I'm excited to be in the city.'

'Not sure it's me, but it's different.' His gruff appearance hid a softer side to his personality that had been coaxed out when he met Holly, was reunited with his son, Albie, and got his life back on track. Now, nobody would really understand the pain he'd been through. He had integrated back into the local community of Inglenook Falls and was a pleasure to be around these days.

'It's only four weeks, then you never have to come back to the city if you hate it,' she told him.

His stubble was all the more visible now the sun had crept up into the sky, hovering somewhere behind the tall buildings that dwarfed the market stalls. 'Who knows, I might enjoy it. That's what Holly keeps telling me.'

Holly was good for him. She was confident, she didn't hold back when she wanted to say something, and Cleo couldn't imagine either of them without the other. 'Is she coming today?'

'She's already taking photos.'

'Typical,' Cleo grinned. Holly had a love of photography that doubled as work and no doubt she'd soon be capturing shots of the market traders getting ready, faces anticipating what was to come, the joy of Christmas right around the corner. You never know, she may have even photographed some of them already and Cleo almost wished she'd done more than wound her dark blonde hair up into a top knot. Mind you, it was so cold it wouldn't be long before she tugged the band out and put a woolly hat on her head instead. Already, whenever the wind found its way inside the chalet it licked around her ears promising more.

Mitch went back to his own stall, leaving Cleo to finish setting up. And before long, the bell to mark the start of trading was accompanied by a whoop from the traders that Cleo joined in with and it was all systems go. People had been milling and perusing stalls, some ready to pounce on purchases, others happy to take it all in. And Cleo already suspected there wouldn't be much chance to take out her knitting and sit on the fold-up chair at the back of the chalet while she waited for business to get going.

Cleo put another purchase into a paper bag for her customer. 'Be sure to hand-wash or put it in the machine on the wool cycle,' she advised after she took the credit card payment for a deep-teal sweater she'd knitted herself. She and Mitch had compared notes on the drive this morning. Cleo didn't sell a huge number of ready-made products at the Little Knitting Box, it was mostly yarns and haberdashery, so all year round with holiday markets in mind she was continuously building up as much stock as possible. Mitch was hard at it three hundred and sixty-five days of the year too, cultivating trees in their infancy, others in maturity. Neither of them did much outsourcing, preferring to throw their own energies into businesses that were their passion as much as their livelihood.

'You'll have to get the kids knitting, make a production line.' It was Dylan, ducking to avoid the top of the chalet doorway as he stepped inside.

'What are you doing here?' A smile spread across Cleo's face at the sight of the handsome man with green eyes and dark-blond, dishevelled hair who'd won her over in a second three years ago when he'd walked her home from her friend's party and kissed her against a tree. He was still as devastatingly attractive now as he was then, as amazing as he'd been the day he proposed in front of all their family and friends at the Little Knitting Box last December. Some days his daughter Ruby seemed all for the idea of making Cleo an official fixture in her life, other days she scowled across the room or was deliberately obstinate. Dylan assumed the delay to their wedding plans was all down to their hectic lives with Cleo's knitting business and his web design company, but it wasn't strictly true. Cleo never wanted to get married unless everyone was one hundred per cent for it but she didn't want to cause waves and tell Dylan that Ruby might not be as on board as he thought. Dylan and Ruby were close. She never wanted him to have to choose to please one over the other.

'I couldn't let my favourite fiancée hit the Manhattan streets without a bit of support.' He took her in his arms and kissed her, not in the least bit bothered by the onlooking customers.

'Gotcha!' Holly had snapped them, of course, her sharp blue eyes missing nothing.

'Holly, what are you like?' Cleo called after their friend, although she could only see the back of her auburn hair as she moved on to capture something else at the Garland Street markets. 'Where are Emily and Tabitha?' she asked Dylan.

'Your gramps and Elaine have come to our place to be childminders for a few hours. I know you worry your gramps is getting too old, but they'll be fine, and they said it's like an early Christmas present to have the grandkids.'

'Yeah, well, we'll see how they feel about it when you get home. Tabitha has taken to using the word "no" at the top of her voice and stamping her foot whenever she's asked anything. Little terror.'

'She's cute when she does it though.'

She furrowed her brow. 'Don't let her know you think that or she'll wrap you around her little finger.' Just like older sister Ruby who was becoming more and more like Prue, her mum. Dylan's ex-wife had always liked to get her own way. Cleo wondered how much of the current unrest Dylan picked up on, whether he could see what she could – how thick as thieves Ruby and Prue were, especially since Cleo and Dylan had started to discuss the wedding more seriously. Ruby had been so excited when they got engaged but it was as though the last calendar year had given her time to rethink and, now, Cleo wasn't sure Ruby wanted the union to happen at all. In fact, she was convinced Prue must be feeding all kinds of thoughts into Ruby's head.

'Don't worry,' said Dylan. 'Jacob is being the doting big brother and puts Tabitha in her place.'

Jacob, unlike Ruby, seemed unphased that his dad was going to marry someone who wasn't his mum. And he was young enough at seven – almost eight as he liked to remind them – to still want his cuddles, which made Cleo feel as though this would all work out in the end.

'You know how you could really support me?' In Dylan's arms, she looked up at the man she'd trusted with her past and her future.

'How's that?'

'Grab me a hot chocolate from somewhere, it's freezing in here.'

'I'll see what I can do.' He left her chatting with a customer trying to decide between a dusk-pink scarf or the same pattern in cream.

As soon as he returned, Cleo welcomed the hot chocolate Dylan had sourced, the steam swirling from the tiny spout on the lid and instantly warming her. Hands clutched around the vessel, she sipped the liquid gingerly. 'I really needed this, thank you.'

Dylan took charge of the hot chocolate when another customer plucked the fawn scarf for her husband's Christmas gift this year. 'It's busy, are you happy?' he asked as he handed Cleo back her drink.

'I had no idea what it would be like. I wondered whether it would be quiet because it's new, but a few customers have told me flyers have been circulating around Manhattan for weeks.'

'And how is it being back in the city?' He grinned. 'Come on, I know you. You've always missed the buzz.'

'I couldn't live here again, I love where I am now. But it is nice to be in amongst the busyness again,' she admitted – although she refrained from saying how much she needed to have time away from Ruby at the moment.

'When does Amelia arrive?'

'She should've landed by now; I'm hoping she'll start in the next couple of days. I've already come up with a bit of a rota for me, Kaisha, Amelia, and a couple of other helpers I found via Kaisha.' Her assistant had once been at the highly regarded New York

University and had many friends dotted about, all as charming as Cleo's colourful assistant herself and who all, thankfully, worked just as hard as Kaisha, glad to earn extra cash in the holiday season.

'It's pretty full on.'

When he frowned she said simply, 'Bit late now, I'm signed up until Christmas Eve.' She sold a pair of cream gloves to a woman who wanted to take off the tag and wear them right away. When the woman moved on Cleo put a hand to Dylan's cheek. 'I'll cope, don't you worry about me.' It was harder being here though. Not only did she have to travel into Manhattan, she also couldn't duck over to her store if things fell quiet or to help out when she was needed. She filled him in on numbers sold.

'Now that's impressive, and on day one.'

'It'll help fund our wedding.' It was nice to be able to talk about the wedding without little ears picking up on it and directing attention elsewhere. When they'd begun to talk about venues last week Ruby had stubbed her toe on the bottom of the stairs and wailed until Dylan went running; when Cleo mentioned ring designs to Dylan a couple of nights ago Ruby had mysteriously come into their bedroom with a tummy ache, tucking herself in bed between the both of them.

'If it ever happens,' he teased. 'I'm doing my best to make an honest woman of you, Cleo.'

'I promise it'll happen.' Maybe he'd see for himself what Ruby was doing and they could find a way to deal with it together.

'You need a date, something to head towards. If we don't set a date then we'll put it behind everything else we've got going on.'

'Ruby is fussing that I'll make her wear a horrible colour.' That was another thing. If they ever did enter into a discussion, Ruby did her best to be as unamenable as possible.

'She's ten, she's starting to assert herself, that's all.'

'I get the feeling Prue has been causing trouble.'

'In what way?'

'Ruby and I got along famously for a long time but, lately, she seems against the wedding. That's why I've been stalling,' she admitted sheepishly.

'Are you sure you're not reading too much into it?'

She reminded him about the tummy-ache incident and sharing their bed, then about the mysterious toe stubbing, where there was no blood, no bruise, and she was running around the house shortly afterwards as though nothing had happened at all. 'She also seems to criticise me in whatever way she can.'

'Ruby? No way, she adores you.'

'Dylan, I love you, but you need to open your eyes.'

He shook his head. 'I'm sorry, I'll talk to her.'

'Or perhaps we should wait for it to settle down.'

'What else has she said?' He saw right through her obvious hesitation. 'You may as well tell me or I'll be blinkered forever more.'

'Yesterday she made a remark about my hair needing a wash. The day before she moaned about the banana cranberry muffins I made for them to take to school.'

'She loves those.'

'Not any more. Apparently she hates cranberries – she picked every last one of them out while I was standing there.'

He reached out and touched his fingers to her cheek. 'She'll come around.'

'I hope so.'

'And in the meantime, try not to worry. You've got enough on your plate as it is.'

Should she mention seeing a little smirk from Ruby when Dylan and Cleo had bickered about her taking on the extra workload of a market stall? And it wouldn't be the first time that look of triumph had passed over Ruby's face either. It had reminded Cleo of Prue when she'd come to the Little Knitting Box in the West

Village, her newly appointed job giving her the task of gleefully announcing that the extension to the lease for the rental premises hadn't been granted as Cleo had believed and that she would have to vacate sooner than expected.

Cleo decided she'd said enough for now and instead told Dylan about his son, who still loved his cuddles from Cleo. 'Jacob can't wait to put on a little suit and be the page boy and ring bearer.'

'He tried a suit jacket of mine the other day and it was like looking at one of the seven dwarfs – sleeves hanging down to the floor, the rest of the jacket to his ankles.' Dylan's smile was back, the crease of worry gone from his forehead for now. 'And don't think Tabitha and Emily won't want to be involved.'

'Tabitha is only interested in wearing fairy dresses, although that could work, but Emily has a very limited eight-word vocabulary so far and she won't even realise what's going on.'

'She will at the rate we're going – she'll be an adult.'

'Very funny.' What she didn't want to do was have a wedding where one of Dylan's children was miserable in all of the photos but more than that, she didn't want to be the object of Ruby's resentment.

'We'll have to include Emily,' Dylan went on, not fully realising how complicated this already was. 'Otherwise in years to come, when she looks back at the photos, we'll be facing the consequences.'

Cleo's original arrival in New York was as a twenty-nine-year-old divorcee starting over following a disastrous marriage and, back then, she'd never once thought she'd have all this: a man she was as in love with as the day they began going steady; a blended family with four kids she adored despite any angst they brought her; and a business she loved with a passion that bordered on the unhealthy when she tried to branch out with things like Christmas markets in Manhattan as if she didn't already have far too much to do. But perhaps she'd simply got avoidance tactics down to a tee.

'What do you think to a winter wedding?' She floated the idea to Dylan while handing change to a customer who had, after much debate, gone with the navy, long, cashmere sweater instead of the fawn. Perhaps if they made firmer plans then Ruby would have some time to get used to the idea and she'd work through her grievances, whatever they might be.

'I think even by your standards you'd be pushing it to fit it in,' Dylan replied.

'Not this year, even I'm not that insane. I was thinking next year.'

'I didn't want to wait that long. Why not early spring?'

'Ruby needs time, Dylan, and this will give her that. And besides, my dad and Teresa have already booked to come over next Christmas.'

'You never said.'

'I only got the text late last night and you were asleep when I left this morning. They booked yesterday as soon as the new fares were released.' Once upon a time Cleo hadn't got along with her stepmother Teresa, but now she appreciated how happy she made her dad and they'd gradually become friends who spoke on the phone regularly.

'I guess it would make sense for the wedding to wait until then if they're already coming.'

'Exactly. And do you realise, it's supposed to be the girl pressuring the boy to hurry up and get married, not this way around?'

'Since when have we ever done anything conventional?'

'Good point.' She pulled the lapels of his coat so he came towards her and she kissed him decisively. 'Next winter it is.'

'We need to lock in a date, book a venue.'

'Any ideas?'

'You mean you don't spend every waking moment planning where we'll get married?' He put a hand against his strong chest beneath his coat. 'I'm shocked, offended.'

'Get away with you,' she grinned. 'Can we keep it to ourselves for now, tell the kids once we fix the date?'

'I'll do anything to get you down that aisle.'

'Great, and I'll add wedding to my never-ending to-do list.'

'As long as it's ahead of markets or knitting, that's fine.'

Cleo wanted to find a venue, set the date, and then she could deal with Ruby and the emotions that seemed to have gone on spin cycle inside the ten-year-old, probably with a big push of the button from Prue.

Rushed off her feet for the rest of the day, Cleo managed to eat her sandwich between taking payments, putting out more stock from the boxed-up supplies she'd brought with her today in Mitch's truck, and answering questions about the sizing of the women's cashmere and merino socks, and by the time the moon came out from its hiding place high above the cold Manhattan streets, she'd had a text from her friend Amelia to say she was here, in New York City, and couldn't wait to meet up.

And Amelia was a pro when it came to managing kids. Cleo had always been fiercely independent but even she wouldn't mind admitting that welcoming Amelia was going to be a bit like greeting a fairy godmother who, with one wave of her wand, could eradicate any misgivings Cleo was having right now. Amelia was used to dealing with problem kids and all Cleo hoped was that she could offer some advice when it came to Ruby, who had told her the other day that if she kept frowning like that the wind would blow through town and her face would stay that way forever. Cleo had been left in no doubt the phrase came right from Prue along with the attitude, and it was time to sort things out.

Only then would she be happy to get married.

2

AMELIA

'It's positively tropical,' Amelia laughed once the flight attendant had made the announcement to passengers that local time here at JFK airport, New York, was three o'clock in the afternoon and the temperature was a shivering two degrees.

Her attempt to inject humour was lost and she got nothing more than a grunt from her nephew, Kyle, whose gaze had been fixed either on his phone or out of the window for the last eight hours, unless he heard the offer of food, in which case he was straight on it.

'Well, I'm glad I've got my scarf and coat,' she smiled, nerves making her more vocal as usual. Her ex-boyfriend Paul had always told her she talked too much when she was nervous, as though she processed her thoughts out loud rather than in her head. 'I can't believe we're here, are you excited?' She watched Kyle, slumped in his seat as the plane taxied to the gate. It would soon be time to disembark into a city she'd only ever dreamed of or seen in films and she wasn't going to let her spirits be dampened by a sulky seventeen-year-old at her side. At least Cleo had replied to her text to say they'd arrived with enthusiasm, and all of a sudden she was glad that on the other side of the world she'd have a good friend to talk to. She suspected she'd need one with Kyle in tow.

'Yeah, it's gonna be a blast,' he muttered, which was at least something. And it was the longest sentence he'd said to her since his mum, Connie, had left her house in London to set off back to Cornwall. Amelia had tried not to resent the fact that Connie was socialising and about to have freedom when she herself was taking Kyle away to try to make the kid see sense, realise he couldn't throw his life away by drifting along now he'd left school with no job and absolutely no direction. He'd been getting in trouble too and Connie was at the end of her tether. It would've been easy for Amelia to dismiss Kyle as not being her problem, but she'd never been that sort of auntie. Ever since Kyle was a baby they'd been close and she cared what happened to him, so regardless of how frustrating it was to be relied on yet again, she only hoped these four weeks away could do some good. She'd planned on having some time with Kyle anyway, seeing as she suddenly had leave from her job, and when Cleo suggested she have a holiday and come here to New York she thought Kyle tagging along could be a positive move.

She hoped she didn't end up regretting her generosity.

'It's just over three weeks until Christmas,' she chimed, perhaps a little too eagerly. 'The city will be festive, we might even get snow.'

'I hope not. Can't stand the stuff. Don't get hardly any in Cornwall, it's about the only good thing about living there.'

'Come on, Kyle, give me something. A little smile, a bit of enthusiasm.' Nothing. 'Snow will make New York really Christmassy.'

'With snow you get slush, ugly grey slush. Cars stop moving, everyone is sick and snivelling from the cold.'

'It can also be very beautiful,' she batted back as she ran a hand through her dark, wavy hair which still smelt of the lavender shampoo she'd used that morning. She didn't feel quite as hideous as she often felt after travel, mainly because she'd escaped to use the bathroom right before the beep and the light came on above where they were sitting to ensure they and other passengers remained in their seats ready for landing. She'd brushed her teeth to freshen up, added a thin coat of mascara to open up her tired green eyes and put on a slick of red lipstick so she could feel like herself, even if only for a moment. At least it had gone some way to making her feel like the Amelia who was in control rather than the Amelia who wondered what on earth she was doing bringing a surly teen on holiday with her.

'I blame your dreamy vision of snow, which causes chaos and sucks, on all those soppy movies you watch,' said Kyle. 'Mum told me,' he shrugged by way of explanation. 'She joked you'd be making me watch them every night.'

Guilty. She did like snuggling up in front of a good Hallmark movie with a guaranteed happy ever after – and more often than not it involved snow, which never caused the couple any problems other than to inject a bit of magic for them. Snow in those movies never made the characters shiver, or ruined their hair or make-up; they never fell over and hurt themselves. Life for those characters never presented much of a problem that couldn't be solved by a kiss and a cuddle, but real life came with a huge amount of crap, the cuts and bruises and scrapes that everyone had to go through, including Kyle.

Amelia gathered up her things from the seat pocket in front: a bottle of water, a packet of tissues, and her book she hadn't turned a page of, far too hooked by the entertainment system and the list of movies. She wondered briefly what her colleagues were doing right now, how the kids she'd been involved with were doing. She had a busy job in London as a youth worker for the council, a job she'd scored because of her excellent behaviour-management skills and affinity with young people from different backgrounds who needed structured support to stay on the right path. What the job description hadn't specified was getting too emotionally involved. On top of the job stress, Amelia had been trying to sort out her flat near Brixton so it would feel like home after she'd rented it out to move in with Paul. At the time she'd tried to persuade him it would be much nicer to live in the grittier and lively Brixton that she'd grown to love than in leafy Forest Hill, where he had a gated detached house with access to a tennis court, but he'd been more than prepared to share his home with her and even gave her free rein with the decor when she moved in.

Shuffling in a herd down the aisle to the freedom of the plane's door, she knew that for these four weeks she could leave behind all her pressures at home, put to the back of her mind the redecorating she had to do, the new kitchen floor she needed to fund after a minor flood had damaged the tiles beyond repair.

Amelia thanked the hostess after Kyle walked past the woman with his eyes fixed to the ground, and she kept on his tail, reminding herself she'd volunteered to bring him here.

She must've lost her mind.

Then again, Kyle had already had to deal with plenty. The death of Connie's husband had knocked her sister's world sideways, but although Connie had wobbled, she'd managed not to topple over completely from the knock – whereas Kyle had never been the same again. He'd worshipped his father, Stuart, and losing him had changed the kid forever. If Amelia ever grew frustrated with Kyle's attitude to her, to life, to anything, recalling what he'd gone through was a harsh reminder that he could never go back to being the happy-go-lucky boy he once was. Amelia and Connie had had the luxury of two parents being there for them right up until five years ago, when they'd both passed away within twenty-three months of each other, and Amelia couldn't imagine how different their lives might have been without that kind of stability.

Paul and Kyle had never got on. Paul had never appreciated the way Connie expected Amelia to pick up the pieces when it came to her nephew. He was right, in some respects, but Amelia had never been able to turn Kyle away or say no to her sister, whose life had endured plenty of knocks already too. Paul had always blamed Amelia's empathetic nature, but she wondered, was that something she ever wanted to change? When she was with Paul she sometimes wanted to explain to him, a man who still had both parents and plenty of extended family who gathered on a regular basis, that not everyone was as lucky. Sometimes a kid needed someone else to step in for a while. But when they'd argued about it, and more so now she was on the other side of the world with Kyle, Amelia wondered why she'd never ever been able to say no to her sister.

Amelia absorbed the sound of American accents as they emerged from the plane to a city that had always felt impossibly out of reach. Her heart sank when they saw the queue at JFK's passport control. Kyle when he had something to do was hard company enough, but Kyle and her stuck in a long line, with him barely managing to utter more than a quick word, was going to be agony.

She shuffled forward whenever the queue allowed and her patience began to wane. 'We've got a month together, Kyle, we may as well try to get on.'

'What's the point? I know you didn't want me here, you're doing it because you have to, to help Mum out.'

'I am helping her out, yes. But it was my idea for you to come on this holiday, not her suggestion.'

'Admit it, you'd rather be on your own than have me tagging along.'

'That's not true.'

He shook his head with all the anger she'd seen too often at work from kids under her watch. It was always a toss-up as to whether you tried to reason with them or let them settle before you made the effort. She went for the former. 'This is a favour to Connie and it's also a favour to you. You and your mum clash, I don't need to point that out, but you've reached a crossroads and you both need space.' She'd heard Connie more than once say she was close to throwing him out of the house, but she wasn't going to tell him that.

'You drew the short straw.'

'Then it's up to you to fix that,' she said as they progressed in the queue. 'Make this a good experience, for both of us.'

'Not much of a good experience for you if you have to work at the markets. Who is this Cleo anyway?'

A little bit of sympathy from his direction and an interest in conversing was a step in the right direction. 'I worked at her aunt and uncle's knitting shop in the Cotswolds.'

'You knit?'

She shook her head. 'No, I'm rubbish. But I was a good Saturday girl. I served customers, cleaned floors, surfaces, took deliveries.'

'Sounds riveting.'

Ignoring his remark, she said, 'Cleo and I have been friends ever since and it worked out well being able to help at the markets, not to mention the free accommodation. Do you know how lucky we are with that?'

'Sure.' He didn't sound convinced.

'I'm looking forward to it in a way. The markets won't be proper work, it's not my usual job, and I certainly won't have to put in the long days.'

'You trust me bumming around the city while you're working?' He seemed doubtful but she couldn't totally read his expression behind the curtain of long ebony hair that was just like his mother's. Silky smooth, it suited him and complemented the dark skin he'd inherited from his father; so like his dad, Kyle was a constant reminder that Stuart wasn't with them any more.

'You won't be bumming around.' Cleo and her friends had also come up with a favour Kyle could do for them in return for their hospitality. He probably thought he'd be getting free rein around Manhattan for four weeks, no adults to nag him, no chores to do. Amelia wasn't that much of a mug, but she deliberately hadn't told Kyle about the work she had arranged for him, knowing he'd be likely to go walkabout and not get on the plane. Connie didn't need that, and Amelia hadn't wanted to get roped into looking for him at the last minute with the risk of missing her flight.

'Hanging around, then.'

'We'll do plenty of tourist things,' she assured him.

'You're not going to expect me to be with you every minute of the day, are you? Oh Jesus, you are. You're going to have me on the clock, track my every move, report back to Mum – not that she cares. She'll be glad to see the back of me for a while. Bet she thinks all her Christmases have come at once.'

He could do a runner here but the chances of that were unlikely so she braved telling him what she had planned. She hoped he wasn't going to freak out and make a scene at passport control that would result in them being detained like in one of those border-patrol shows, or their body cavities being searched. 'In exchange for the apartment in the East Village we'll *both* be helping out at the markets.'

Face stony, he stared at her. 'No way. I'm not working on a la-di-da wool stall selling ugly jumpers.'

If he wasn't so volatile she'd have a bit of a joke with him, wind him up, but it wasn't worth the risk. 'You won't be on the wool stall. Cleo has a lot of close friends doing her favours for us this holiday, and her friend Mitch has said he could use help with selling Christmas trees.'

'Do I get to cut the trees down, with a chainsaw?' He leapt into boy mode and mimicked using a chainsaw with his hands.

'Behave, don't draw attention to us.' Something about airports and security always made Amelia nervous despite being totally innocent. Whenever she and Paul had travelled somewhere he'd insisted they do it smartly dressed so they looked like professionals rather than anyone who was up to no good. She'd seen his point after a friend of theirs was strip-searched before boarding a flight to Thailand. 'You'll be in the city at the Garland Street markets.' Near me, where I can keep an eye on you, although she kept that part to herself.

'Figures.' He'd seen right through her.

'If you play your cards right Mitch might want a hand at his Christmas tree farm out in Inglenook Falls, but you'll have to prove yourself first.' She put it back on him, left him in control rather than bossing him about, and he took her suggestion well, the corners of his mouth not looking quite so downturned. Dealing with trees and the possibility of getting close to a chainsaw was clearly manlier than handling soft, luxurious wool, or yarn as it was known in America. It was going to take her a while to get used to the different lingo, but it was exciting too. She'd never done much travel on her own – the last few long-haul trips had been with Paul when he went on business – and now they were here, she wondered why she'd left it so long to be more adventurous.

They inched forward in the queue and finally reached the front. 'Don't give them any attitude,' she whispered to Kyle, referencing the security men standing to attention. Her work persona was never far from the surface.

'Don't draw attention, don't give them attitude,' he mimicked. 'I'm not a total dumb arse.' And off he went to the booth where they checked the passport and your fingerprints before she had a chance to reprimand him for his language.

This trip to New York was supposed to take her away from her job; she'd have to make more of an effort to switch off, but that was hard when it was family. She'd helped out with Kyle in the early days, which she hadn't minded at all; in fact she'd enjoyed it. But the favours had long continued as Kyle got older, and although Amelia valued the bond she'd made with her nephew, the child-minding hadn't been done entirely without rancour. It's just that as time went on Amelia had found it more and more difficult to turn down the requests. Her job in those days as a home-based telesales executive had been ideal in many ways. When she was feeling unwell she could stay in her pyjamas all day, if she had a cold there was nobody to offend with her constant nose-blowing and sneez-ing, but it also meant that others didn't quite see her job in the same light as their own. Connie had assumed that because Amelia was based at home she could jump through hoops to keep her sister's life running as smoothly as possible. Amelia was on hand to take Kyle when he was too sick to go to school, she was there to meet him at the school gate if Connie was held up in a meeting, and if Stuart was working overtime and between them they hadn't coordi-nated childcare, there was Amelia yet again. But every time she was asked, Amelia acquiesced. It was what family did, wasn't it? And after Stuart died, how could she possibly say no to Connie?

By the time they were both through immigration and making their way towards baggage claim Kyle added, 'I do know not to mouth off at an airport. I'm seventeen, I've been out in public before.'

Surrounded by hoards who'd disembarked just like them and were waiting to make sure their luggage had made it as far as they had across the globe, Kyle found both cases on the conveyor belt, yanked them off, and it was time to make their way into Manhattan.

She pulled up the handle on her suitcase so she could wheel it along the ground behind her. 'What's making you smile so much?'

He nodded towards two police officers stood back from the baggage carousel. 'I thought that was a myth, cops and doughnuts.'

Both officers were enjoying a sugary snack that looked rather tempting right now. The food on the flight hadn't been great, although doughnuts weren't much better, and she couldn't wait to have something decent.

'Already this city is way more exciting than boring old Cornwall,' he grinned and Amelia had a sudden pang that as hard as this was going to be, it was the right thing to do.

'Your mum did a lot of travelling after she left school,' she said. 'I bet she'd love to help you plan a big trip like she did. She was away for ten months, she saw loads of Europe, far more than I ever have.'

Kyle let her get away with her subtle way of bringing his mum into the conversation and asked, 'Why did you never go?'

'I guess I never got round to it. We both got some money when we turned twenty-one, Connie used hers for travel, I used mine to put myself through university and change career.'

'I forget you didn't always work with lowlifes like me.'

'You're not a lowlife. But yes, I wasn't always doing the same job. I was once a telesales exec, which sounds far grander than it really was.'

'Why do it if you weren't into it?'

'I had no idea what to do so I got a job quick.'

'Not necessarily a bad thing; it's responsible.'

'I should've taken time to think about what I really wanted. But what it did do was show me how much difference it can make when you finally find a profession you enjoy.'

'It's still work.'

'It is, but the days go a lot quicker if you've got a passion for something. Don't you have any passions, desires to follow a career?'

'Not really.' His brow creased in frustration. 'I'd like to see a bit of the world one day.'

'Then you need to start saving.'

'Got to find a job first. Can't save thin air, can I?'

She'd forgotten cockiness was a personality trait of seventeen-year-old boys and Kyle hadn't missed out on that part of his personal resume.

'You could always continue your studies,' she suggested as they made their way towards the AirTrain that would take them from JFK to Jamaica Station, where they would connect to another train to whisk them to Manhattan.

'I'd rather have the money.'

'Take it from someone who knows, career isn't always instantaneous, think of the bigger picture.'

He reverted to grunts and shrugs as they boarded the air train.

'I can help you, you know.' She rested her bag on top of her case as she held on to the nearest pole for support when the train began to move.

'That's because you're a do-gooder.'

She was about to get defensive but perhaps Kyle remembered some of the special times they'd had over the years, because he was grinning when he said it. When he was ten she'd taken him to a theme park and ridden all the roller-coasters his mum was too afraid to try; before Connie relocated them to Cornwall they'd gone bowling each week or to the movies or for pizza, anything to keep him chatting and try to keep him in the present. And when he started getting into a lot of trouble, rather than shutting him out Amelia had done her best to be there as an outlet if he needed to talk – he certainly hadn't been talking to his mum at the time.

'I'm not a do-gooder, but I do care.' She left it at that. They didn't talk much for the rest of the journey although the second they reached Penn Station, Kyle became more animated. She wanted to take him back to England remade. Perhaps that was a little hopeful, given she only had four weeks, but even if he had a hint of direction after this trip, it would be a start. She'd wondered as their plane climbed higher in the air to cruise above thirty-five thousand feet whether she was treating him like another work project, but one she could be very vocal with when it came to her opinions on how his parent treated him. That kind of behaviour hadn't gone down so well with one of her most recent cases and when she returned she'd have to remember to maintain a professional distance or she might not get away with being sent on an enforced holiday; if she wasn't careful it could end up being a more permanent arrangement.

They hauled their luggage off the train at Penn Station, wheeled it towards the escalators, and headed up to the bustling streets of New York City. Iconic yellow taxis honked their horns as they moved the best they could in the traffic, a cyclist courier zipped dangerously in and out of vehicles, crowds filled the pavement, and having suitcases in tow was an instant disadvantage. Amelia couldn't wait for it to be dark later, to venture out into Manhattan to see the Christmas lights. She wanted to see Central Park, the Rocke-feller Center, The Plaza hotel, Times Square, Madison Avenue... everything. She wanted to squeal with excitement at all the possi-bilities in a city that already made her feel as though they'd stepped onto a film set, but she knew Kyle wouldn't appreciate it.

'Don't we get the subway or something?' Kyle asked when she got out her map to check the route to the apartment.

'I'd rather see the city.'

'So do I, but I don't want to drag my case around with me.'

'Come on, it's an adventure. This way.'

He reluctantly followed on, daylight beginning to fade unlike Amelia's energy. By her estimations it would only take about half an hour to walk to the apartment on East 24th Street, not far from Madison Square Park.

'At least it's not raining,' Kyle conceded.

'The power of positivity.'

'Bloody freezing though.'

She shook her head. Hopefully by the end of their stay he'd be glass-half-full, talkative and more like his old self, the Kyle she loved dearly rather than this sullen teen with a big, angry chip on his shoulder.

When Kyle expressed an interest in a refreshment at a nearby doughnut stall, she urged him to carry on walking. 'Madison Square Park is right near the apartment and I've heard they do great burgers at the Shake Shack. We could grab a takeout to eat al fresco.'

He harrumphed and on they went, manhandling their luggage up and down curbs, across roads, and finally, as the sun began to set and darkness descended, they reached the park.

A smile spread across Amelia's face. 'Look at the tree.'

'It's massive.'

High praise indeed. There in Madison Square Park, with the famous Flatiron Building in the background, was the most impressive Norway spruce lit up with hundreds of soft white lights. 'First Christmas tree I've seen this year,' said Amelia.

'You'll probably be fed up of them after this trip. And I saw three on the way here.'

'Why didn't you point them out to me?' She'd been too focused on not losing her way on the unfamiliar streets, worried in case Kyle wandered off like a toddler rather than the near-adult he really was. It was why she knew she'd have to tread carefully. Push him too much and he'd take off – he'd done it to her sister enough times.

'I'm starving.' His eyes had already drifted away from the tree and towards the Shake Shack and when they joined the queue they debated whether they'd be able to find anywhere to sit in the park tonight given how busy it was. Picnic-style tables and chairs were plentiful, but not a single one was empty.

They were handed menus and Amelia soon decided on a burger

with bacon and peppers, Kyle of course wanted a double and chose the cheeseburger, and they ordered a couple of portions of fries too.

'Quick, grab that table.' She spotted a young couple standing up about to leave one of the many busy tables right next to a flowerbed. 'You take the cases, I'll wait here for the order and bring it over.'

Service was speedy and before long, with a tray in front of her and her tummy rumbling in anticipation, Amelia bustled past the people still waiting to order and went to join Kyle. He'd got the table but he'd also attracted the attention of some guy who seemed to be giving him a piece of his mind.

'Everything all right?' She set down the tray and stood next to Kyle and this man, ready to go between them if either put their hands on the other one. It had looked heated from a distance and the conversation up this close had definitely taken a turn for the worse.

'He's a thief.' The man jabbed an accusing finger in Kyle's direction.

Good job it hadn't made contact with Kyle because given past behaviour it would've no doubt ended up in a fist fight and although this guy was tall, chunky enough to have a bit of muscle on him, Kyle had youth on his side and had to be half the man's age.

Please don't let them be in trouble on their first day in the city. They hadn't even reached the apartment yet.

She stood her ground, never afraid to speak up. 'I hope you've got a good reason for your accusations.' She'd met enough people like this one in her job, men and women who leapt to conclusions and assumed the worst.

'I'm not a thief.' Kyle looked at her briefly before turning his glare back to his accuser.

The accuser looked Kyle in the eye. 'You really don't recognise me?'

'I've never seen you before in my life.'

'Yes you have. I met you in St Ives once.'

Judging by Kyle's face, a realisation had dawned.

The man turned to Amelia. 'He stole my wallet when I was down in Cornwall on holiday in the summer. I caught him at it too and I thought I'd give him another chance, told him to hop it before I called the police.'

'And now you want revenge, is that it?' Amelia demanded as Kyle's reaction told her this man's claims held an element of truth. 'Bit late now, you should've done something at the time. I'm not condoning what he did, and I thank you for not pressing charges, but that doesn't give you the right to start on him here.' Talk about a small bloody world. Bet Kyle never thought he'd lay eyes on this guy again.

'The woman who left this table dropped some money and your kid scooped it up. I saw it with my own eyes. I've never seen anyone move so fast. And he made no attempt to return it.'

'Not true!' When Kyle yelled, Amelia did her best to calm the fire that was raging inside him.

She'd give him the benefit of the doubt; she had to. 'What happened, Kyle?' She held up a hand when the man tried to talk again. And she didn't bother correcting his reference to Kyle as hers; she'd had it plenty over the years and didn't mind one bit. It made her feel like most other women her age – well, she'd have had to be pregnant as a teenager to have Kyle, but still, it was nice to be thought of as someone who had a family of their own rather than the lonely old spinster she was starting to become, with nothing but work and meals for one to look forward to and the odd trip to the pub when the coupled-up friends who lived locally were allowed out on their own.

Kyle at least matched her calmer tone when he replied to her. Over the last year she'd been trying to educate him about thinking before he reacted, something she knew he found a constant battle. 'I came to get the table before someone else did, and the girl who was sitting here dropped a twenty. I picked it up and was about to run after her when I realised our luggage was at the table with nobody to watch it. I didn't think you'd want to lose our stuff on day one of our holiday, so I hesitated, and he started having a go at me.'

'A likely story,' the man muttered, his dark eyes anticipating more trouble.

Amelia stood between him and Kyle. 'Kyle has explained his side of the story, so unless you have proof to show otherwise, I suggest you leave us to our meal.' And bugger off. 'We'll stay here until we've eaten. If the girl comes back we will pass her the twenty; if she doesn't, rest assured it'll go in the first charity collection we see.'

He harrumphed as though he wanted to say *Bullshit!* but thought he'd better be more polite.

'You have a nice day!' she called sarcastically when he walked away. She used the best American accent she could muster and the filthy look she got in return suggested she hadn't made a friend.

When she sat down, Kyle was clearly doing his best not to smile. 'What's so funny?'

'Auntie Amelia, you're a badass!' He put up a hand and she couldn't help smiling and high-fived him back.

'Did you really steal from him in Cornwall?' The fact he wasn't meeting her eye was enough of an answer. 'Kyle...'

'It was in the summer, I haven't done anything like that since, promise.'

'And how many times have you done that sort of thing?' She dismissed her own question with a shake of her head. 'Actually, I don't want to know. I only want you to promise all that has stopped. You're a good kid, do your best not to prove me wrong.' It was the firmest she'd been with him in a long time and she was expecting it to backfire but, instead, she watched as he calmly unwrapped the burger and took a generous bite.

'I won't do it again. Derek told me all sorts of things about being inside. No way would I do that to myself.'

She started on her own food, grateful to be miles away from Kyle's so-called friends.

'For the record, Auntie Amelia, this time I'm telling the truth.'

She looked him in the eye. 'I know you are. And can we make a deal?'

'What's that?'

'For this holiday you call me Amelia. Auntie makes me feel too old now.' Amelia also sounded more of a friend, less of an authority figure, and perhaps he'd respond better this way. She was willing to try anything.

The twenty was still in full view, its corner beneath the box of fries so it didn't blow away in the winter winds that seemed to be picking up now, reminding them of the season they were in. 'If the girl comes back we'll pass her the money,' said Amelia. 'Otherwise, charity, like I told that horrible man.' Who hadn't exactly been hit with the ugly stick.

'Not a collection bucket though, you never know whether the person holding it pots some of the cash.'

The burger warmed her hands and the peppers were delicious, smothered in a special dressing. 'That isn't very trusting.'

'Yeah, well, when you've been doubted enough times in your life it kind of makes you a bit pessimistic.'

It was a shame for kids like Kyle who had to prove themselves to all those who didn't believe in them. This evening was supposed to be pleasant, a stop on their way to their accommodation. They should be smiling and chatting below magical rows of twinkly lights and bunting that looped from the Shake Shack across the sky above them, not defending Kyle's honour to someone who had adopted the guilty-until-proven-innocent philosophy.

During their time here Amelia would love to reach Kyle in a way nobody had managed to do in the last few years, and she needed him to learn to believe in himself even though she wasn't the best role model in that respect. Because while she was assertive and even a bit pushy at work, when it came to life outside that environment she didn't have the same confidence. Paul had ended things with her because he said she never put their relationship first. Maybe if she'd been more headstrong and had learnt to say no to her sister, no to overtime demands at work, been more invested in their relationship, they'd still be together and she'd be well on her way to having a family of her own. Until now she hadn't really seen how it must have made Paul feel, to come second best.

And now it was too late. He hadn't called or emailed her; he'd gone from her life almost as quickly as he'd come into it.

3

NATHAN

'This place is dreamy.' Scarlett looked up above them at the lights looping in the sky in Madison Square Park. 'I love all the bunting too.'

'Well done for picking a table with a view of the tree.'

She snapped back to teen mode, which meant a shrug as though his comments didn't matter much at all. 'You took ages.'

'That's because I caught some kid stealing. He thought it was okay to pick up a twenty dollar note dropped by a woman when she left the table. He claimed he hesitated about running after the girl because he had luggage with him and didn't want it nicked.'

'And did he have luggage?'

'Yeah,' Nathan admitted. 'But I still didn't believe him.'

'Just because your wallet was stolen once, doesn't mean everyone's out to get you.'

'I beg to differ. It was the same boy.'

'What are you talking about?'

'Same kid, from Cornwall.'

'No way.'

He harrumphed. 'I saw the panic in his eyes when he recognised me too. Guilty.'

'Dad, you can be scary sometimes, doesn't mean this time he wasn't telling the truth.'

'Your problem is you're too innocent, you haven't been out in the real world as long as I have.'

'Here we go again, the Dad lecture.' She rolled her eyes.

When the buzzer he'd brought to the table vibrated it at least stopped a fight in its tracks and he went to grab the burgers and fries they'd ordered. They were sharing cheese fries at Scarlett's insistence, and seeing as he wanted this to be the trip of a lifetime for his daughter, he wasn't going to argue. At least not on day one, at least not about something so petty.

All animosity had gone when he set down the food and they tucked in. He'd been absent far too often as Scarlett was growing up, and ever since it had become just the two of them he'd spent every waking moment wishing he could make it up to her. He hoped this holiday was a start. Here in New York for the first time, they were embarking on the longest holiday they'd ever taken together. Finances were good – Nathan had worked hard over the years – but he'd decided that with Scarlett having finished her GCSEs and in her first year of sixth form, he didn't have long left to whisk her away and try to rebuild bridges before she lost interest in him altogether. He got the impression she'd do her A levels, go off to university, and never look back. And the thought of that scared him every single day.

Every year, around this time with Christmas fast approaching, Scarlett showed a softer side and would spend more time with her dad, less hidden away in her room. She didn't have a television up there but she adored Christmas movies and so it was either be together with your uncool dad or miss out. Thankfully she always chose the former and they'd exhaust all their favourites, sitting together on the worn maroon sofa in their two-up two-down home in Hove, East Sussex. They'd write the titles of all their favourite movies and jumble them up, then pick one. It was always a winner, no matter what it turned out to be. And with some set in New York, they'd got to talking about the city that never sleeps and last year he'd begun to wonder whether it might be time to plan a visit. He'd been on Facebook, scrolling through friends' updates, and saw his ex-colleague Myles Cunningham's post from earlier in the year with Central Park buried under snow, him and his wife, Darcy, posing for a selfie as they rode in a horse-drawn carriage, and another picture of them indulging in cupcakes from a famous bakery that according to Scarlett was featured in *Sex and the City*. Nathan also remembered that Myles had had a strained relationship with his father and although they were on good terms now, Myles could've easily come here to New York and severed all ties.

Nathan never wanted that to happen with Scarlett, and with no mum or siblings to help mend rifts, it was all down to him.

'Are you going to meet up with your friend while we're here?' Scarlett took a bunch of fries from the cardboard container and dipped them into the tomato sauce.

'Of course. But he's busy, he works hard.'

'That's the job, right?'

He shuddered, remembering how he'd yelled that at Dawn more than once when Scarlett was young. It was true, a job as an investment banker didn't come without a lot of hard work and commitment. Often, he'd been in meetings, and that was why he was putting in more hours, but at other times he'd been socialising and avoiding the responsibilities waiting for him when he got home. 'It's hard work, but well paid, so all worth it.' He hoped his summation would stop this from escalating into an argument. 'And I'm sure Myles and I will get together soon – I need to buy him a drink to thank him for his help in finding us a good hotel.' Myles's wife, Darcy, co-managed the Inglenook Inn where they were staying, and earlier they'd got to meet her when they checked in. Darcy had captured Myles's heart when he'd never once so much as hinted he was the type to settle down, and Nathan found she was every bit as kind and welcoming as he'd been told.

'I'm so glad I got out of school already,' said Scarlett, dragging another fry through the sauce.

'Don't get used to it. You'll have to work extra hard when we're back.'

'Relax, Dad, we get three weeks anyway, I'm only missing five days.'

Nathan had taken leave from work and had it agreed by the powers that be at Scarlett's private school, for which he paid through the nose, that she could have the extra time off. He'd expected them to make a fuss and was ready with arguments about how this trip would be educational, but they'd not objected at all. Maybe that was one thing that truly was all about the money. And, now, he hoped this would be a trip that cemented their relationship some more. If he could, he'd give his daughter the world. Except of course he couldn't, because Dawn wasn't around any more.

He bit into his double cheeseburger that oozed with flavour and left him in no doubt as to whether he'd have a few more of these before they returned to the UK in a month's time right before New Year's. 'Valerie at work was right, these are the best burgers ever.'

'Valerie seems nice,' said Scarlett with a hint of mischief he chose to ignore. Scarlett had met Valerie at the office a few weeks ago when she came in to collect Nathan's house key after losing her own, and Nathan hadn't missed the way his daughter had looked at the woman, hoping that perhaps there was something going on romantically between the two of them.

'She's coming to New York. And she'll be staying at the same inn as us for Christmas.'

'Are you and she...?'

'Don't get any ideas, we're just colleagues. She's planned a last-minute trip and I sorted the accommodation side out for her, put her in touch with the manager of the inn. That's all,' he reiterated.

'Are you sure? She always seems to be after you.'

'If you're referring to the phone discussions we have, or when we go out for drinks, that's because we're friends.' And Valerie had a daughter slightly younger than Scarlett who was doing the same things as Scarlett, pushing her parent away, making her wonder if one day she'd leave for good. Between them they weren't sure whether it was regular teen behaviour or if their daughters were being particularly brutal. But he and Valerie understood each other and it was a relief to have another adult who completely got where he was coming from.

'Can you believe we're actually here, in Manhattan?' He directed the conversation away from his love life, smiled across at his daughter and she didn't glare at him or roll her eyes as she might have done at home.

She grinned, a megawatt smile in place. 'Thank you for bringing me here.' She offered him the last of the cheesy fries but he declined. 'It's amazing, and all decked out for Christmas too. I feel like a kid again.'

'You'll be wanting a stocking on Christmas morning next.'

'Of course I will. I'll never be too old for a Christmas stocking.'

'I'd better get thinking of some gift ideas then.'

'Don't let me down.'

He'd done that too many times, he never wanted to again. 'I won't. Are you happy with the Inglenook Inn?'

'I love it. I'm so glad it's a brownstone, I feel like a proper New

Yorker. I thought we'd be staying in a dive of a bed and breakfast. Remember that place you took us to on the Isle of Wight a few years ago?'

'How could I forget?' It was what you might class as an epic fail. Run by an odd couple who liked to bicker in front of their guests, the accommodation had a poky bathroom with cracked tiles and a stained sink that made him gag when he cleaned his teeth, and the owner insisted on vacuuming first thing every morning, usually when they were still in bed, the vacuum whacking up against their door every time she moved it back and forth across the carpet outside.

Their accommodation here in New York was everything he'd hoped for. He'd seen enough pictures on the website for the Inglenook Inn to know that it would be, but he hadn't shared them with Scarlett – he'd wanted to see her face as they crossed the city in a cab, made their way to Greenwich Village, and saw the exterior of the brownstone building they were going to stay in. And her reaction hadn't been a disappointment. She'd been in disbelief, gasping, saying she felt like Carrie from *Sex and the City* – he dreaded to think which of the female characters that one was – and inside they'd been greeted by Darcy in the communal lounge at the front with its stunning Christmas tree that could be seen from the street outside and an inviting, cosy fireplace that guests were free to enjoy should they want to, perhaps with a drink from the small bar in the corner near the office desk. Nathan already had his eye on that if Scarlett turned the teenage angst to full volume during their holiday, and it was slightly less sad than getting a bottle of something in a brown paper bag and drinking it all alone. On the top floor of the inn was their suite, which was enormous and ideal for a man and a teen who really didn't want to be living on top of each other for the duration of their stay, and Nathan was kind of glad he'd missed out on staying at Myles and Darcy's rental property in the East Village, which had already been reserved for another friend. The Inglenook Inn was perfectly situated, they'd got a reasonable discount for their stay, and Darcy was a hostess who had already made them feel more than welcome with the little tray of treats in the suite upon arrival. Scarlett and he had devoured the croissants with jam and some fresh fruit before unpacking and finally setting off here to Madison Square Park.

They finished their burgers and fries and it was time to do some more exploring. Scarlett took a ton of photos of the tree in the park first, the Shake Shack itself, bystanders and characters she thought looked interesting. 'Where to next?' she asked when she finally put her phone away. No doubt she'd be posting the photographs all over Instagram later tonight, but it was good to see the enthusiasm.

'What would you like to do?'

'Everything,' she grinned.

'Let's leave the art galleries for now.'

'I know you're not keen, I can do those on my own.'

'No, I'll go. This is a holiday together. I'm looking forward to it.'

'Liar.'

'Okay, so I'm not a massive art lover. But I do want to see the Met.'

'There's so much to see,' she told him as they wandered a bit aimlessly. 'Not just the major venues, but other things – the Whitney, The Met Cloisters, I want to see street art in Freeman Alley, Eduardo Kobra's technicolour murals around the city.'

'The what?'

After she explained, he concluded, 'You mean graffiti.'

'It's not graffiti, it's art. It's a whole project; they're huge, iconic works. One is of Gandhi and Mother Teresa, there's one of Albert Einstein. He did another called 'The Braves of 9/11' – it's a seven-storey work of art depicting a kneeling firefighter, and the number on the fireman's helmet is the number of firefighters who lost their lives.'

Nathan registered her frown at his apparent ignorance and the personal angle she'd hit him with to perhaps try to persuade him not to dismiss art as frivolous, something that didn't matter. 'You've done your research, and we will make time for as much as we can.' But he wanted to head off any argument about her future career aspirations, at least for the time being. 'It's the first night, we need to do something we'd both like.'

'How about checking out some movie or TV locations?'

'Anything in mind?'

'We could see Carrie's brownstone on the way back to the Inglenook Inn, and the *Friends* apartment building is down that way too.' She took out the paper fold-up map of the city he'd given her that she'd resolutely refused to use but that she'd soon changed her mind about when she realised using an app on her phone would deplete the charge and she wouldn't be able to take so many photos.

He turned the map the right way up. 'Remember we're here for a month. Perhaps we don't need to do it all tonight.'

'What should we start with?'

'Central Park.'

'Central Park is huge.'

'I'm not suggesting we do all of it right now.'

'I hate to point out the obvious, but it's dark.' Although her frown lifted quickly when she said, 'We could ice-skate.'

'I was thinking more of a horse and carriage ride.'

'One of those too, but ice-skating tonight. Please, Dad. I watched *Serendipity* last week and they were at the Wollman Rink and I really want to go. We'd be seeing Central Park plus a movie location so we're both happy.'

He had no desire to attempt balancing on two thin blades and end up spending more time on his arse than upright, but he wanted to make her happy. 'I wouldn't class it as something I want to do, but... go on, let's do it. But it's only fair to warn you that I've never done it before.'

'Not even on all those ski holidays you've been on with mates over the years?'

Ouch. Those ski holidays had been when she was younger; he'd left her with her mum and just buggered off. He was older and wiser now, but back then nobody had been able to get through to him. Not Dawn, not his parents, and definitely not Scarlett, even when she'd been upset that Daddy was going away. 'Not even then. We skied, we ate, but a load of blokes hitting the ice-skating rinks?' He screwed up his nose.

'About time you gave it a try then. Live a little, Dad.'

He frowned and, with an accepting shake of her head that indicated she was already anticipating the cringeworthy dad behaviour she was about to endure, she helped him scoop up their rubbish to drop in the bin on their way past. 'It's going to be fun watching you.'

* * *

'This isn't like the movies,' Scarlett declared as they ventured onto the rink, her standing freely, him gripping hold of the sides for dear life. 'In the movies the couple usually has the rink pretty much to themselves, or else they have a lot of free space, and one of them isn't afraid to let go of the edge.' She moved out the way of a group of lads who surely must play ice hockey in their spare time given how adept they were at zigzagging their way around, twisting and turning whenever it took their fancy. 'Come on, let go, you can do it.'

'I'm not ready,' he said through gritted teeth.

'I'm going to do a lap.' She was laughing, he could tell, and not making a very good job of hiding it.

When Scarlett turned fourteen he'd taken her and three of her closest friends up to Bath for the Christmas markets and he had hung out in coffee shops while they perused the stalls. They all met up near the Circus and they'd begged him to extend their leaving time and go to the outdoor rink in the park. Every one of them had taken to the ice and within minutes made it look so easy.

Right now, with these wretched blades on his feet, he swore it was the bravery of youth versus the loss of courage with each year you grew older that made him so useless at this.

All too soon Scarlett had navigated the circumference of the Wollman Rink and come back to his side. 'You can't spend the entire evening standing here.'

He'd moved about a metre, cautiously, his hands never leaving the sides.

'I can hold your hand if you like.'

'Then I'll make us both fall down.' But she was holding out her hand, a gesture of closeness he wanted to make the most of. 'Slow-ly,' he urged as they set off, her gliding, him stepping a little like a demented penguin.

They stuck close to the sides of the rink and when he wobbled he reached out to steady himself, and by some minor miracle they eventually made it all the way around.

'You're not bad for an old man,' she smiled. 'Look out, Dad!' Scarlett tugged him to the side, out of the way of a family of four who had joined hands and were about to take them out.

His arms whipped around, he dropped her hand and slumped in a heap against the side of the rink. He groaned. 'I need to hire this place for a private session, there are far too many people.' But when he tried to get up he kept losing his footing and gradually

Scarlett's giggles became infectious and he couldn't get off the ice because his laughing made him so weak.

Scarlett did her best to show him the easiest way to get back up again after a fall but once he was up he decided he'd had quite enough of balancing on dicey blades and he left her to go round a few more times. He gladly returned his ice-skates before nabbing a nearby bench with a view of the rink poised to take some pictures.

He watched his daughter, this incredible girl with her rich, caramel-brown hair that hung in naturally round ringlets, brown eyes that danced beneath the twinkly lights sparkling against the night sky. It was hard to reconcile this version of his daughter who was becoming a woman with the kid who'd wanted picking up the second he came through the door, the same girl who'd cried the day someone at school told her there was no Santa Claus, the Scarlett who'd let him curl up beside her for weeks after her mum died. Back then they were on exactly the same wavelength; it was as though neither of them dared shut their eyes in case more of their world fell apart by the time they woke up, but gradually they'd got through it. She'd been a sensible, together girl until the last year of her GCSEs when hormones and boys came to the fore and he only hoped she didn't make the same mistakes he had done. But he couldn't tell her that. He couldn't say it because he never wanted her to think that he resented her existence. He'd been absent enough over the years to give that impression and he was doing his best to make it up to her. Scarlett hadn't been planned, not by a long shot, but he couldn't imagine his world without her in it now.

Scarlett waved every time she went past. She was having the time of her life outside in the frosty air that caught him by surprise tonight. It was cold when they'd arrived in the city, but now darkness had fallen, the temperature had dropped too. If this were the movies it would start snowing right now to make things extra perfect, the city backdrop totally spectacular, his arse wouldn't be cold perched on this bench and he'd have become an Olympic ice dancer after one lap of the rink.

But this was real life, and sometimes it was hard. And parenting a teen was the hardest job he'd ever have to do. Maybe this holiday would work and bring them closer together and he could stop over-shadowing Scarlett's every move trying to make up for the past when he hadn't been there enough, or worrying about the future to the extent that he was pushing her away more than anything else.

4

AMELIA

Well rested after an early night at their apartment and relieved of the responsibility of Kyle, at least for tonight while he stayed back after she'd dragged him around Central Park all day in the cold, Amelia negotiated the subway on her own, made a detour to the famous Magnolia Bakery, and found the Inglenook Inn in the heart of Greenwich Village. Dressed for winter in a fawn jumper with a slit up the side, skinny jeans, and boots, along with a smart, wool-blend coat, she plunged herself into the New York pandemonium. The city was so intoxicating that it was hard not to pick up on the vibe that Manhattan was filled with possibilities.

Armed with Christmas-themed cupcakes, Amelia suspected that even if Kyle had some energy left, he'd be reluctant to spend time with three women who'd likely chat the entire evening away, and she wanted to give him enough space to get his head sorted – not so much he got in trouble but enough that she didn't smother him.

'I can't believe you're here.' Cleo hugged her tight the second she stepped inside the beautiful brownstone. 'It's so good to see you. It's been too long.'

'It really has.' She hugged her fiercely and when she pulled back said, 'New York is as amazing as you always told me it was, just like your photos.'

'You've come at the best time of year, in my opinion. Come on, let me introduce you to Darcy.'

Darcy had just finished on the phone and held out a hand in welcome. The professional hotelier, dressed in a navy suit with a crisp, white blouse, her lustrous, chestnut-brown hair pinned up in a chignon, was all smiles. 'Welcome to the Inglenook Inn. It's a pleasure to meet you.' Despite the immaculate attire and air of capability, she was open and friendly and Amelia instantly warmed to her.

'This place is gorgeous.' Amelia looked around her, taking in the interior of the inn, welcoming with its low-lit lounge, the Christmas tree all lit up and visible from the street, the fire in the grate.

'Thank you,' Darcy smiled. 'We're a boutique hotel but try to make it as homely as possible.'

'Much nicer than a huge hotel,' Amelia agreed, removing her coat when Darcy offered to hang it for her and Cleo took a phone call. 'And thanks so much to you and your husband for the loan of your apartment.'

'You're happy with it?'

'It's wonderful, so much space for two of us, I'm incredibly grateful.' She looked around her again, mesmerised by the beauty of the inn. 'Although, I would've been happy coming here too. This place is really special.'

'You bet it is. Now, can I get you something to drink?' Darcy moved towards the small bar in the corner.

'Orange juice for me, please.'

'Are you sure? I have wine, Baileys, I can make a cocktail.'

'Maybe another time. I have a teen in tow and I want to set a good example.'

'Seems to be a theme.'

'What do you mean?'

She fixed the orange juice and dropped in a couple of ice cubes from the bucket on the bar. 'There's a guy staying here with his daughter and he said pretty much the same thing to me earlier when he was waiting here for her to get ready.' She handed Amelia the drink. 'Cleo told me your nephew has had a few problems; I hope this trip works in the way you want it to.'

'Me too.'

They moved over to the sofa nearer the fireplace as Cleo finished up on the phone and put her order in for a diet cola.

'You're not drinking either?' Amelia commented.

'I've been at the market stall most of this afternoon – Kaisha has taken over now but I'll be back to it after this. Darcy kindly lets me take breaks at the Inglenook Inn and it's way better than shivering my behind off at some coffee cart.'

'Everything all right at home?' Darcy asked Cleo, noting her frown when she handed her her drink. She bent down by the fire-side to add another log as the flames bathed the Christmas tree by the window in a soft glow.

'My call was from Ruby, reminding me there's a bake sale at school the day after tomorrow and I need to make cupcakes.'

'I'd buy some if I were you,' said Darcy.

'Apparently it's frowned upon. The other mums make them from scratch, all pretty with swirly icing and little decorations.'

'Other mums probably don't run their own business, have two market stalls, four kids with two of them under the age of five either,' said Amelia, Darcy adding her agreement too. 'I honestly don't know how you do it.'

'I have got four kids,' Cleo replied, 'but I've got a Dylan too.'

'So that's where I'm going wrong,' Amelia grinned. 'I've only met him briefly when you brought him over to the UK but you do seem to have hit the jackpot.'

'He's a good husband and a wonderful father.'

'Amelia is right though,' Darcy put in, 'you have a lot going on – making cupcakes is the least of your worries.'

'I'll manage it. I'll just have to remember to get the ingredients in the morning. I can make them in the apartment kitchen above the Little Knitting Box, that way I'm still at work and multitasking.'

'I'm telling you, this is why God invented places like the Magnolia Bakery,' said Darcy, eyeing the box of cupcakes. 'Because not everyone has time for all that competing crap.' When Cleo opened her mouth to say something she said, 'You know I'm telling the truth, don't you?'

'It's true,' Cleo told Amelia. 'But things with Ruby are delicate enough as it is, I don't want to do anything to upset her.'

'She's trying to push your buttons,' said Darcy and when Amelia's look begged the question, Cleo explained what had been going on at home.

'It sounds like she's reached the age where she's testing you, trying to work out her place in all of this. You'd know what it was like, I remember you telling me about your stepmum Teresa.' It dawned on Amelia that that might be the problem. 'Is that what's behind all this worry?'

'I was a little cow. I made Teresa's life far harder than it ever needed to be and, looking back, it probably made it more difficult for my dad too. But I thought Ruby and I were friends. She was always happy for me to be around, it's only lately she's changed and pushes the boundaries whenever she can.'

'What does Dylan make of it all?' Amelia asked.

'He's brushing it off like she's just going through a stage, which she is, I know that, but from my own experience I know that stage, with all the resentment, can last well into your twenties. He's offered to talk to her but I don't want things to become more difficult, I don't want her to think I'm trying to turn him against her.'

'Why don't you try talking to her yourself, ask her why she's feeling differently?' Amelia suggested. 'It could all stem from one small thing she's blown out of proportion.'

'Maybe. I appreciate any suggestions from you; you've got the experience after all.'

Amelia began to laugh. 'I wouldn't say that, and you might change your mind depending on how I handle Kyle during this trip away.' She watched as Darcy mixed business with pleasure, interacting with another customer who came through the door, answered a phone call as well as liaising with a man called Rupert, the chef at the inn, multitasking almost like second nature to her. 'Darcy's lovely, so professional, so relaxed. I've never been able to carry that off in my own job.'

'She thrives on being busy and she pretty much runs this place when the owner isn't around.'

'Where's the owner?'

Cleo explained Sofia's situation: her daughter in Switzerland, the toing and froing to see her grandchildren. 'Darcy told me earlier that Sofia is thinking of selling up and I think Darcy would love to buy this place. Myles has been working long hours again; I'm a bit worried they're pushing themselves too hard.'

'It's prime real estate here in the city, that's for sure. And such a gorgeous inn.'

'Darcy has worked hard so she's emotionally attached. I just hope she and Myles make the right decision.'

'You don't think they should buy the place?'

'Myles and Darcy are very similar when it comes to career – they both give it their all but sometimes it can mean they neglect their relationship. They've had some ups and downs; they almost didn't get married. They're too nice a couple not to go the distance. They need to remember it's not all about work.' They watched Darcy disappear out of the room with one of her guests who'd just come downstairs.

'Says the woman with the business, the market stalls, the family.'

With a wry smile Cleo conceded, 'Point taken.'

Amelia turned to admire the tree again. 'It's beautiful, I love seeing it from the street, and it smells gorgeous. The pine scent is a real reminder of the season even though Christmas is weeks away.' You couldn't possibly forget the holiday season in a city where in almost every place you looked, each hidden corner, were decorations – twinkly lights, garlands, window displays – some huge, others smaller but no less impressive.

'The tree came from Mitch's farm,' said Cleo.

'The same Mitch you've earmarked for Kyle to give a hand to?'

'The very same. And I'd have set you up with him if he wasn't taken already. He's just your type.'

'Oh yeah, and what type is that?'

'Good-looking, kind, spark of mischief about him.'

She wasn't sure Paul had ever fitted that description, and he had been her type until he ended things. 'I hope he and Kyle get on.'

'Mitch is very kind. He'll have no problem warming to Kyle, and vice versa, I'm sure. And, like me, Mitch needs the help.'

'Are you beginning to think you took on too much this year?'

'Dylan thinks so, and I protested at first but he's right. Having a market stall at Inglenook Falls is more than enough along with the store and running a family. But this was such an exciting opportunity. And it's worked out well that Mitch signed up too – I have transport each way on most days, when it fits in with our timings. Dylan works from home so can get the kids from school, and it's only short-term.'

'But still, it must be exhausting.'

'It is.'

Amelia set her empty glass down on the table. 'How's your grandpa Joe?'

'In his words, he's hanging in there,' Cleo laughed. 'He's getting older but he's doing well, no real serious health issues even though he's slowed down quite a lot.'

'I'll bet he's excited about the wedding.'

'He keeps going on about how he'll be six feet under if Dylan and I put it off much longer.'

'You are taking a while,' Amelia grinned. 'I was kind of hoping I could come for a holiday and be there for your wedding.'

'We're thinking of a winter wedding, next year.'

Amelia couldn't hold back the smile. 'See now you're going to make me have to visit again.'

'Would you come?'

'Try and stop me. I get the feeling one holiday in New York will never be enough, but I'd better start saving.' And sort herself out at work too so she actually had a reliable income. Her behaviour lately hadn't been within the parameters of the job description and while she hadn't wanted to take a month off, it was probably the best idea when it was heavily suggested by her boss in a tone that brooked no argument.

'Anyone new on the horizon?' Cleo ventured. 'Since Paul.'

Amelia shook her head. 'Nobody.'

'Have you heard from him?'

'Not apart from coordinating the collection of my things from the house when we broke up. Nothing since then.'

'Do you miss him?'

'I've been so busy I haven't had much of a chance to think about it but, yes, I do miss him. He was in my life for years, it's hard to adjust.'

'I'm sure it is. And it takes time. How's the flat?'

'Getting there, feeling more like home again. It was weird to be back there after I'd rented it out, but I like it, I love the area. Vikram in the corner shop was delighted I'm back and he's once again the source for my late-night packets of crisps or bottles of wine.'

Cleo laughed out loud. 'Sounds as though you've got the essentials covered. Who needs a man when Vikram can keep you in crisps and wine?'

'Here we go.' Darcy came back through to the lounge with serving plates and Amelia opened up the box of cupcakes. 'See how good they look, Cleo. If I were you I'd pick some up, take them home, and save yourself the bother of baking from scratch. Ruby will love them too.'

Cleo shook her head. 'I can't, I'm going to have to bake,' she insisted.

'Up to you,' Darcy shrugged, 'but take it from someone who has very little time on her hands, I'd be the first in line to buy them rather than spend hours in the kitchen.' She asked Amelia, 'Any preference? You're the guest of honour.'

'I chose three different cakes, happy with any.' She insisted Darcy had first choice as the host, then Cleo, who'd done her a huge favour lining up some work and accommodation, and took the third for herself. Indulging together in their frost-covered cupcakes piled high with swirly icing, red, white, and green sprinkles, edible snowmen, Santa and snowflakes, they talked about life: Amelia's work and her charge at her side for this holiday, Darcy's love of the hotel industry and her investigations when it came to affording to buy the Inglenook Inn herself, Cleo's ability to juggle parenthood with a business and still keep a level head. They giggled at the way Darcy and Myles had met, how they'd detested one another at the start. Amelia thought it all sounded very romantic and if she could have one ounce of these women's happiness to ease the feeling of loneliness, she'd be right on track.

Cleo ducked out to grab takeaway hot drinks for all of them as a special treat. Darcy had a caramel macchiato, Cleo had the same, claiming she needed a good energy boost, and Amelia had gone for a hot chocolate. Back with their orders, Cleo asked Amelia what else she wanted to do while she was in the city.

'I want to see Macy's, Bloomingdale's, the shops along Fifth Avenue, the tree at the Rockefeller Center is a must, the lights on all the famous stores.'

'Don't forget the Winter Village at Bryant Park,' Darcy suggested, 'it's really pretty and they have some great stalls.' When Cleo cleared her throat Darcy added, 'Of course, nowhere near as good as the Garland Street winter markets.'

'Garland Street isn't far from here,' Cleo elaborated. 'There are different stalls, I'm in a good position, and it's really friendly. Small compared to some of the markets in the city, but that makes it extra special, in my humble opinion.'

'Was it expensive to rent a stall?'

'It was, but I'm hoping it'll be more than worth it. It's been easy enough to set up the merchandise, and I've had plenty of footfall so far. I've enlisted help from another school mum to run my stall out in Inglenook Falls too, with Dylan on hand for any problems.'

'And what about Mitch – are you sure he'll have plenty for Kyle to do? It might not go down well if Kyle thinks Mitch is only humouring him by giving him work.'

'Don't worry, there'll be lots for him to do,' Cleo assured her. 'Mitch owns and runs the Christmas tree farm out in Inglenook Falls and this year he's busier than ever with that. He also does a bit of painting and makes picture frames and so the market stall is something new. He has a son who can help out a bit at weekends and another boy, Jude, who can divide his time between Inglenook

Falls and here, but I sense he'll still be crazy busy in the city so don't worry, Kyle won't get bored.'

'How does Kyle feel about helping Mitch with the market stall?' Darcy ventured.

'I don't think he was entirely surprised I'd lined something up for him. And he seemed relieved I wasn't going to make him help out with selling wool and knitting paraphernalia. He was much more willing when I explained his job would involve Christmas trees. He got all excited he might get to use an axe or chainsaw until I explained the trees would be chopped down already and he'd be helping to set up the stall, helping customers make a selection, all the boring stuff I think he'd prefer to avoid. I just hope he behaves himself with Mitch.'

'Mitch won't stand for any trouble,' Darcy put in. 'He'll keep him in line. If I were you I'd be more worried about what a seventeen-year-old boy will make of all the stores you intend to visit.'

'I haven't told him the half of it yet,' Amelia grinned.

'What's Kyle like? Is he all spotty and stroppy? What?' Darcy had earned a look from Cleo. 'From memory my brother Tate was both of those things at that age. He's normal now, we get on well, but at the time it was steer clear unless you wanted your head bitten off.'

Amelia dismissed Cleo's concern that Darcy had insulted her. 'No offence taken. And he no longer has spots, but he *has* got stroppiness in spades. As you already know, he's had some challenges and I'm hoping this holiday will get him away from everything and allow him a bit of perspective. I want him to realise he's a good person, he needs to believe in himself.'

'You're as amazing as this one then.' Darcy tapped Cleo's knee. 'I'm not very good with kids. Myles and I looked after Cleo's baby Tabitha once, it was horrendous.'

'You coped!' Cleo assured her.

'We lost Tabitha's favourite cuddly toy in Central Park.'

Amelia couldn't help but laugh. 'It could've happened to anyone.'

'But it happened to us. We were so stressed.'

'Well, Kyle is beyond cute cuddly toys,' said Amelia, 'but I think I'd sometimes take a baby or toddler wailing rather than the emotional warfare of a teenage boy.'

'Your sister is lucky you're so involved,' said Darcy.

'She is,' Cleo agreed, taking the lid off her takeaway cup and tipping it back to get the last dregs of her drink. 'I was a terrible teen, I remember it well. I was horrible to everyone around me when my mum died, and half the time I didn't even realise I was doing it.'

Amelia relaxed among friends, old and new. And when she finally bundled herself up against the cold again after Rupert made them all a hot cider before they went on their way, Amelia headed back to the apartment, through the swarms of shoppers and commuters, people out to take in the wonders of Christmas in the city, with the feeling this would be a holiday to remember.

She wasn't wrong.

She opened the door to the apartment to find Kyle lounging on the sofa, iPad on his lap, bottle of vodka in one hand. His jaw dropped; he was well aware he'd been caught red-handed.

She snatched the bottle from his hand and at the same time saw a face on the iPad. 'Who's that?'

'A mate.' He clicked to hang up the call but not before Amelia saw the face again, the tattooed neck of Derek, idiot extraordinaire, so-called friend of Kyle's but the biggest bad influence on the planet, who Amelia thought was still under lock and key at Her Majesty's pleasure.

She snatched the iPad away.

'Are you trying to suck all the fun out of my life?' he roared at her.

She held the bottle of vodka aloft, some of it slopping out. 'Damn right I'll put a stop to this sort of fun. You're underage in England, you're well underage here. Where did you even get it?'

'I found it in the back of the kitchen cabinet.'

'So you stole it.'

'You told me yourself, nobody has lived here for a long time. I don't think anyone will miss a bit of vodka.'

'Not really the point, is it?' She screwed the top back on. At least it was half full – he couldn't have had all that much seeing as he wasn't slurring and stood his ground in front of her right now. She'd got well versed at spotting the signs of underage drinking, knowing when someone was spinning her a story. It was par for the course in her job, and she'd seen Kyle drunk before, more than once. No wonder Connie had fallen apart when it happened, because it was horrible. He'd been a mean drunk, out for trouble like the loser mates he'd hooked up with, including the guy he'd just been talking to.

She set the bottle down in the kitchenette. 'You've let me down and we only just got here.'

'I let everyone fucking down! What, do you expect me to hold your hand and skip around New York for the next few weeks?'

'No, but I would hope for a little bit of respect.'

'Yeah, well you shouldn't have any expectations as far as I'm concerned. I told you, I'm not worth bothering about.'

Her attempts to diffuse the situation fell on deaf ears when he stormed off to his bedroom and gave the door an almighty slam.

In the still of the lounge, Amelia sank into the sofa. Right now she wished she had accepted Rupert's offer of a double Baileys, the option Darcy had gone for as she neared the end of her own working day. Then at least it might have softened the blow of finding Kyle.

Over the years, Amelia had built a strong bond with Kyle and for the most part she'd enjoyed having him around. When he was little she'd taken him to the park to play football, she'd pushed him on the swings, even got to know other mums who assumed Kyle was hers. Sometimes she hadn't even corrected them. It wasn't until the last couple of years, when Kyle's life became more problematic and Connie relied on her even more, that Amelia had begun to really question who the parent was supposed to be. But by that time she was so close to Kyle that saying no to her sister would be saying no to him too. And she couldn't bear the thought of that. He didn't have many people in his corner as it was.

Her fingers hovered on her phone as she pondered whether to tell Connie about this, the fact he was in contact with someone who spelled trouble, how she'd caught him with alcohol again.

But she put her phone down, and after doing her teeth took herself off to bed and oblivion.

Maybe tomorrow would be a better day.

5

CLEO

'I hate you!' Ruby shrieked at the top of her voice before running in tears from the kitchen at their home in Connecticut.

Cleo opened the pantry door again in the vain hope that the ingredients to make cupcakes had magically appeared and had been hiding in there all along. They had one egg, no self-raising flour, only demerara sugar and the icing sugar packet was light enough you could've assumed it was empty. She'd meant to check what they had and then go to the store yesterday if necessary, but somehow, in between running the market stalls, the Little Knitting Box, and making sure she'd posted all of her holiday cards to England, it had completely slipped her mind. Ruby had set her alarm this morning to get up extra early and make them before school so they'd be fresh, and she'd been in the kitchen tying on her apron when Cleo sat up in bed remembering what she'd promised. She'd come down to get started and realising they didn't have the ingredients had been like taking a blow to the stomach, the pain enhanced when Ruby screamed at her.

'She didn't mean it.' Dylan's comforting hand rested on Cleo's shoulder. He'd been working in the study but Ruby's voice would've alerted someone from three streets away, it was that loud and venomous.

She shrugged him off. 'I'll drive down to the bakery, see what I can find. I don't have to send twenty-four cupcakes like Ruby wanted, a small container of a few will be enough.' It wouldn't be for Ruby, who was devastated, but it would at least be an effort on her part. She wished Ruby had mentioned the cupcakes again yesterday but she'd been at her mum's after school, no doubt with Prue in her ear about Daddy's other half and how she'd never measure up. There was a brief time Cleo had thought Prue had moved on enough to be mature, to the point where if her own kids were having trouble accepting Cleo, Prue would reason with them and be on Cleo's side. But no such luck. Prue had always liked to cause trouble, and she wouldn't mind betting Ruby would soon be telling her all about this little mishap.

She grabbed her purse and called up the stairs to Ruby, asked her if she'd like to come and help her find something, but she got no answer.

'Leave her to calm down. She needs to shower and get ready for school anyway, and by the time she's done that you'll be back from the bakery with the cakes.' Dylan wrapped Cleo in an enormous hug. It was hard to stay mad at him for long. Not that she really was; it was more frustration that he didn't seem to get how scary it was for her to have Ruby, who had always got on with her famously, suddenly turning against her.

Cleo, thankful the bakery opened so early, didn't take long to return with a good selection of cupcakes, fit for any school bake sale. Some had swirls of chocolate icing on top of fluffy sponge bases, others vanilla, and all of them had pretty stars and heart decorations in silvers and golds. They would sell just as well as anything they made here.

Ruby stayed upstairs until it was time to leave for school. Ordinarily she would've been in the kitchen chatting away, but not today. When she appeared Cleo was transferring the cupcakes from their cardboard carriers to a Tupperware box. She wasn't trying to pass them off as homemade but at least this way Ruby might not feel so uncomfortable. She turned to Ruby waiting for a relieved smile but she didn't get one.

'What's wrong?' Cleo asked as Ruby's face fell when she saw the cupcakes.

'They're not Christmas cupcakes.'

That hadn't been in the brief. 'No, you didn't mention they should be.'

'Duh, it's nearly Christmas. And I told you.' She hadn't. 'Now I'm going to look stupid, because I'll be the only one who forgot.' Her little voice shook and rose as she hurled accusations.

'Ruby, that's enough.' Dylan had come into the kitchen and judging by his face was surprised at how much his daughter was acting up.

'I told her, Dad. I told her they had to be Christmas cupcakes.'

'Whether you did or you didn't isn't really important, you still shouldn't talk to Cleo that way.'

Face screwed up in anger, Ruby snatched up her packed lunch and made for the door.

Cleo and Dylan exchanged a look. 'We need to talk to her.' He'd echoed Cleo's thoughts and she didn't dissuade him this time. But where did they start? 'She can't keep being like this.' His lips brushed her cheek before he followed after Ruby with the Tupperware container.

When the house was quiet Cleo wished she could put her feet up, have a tea or a coffee, or even go back to bed for an hour. But not today. Kaisha was in the city minding the stall and she'd join her later, so first up was a stint at the Inglenook Falls markets ensuring they had plenty of stock at the ready, and then she needed to order in supplies for the Little Knitting Box, restock some of the shelves in there, and make sure her seasonal employee Brianna was set for the day. Even with the extra staff she'd taken on this year, the season and the markets were big money-makers and they'd have plenty for their wedding and a nice honeymoon too. It was part of the reason she'd opted to be so crazy busy, not wanting them to miss out on getting away somewhere, just the two of them. And if Prue dug her heels in and was difficult about having Jacob and Ruby while they were away, her dad had told her on the phone last night when she mentioned the wedding in a year's time that he would be happy to fulfil his grandparenting duties during their visit. It was a lot though, four kids at once, and she'd rather not do it to him unless she had to.

Cleo started at the Inglenook Falls markets and helped local Trish set up. Trish had been in the store one day and volunteered her services on a casual basis as and when Cleo needed her and Cleo had snapped her up. Her kids were older, she didn't have to disappear for the school run, and she knew her stuff when it came to knitting. They unpacked stock from the boxes they'd hauled over from the store, uncovered existing stock from yesterday that they had put a dust sheet over at night before locking up the little hut, and Cleo left confident Trish had everything in hand.

Over at the Little Knitting Box next, Cleo opened up for Brianna and between them they had the shelves tidied, yarn supplies replenished, and Cleo disappeared up to the apartment above so she could log on to the computer and pay invoices as well as reordering. She went onto her Facebook account and responded to a couple of messages and was about to log off when something in her news feed caught her eye. It was Prue and Ruby, photographed at today's bake sale already. Prue must've had someone else take the picture and Cleo tried her best not to let it bother her. They were mother and daughter, their bond was strong and she respected that.

What she didn't approve of, and she knew Dylan shared the sentiment, was Prue stirring up trouble behind their backs.

Ruby had on a new coat, something that instantly niggled Cleo because she'd already been told to make do with the one she had for this season. It fitted her, it was warm, and they weren't going to buy another just because she fancied a change. Prue must've had other ideas and Ruby wouldn't have had to say much for Prue to leap in and buy her the heavy red wool coat she'd been admiring in an online catalogue last month, thus making her the good guy and Cleo the baddie. Prue's behaviour, never mind Ruby's, rankled Cleo. Dylan was a good dad, he never poisoned his kids' minds against his ex-wife even when she blatantly did something untoward like messing him around with times when she could have them or not turning up when she should. She'd done it a couple of months ago and Dylan had had to calm a tearful Ruby when instead of having her daughter for a sleepover, Prue attended a glam party in the city. But even then he hadn't said he agreed that it was a terrible thing to do; he'd comforted Ruby and said he was sure her mum wouldn't have gone if it wasn't really important. Now the kids were getting older, maybe it was time to be a little more honest about Prue and not keep covering for her when she let Ruby and Jacob down.

Cleo looked at the photograph, at Ruby's smiling face. She looked happy enough. Their talk tonight might help to iron out a few issues – who knew, maybe Ruby would get enthusiastic about the wedding and even want to be more involved.

With the Inglenook Falls markets done, the store dealt with and the ordering complete, it was into the city for Cleo. Amelia was going to start helping out tomorrow, so today it was all systems go the second she arrived. Mitch had taken boxes of stock there for her – they still had plenty locked in the chalet overnight from yesterday so it was only a small replenishment – and Kaisha said the morning had been steady. The afternoon was a mad rush from noon until sundown and Kaisha had stayed on to help, but both of them buzzed at the excitement of it all.

When she finally put the key in the lock to their home that evening, Cleo was exhausted. But at least there was laughter and chatter coming from the kitchen – that had to be a good sign.

'Hello,' she called out as she hung up her coat next to Ruby's brand-new red one and made her way in to join her family.

'You're home,' Dylan smiled when he saw her come in. He had the extractor fan going above the cooker while he made Bolognese, Ruby and Jacob's favourite, and Jacob clutched a big bunch of dried spaghetti trying to assess how much was enough.

'Twice that amount will be good,' Cleo told him and leaned down to kiss him on the forehead. 'How was school?'

'Good, I got to eat cake from the bake sale.'

'How many did you have?'

'Two,' he said with confidence.

Cleo picked up Tabitha, who had come charging through from the playroom when she heard her mummy's voice, and cuddled her tiny form against her. Her cheeks were rosy but cold; she'd likely been leaning on the window as she played with her doll's house again. Emily had a rusk and was strapped in the high chair, happy enough. She'd always been placid, didn't demand to be picked up unless she was upset or not feeling well. Cleo guessed it was the chaos in a family with four kids that gave her a natural assumption she'd have to be patient.

'And how many did you eat, Ruby?' Cleo walked over to the table where Ruby was drawing a picture of the bake sale to go with the written account she'd already done beneath.

'Two,' she admitted, changing her coloured pen from red to brown.

'What flavour did you go for?'

'Chocolate.'

'One of ours?'

'No, it was a reindeer, Tyler's mum made them.'

Tyler's mum had one child, didn't work, and a husband whose only worry should be the gardener who spent an awful lot of time round their house supposedly working on land that was no bigger than a postage stamp.

'You weren't too embarrassed supplying non-Christmas-themed cupcakes?' she asked. 'I'm sorry again, Ruby.'

Ruby shrugged. 'Doesn't matter.'

It was then that Cleo spotted the Tupperware container next to Ruby's school bag and it was still full. 'Did you even take them in and give them to your teacher?'

'I was going to talk to you about that.' Dylan appeared at her side with a spoon that he thrust towards Cleo's mouth so she could taste the bolognese. He was trying to win her over and stop a fight, she suspected, and what better way to do it than this? He was good in the kitchen and he generally took over the lion's share of deciding what to have for dinner as well as preparing and cooking it.

'Talk to me about what? Did you leave them in the car?' She looked at Ruby again but she was determined to keep colouring and fixed her eyes to the page.

'She left them in the car,' Dylan confirmed.

Cleo shifted Tabitha to her other hip. 'Then it must've been worse because you would've been the only person not to bring any, surely.'

'Mom made some,' Ruby blurted out, and when Dylan looked the other way Cleo knew Prue had scored another win at making her look like the baddie.

Cleo set Tabitha down when she began to wiggle and let her toddle off towards the playroom again. She joined Dylan by the stove, where he was holding one end of the handful of spaghetti in the boiling water and waiting for it to soften so he could fold the rest in. 'Since when did Prue bake?'

'I doubt she did, the cakes looked shop-bought to me.'

'But they were Christmas-themed. Prue wins again.' She took out a glass from the cupboard and poured a generous measure of red wine.

Dylan turned the heat down now the pasta was cooking, set the button to go on the timer, and gently coaxed her out into the hall, and out of earshot. 'It's not about winning or losing.'

'Isn't it?'

'No, of course not. Prue is her mom, I can't change that. But Ruby loves you. She's being difficult right now but we'll get through this.'

'She never mentioned the cupcakes had to be Christmas-themed, you know.'

'I didn't hear her say it either, but thank you for not arguing the point. Prue would've done.'

They went back through to the kitchen and Cleo entertained Emily with a game of peekaboo from behind the table, making her giggle with glee. Even Ruby seemed amused by her youngest sister and cracked a bit of a smile, something of a rarity in Cleo's presence these days.

When they were eating dinner Cleo asked, 'What were the cupcakes that your mum brought like?' Might as well pretend it didn't bother her.

Jacob was first to describe them when Ruby looked less than enthused and Cleo went along with it as she heard all about the cupcakes with their peppermint frosting topped with red, green and white sprinkles. 'Well, I guess neither of you will want one of our cupcakes for dessert, seeing as you've had two each anyway.'

Jacob's face fell. 'What if I eat all my dinner?'

She sucked the air in through her teeth. 'I suppose I might

consider it if you don't leave anything on your plate – that includes not picking out pieces of mushroom.'

He weighed up whether it would be worth it or not and then re-added a few tiny pieces of the mushroom he'd already scraped to the side of his plate.

'Ruby, that goes for you too.' Dylan nodded towards the pieces of mushroom his daughter had picked out. Whenever Cleo chopped the ingredients for their favourite meal she always remembered to chop the much-hated vegetable so small the kids would never be able to find it, but Dylan frequently forgot.

'I don't want one.'

'Fine,' said Cleo a little too harshly, earning her a look from Dylan. She ate the rest of her dinner in silence unless she was talking to Emily, who sat contentedly in her high chair and didn't need any persuasion although some of the dinner inevitably ended up in her hair every time, with tonight being no exception.

Cleo was tired. She didn't have time for melodramatics; it had been a long day, and the second Tabitha and Emily were finished, she took Emily upstairs for her bath. Getting out of the way with the two easier girls and a glass of wine was a godsend until Ruby came and knocked on the door.

'Daddy sent me up,' she said sullenly.

'Why?'

Ruby looked at the floor. 'I'm sorry I was rude.'

'I do my best, Ruby.' She looked away from her and squeezed the rubber duck in the bath so that it gently squirted water against Emily's chest, making her grin and squeal in delight. She could sense Ruby was still there but she didn't know what else to say. She was fed up being the enemy, too tired to justify herself.

Ruby knelt down beside her and began talking to her little sister. She even picked up the multicoloured plastic umbrella that had raindrop-shaped holes in it to let the water pour out and moved it over Emily's head. Cleo couldn't help but join in with the laughter as Emily gasped in shock at the water in her face before she clapped her hands together at her entertaining half-sister.

'You've got a new coat I see,' said Cleo.

'Mom says she got it on sale. She bought one for Jacob too.'

'Right.' Prue sure liked to bend the truth. Cleo bet there was no sale at all.

Emily soon started fussing and Cleo scooped her out and into her hooded bath towel that was laid on the floor.

'Can I wrap her?' Ruby, who'd been aloof when it came to paying her sisters attention in the last week or so, suddenly wanted to be a part of it all again. Cleo suspected the kid didn't know which way to turn, whether to make Cleo the antagonist and, by association, the babies she'd brought into the world, or whether they could all turn out to be on the same side.

Cleo let Ruby wrap Emily and instead of trying to talk to her about how she was feeling when it came to the bigger picture, her position in her life, they sang to Emily as Ruby helped put her diaper on and Cleo found an outfit for bed. Dylan had taken over with Tabitha's bedtime routine and left them to it, which was probably the best way.

'Thank you for helping, Ruby.' They were sitting in the nursery with soft lullabies playing in the background to help settle Emily before they put her in her cot. Tabitha wouldn't be too far behind, then Ruby and Jacob an hour later. They'd all mastered the routine by now. They had to. Their household would be chaos otherwise.

Ruby let Emily toddle over to her and sit on her lap on the floor.

'I wanted to talk to you, Ruby.'

'About the cakes.'

'Not really about the cakes. More about me and you.'

Ruby had picked up one of Emily's favourite books with a story about a cow and furry animals on each page to touch.

Cleo took her silence as a green light to come out with it. 'I thought we always got on very well. I thought you were happy for me to be a part of your lives – yours, your dad's, Jacob's.'

Ruby shrugged. 'I am.'

'You don't seem it.'

'Mom says blended families never work because you'll always treat me and Jacob differently.'

Cleo tried not to let her temper rise. She'd been right to think Prue had played a part in Ruby's altered mood. 'Differently to Emily and Tabitha?'

Ruby's eyes were glistening with tears and she'd done a good job at hiding it as she played with Emily and the dolly she'd picked up.

'Ruby, please look at me.' Cleo scooped Emily onto her lap for a cuddle and then put the dolly in front of her. She waited for eye contact from Ruby before she continued. 'The only thing that is different is that you already have a mum. But to me, you and Jacob are still my children. You might not call me mum, I may not have grown you in my tummy, but you are just as important to me as Tabitha and Emily.' She could throttle Prue, and Dylan possibly would when she relayed this little gem of a conversation. 'Is this why you've been a bit strange lately?'

'I didn't think you'd notice.'

'Of course I notice. I notice all of our children. Remember the Halloween costumes I made this year?' Ruby's face said she had no idea where this was going. 'I spent hours on yours and Jacob's, then Emily's and Tabitha's I picked up from a second-hand store because I'd forgotten. It doesn't mean I love Emily and Tabitha less than you guys. And then last week when I left Emily's favourite blanket at my gramps' house and made her cry, that wasn't because I love her any less. And today when I bought the wrong cupcakes that weren't Christmas-themed, it was because I'm trying to do a thousand things at once, it's no reflection on the way I feel about you.'

Sheepishly Ruby fiddled with the corner of the shaggy rug on the floor, the surface Emily loved to crawl through and squish her face against. 'I never said they were supposed to be Christmas cupcakes.'

'I know you didn't,' Cleo said softly, reaching out to tug at Ruby's hand until Ruby came and sat next to her and Emily. 'Tell you what, let's get the girls to bed, your daddy can hang with Jacob, then how about you and I watch the end of the Santa Claus movie?'

'But it's a school night.'

'I think we can make the exception just this once.'

'Can we eat one of your cupcakes?'

'Did you eat all of your dinner? I can't treat you any differently to Jacob.'

'I ate it all, ask Dad.'

'No need.' She lowered Emily into her cot and turned on the mobile above.

When they were down in the lounge room with the movie playing and the empty paper cases from their cupcakes discarded, Cleo felt Ruby snuggle up next to her as she'd done plenty of times before, just not in the last couple of weeks since talk about finally getting moving with wedding organisation had started.

Cleo had never liked Prue all that much but she tolerated her, so did Dylan, because she'd always be in their lives. But if she was intent on causing trouble by feeding Ruby with false information then they'd have their work cut out for them. She only hoped tonight was a step in the right direction. She wanted to get married surrounded by family and friends who were happy for them; she didn't want anyone thinking this was a terrible mistake.

6

NATHAN

Nathan carefully sat himself down at the breakfast table in the dining room at the Inglenook Inn, and Scarlett didn't miss a thing.

'What's going on with you? Why are you moving like an old man?' She thanked Rupert for the pancakes she'd ordered for both of them while Nathan had finished up in the shower.

'Nothing,' he said.

'Liar. Don't tell me you're still hurting from the ice-skating the other day.'

'My body isn't built for those sorts of activities. I used muscles I didn't even know I had, but it's the bruise on my arse that's the problem.'

'I'll take your word for it, don't do anything crazy like try to show me.'

He tucked in to the double blueberry pancakes and a large glass of juice. 'You were always covered in bruises when you were little. So many of my photos are ruined because of your legs.'

She rolled her eyes and changed the subject by asking what the plan was for today.

'Nothing that involves me balancing on two wafer-thin blades.'

'That's a shame. One of my aims is to skate in every rink in the city before we leave.'

She almost had him fooled. 'Very funny. I don't mind being the photographer if you really want to do it.'

'I'd like to go at least one more time, but not yet, my legs are a bit achy too.'

'Ah, so youth didn't win this time round.'

'You run a lot, your legs should take it.'

'And you haven't run for a long time. Why did you lose interest?'

'You kept going in the rain, I had to do cross country at school – I guess the novelty wore off.'

Or maybe her interest in spending time with her dad was starting to wane, and maybe there was nothing he could do about it. He wondered how much of it was down to her age and how much was because she still resented his disastrous parenting in the early years, some of which she could still remember. She didn't talk about it often but occasionally she made a remark that left him wanting to ask more yet not wanting to know in case the answer upset him. A few weeks ago she'd made a comment about him not showing up to her nativity play once – she'd said that in front of some good friends of the family who had a younger child proud to be playing the Virgin Mary this year. And a few months ago Scarlett had told him to stop worrying about her so much, she was a big girl now, and she'd made an underhand remark about how he should've used up all his worrying in the younger years when she actually needed it.

'Why don't we start with Lower Manhattan this morning?' he suggested.

'The 9/11 memorial? Are you sure?'

'Why wouldn't I be?'

'Because I know you, Dad.'

She didn't miss much. Her uncle Robbie, his brother, would've loved this girl had he ever got to meet her, but he'd been killed on that fateful day. Not in the terror attacks but when he was knocked over by a car at a zebra crossing in a sleepy village back in England. There wasn't ever a chance the anniversary of his death would go by without Nathan and his family remembering it, turning their minds back to the call that had come to say he was in the hospital. The world would remember 9/11 and with every anniversary, Nathan's family had their own private pain on top of the shock and devastation shared with so many others.

'I'll be fine,' he assured Scarlett.

'No you won't. You lost your brother, it'll never be *fine*.'

Memories resurfaced and it always helped to talk about them. 'Do you know, he was your nan's little cling-on when we were growing up.'

'I can't imagine that. He always sounded really independent.'

He'd said so much about his brother over the years it was as though Scarlett knew Robbie too. 'I've no idea when it changed. Mum says that one minute he was clinging to her leg not wanting to be separated, the next he'd gone off to high school and barely turned back. He had a fiery ambition; he travelled all over the world and he had a ten-year career plan with ideas of retiring in the wilderness of Canada of all places.'

'I wish I'd met him.'

'Yeah, me too. He was a good guy. A little terror when he was younger though. He was forever playing pranks at school, getting into trouble. He did the classic whoopee cushion on the teacher's chair, the cling film over the toilet bowl in the *girls'* toilet. I'm serious,' he said at Scarlett's shock. 'And he once set off the school fire alarm because he hadn't revised for his physics test and with it being the end of the day knew they'd have to postpone it.'

'You must miss him a lot.' Scarlett finished her last mouthful of pancake and declared she was too full for anything else, even another drink. 'Were you jealous he did so much and you were stuck at home being a parent?'

'Of course not. Well, maybe just a little.' She didn't come back with a rebuke, comment on his bad parenting she either recalled or had heard about. 'But he was very different to me. He never could've stuck an office job, especially one that had the long hours I was faced with. You know, Robbie asked your mum out once.'

'No way.'

'They went to a dance. She was way too young for him – her parents were not happy at all, ours weren't that impressed either.'

'Did they date after that?'

'No, Dawn says she came to her senses quickly and chose the right brother.' He smiled. 'I never told Robbie that, I didn't want to upset him, but I think he kind of knew anyway. Your mum was a homebody; she wasn't interested in travelling the world and leaving all that she knew. He got over her pretty quick. Two weeks later and he was dating Sara, one of the hottest and most experienced – if you know what I mean – barmaids at the local pub. I think he was pretty happy.'

'Ew, Dad. That's too much information.'

'I wish you could've met him. He'd have loved you. That, or he would've led you astray.' He demolished his pancakes quick enough and the juice too. 'Robbie was also all about seizing the day, so come on, let's go before I get too miserable. We could do Ground Zero then walk the Brooklyn Bridge and leave all the busyness behind.'

'You've a funny idea of what leaving busyness behind actually means. From what I've heard, the Brooklyn Bridge will be a sea of people.'

'I might have to make you hold my hand so you don't get lost.'

'No chance.' But she smiled at his suggestion. 'We'll walk over the bridge, find somewhere for lunch.'

They were soon out and about for father-and-daughter time. Here in a city where they knew nobody, where there wasn't the pressure of friends or school, it was great to see Scarlett so vibrant and enjoying herself. She had an energy she lacked at home and despite the winter chill that hung amongst the skyscrapers and followed them down every street, she was full of enthusiasm, ready for adventure. It reminded him of the little girl she'd once been, the fact that the same girl was still in there somewhere.

Ground Zero was a sombre affair and while the memorial was impressive and tasteful, it didn't detract from the flood of emotion he felt seeing all those names engraved into the stone. It was confronting, yet people went about their everyday lives around it, talking and laughing, some leaning up against the memorial and the names of the victims. A strong beam of sunlight made him catch his breath. It didn't matter how a person was taken from you, the resulting effect was the same. Devastation, pain, a wondering of how you could possibly go on.

They didn't hang around long and, with a coffee each from the first cart they saw, Nathan led the way to the Brooklyn Bridge, negotiating the throng of pedestrians, the traffic fumes that were part of this vibrant city. And after they'd thrown their empty cups in the bin, Scarlett asked, 'Ready to see Brooklyn?'

He pulled her into a hug and she didn't resist. 'You bet,' he whispered into her hair.

Seeing the pain his parents were in when they lost Robbie was something Nathan never, ever forgot. The family home was blanketed in sadness, stifled with an inability to carry on. And it was Robbie who had been in his head when Dawn died, telling Nathan to step up and be a real man and stop shirking his responsibilities. He could imagine his brother saying those exact words because Robbie had always been independent, daring, a bit on the wild side, but he never forgot birthdays or family celebrations and when he was home he immersed himself in everyone around him and had no problem showing love and appreciation. Nathan had always wanted to be like him as a kid and when he was left as a single parent, something inside his head snapped. Instead of resisting parenthood, he embraced it; instead of being afraid, he leapt in and got on with it. And, for the most part, he was convinced it had worked.

The Brooklyn Bridge afforded spectacular views of the Manhattan skyline, the feeling of openness near the water, although the cold winds soon had them craving a warm café for lunch. They were swallowed in crowds, they posed for a selfie with the wind whipping Scarlett's hair around her face as she desperately attempted to hold it back. And when they eventually reached the other side she suggested they go see 'The Braves of 9/11' street art.

Nathan was no art lover but standing there, looking up at the building towering above them, the artwork on the side that spoke of the heartache, the sorrow, the pain, the bravery and courage, it almost swallowed him whole and he could see the emotion on Scarlett's face, feel it through the grip of her gloved hand in his. The details and the depth of feeling captured by this artist, were something else with its bright, vivid colours. It was hard to reconcile misery and devastation with the hope that this mural somehow magically gave.

Scarlett took photographs while he waited and when they were done he hailed a cab to take them all the way up the Upper West Side of Manhattan.

Nathan led the way when they got out of the cab until they were standing in front of a picturesque café Scarlett had seen in one of her favourite movies.

A broad smile had her turning to him. 'You've Got Mail!' Out front of Cafe Lalo she threw her arms around him. 'Can we go in?'

'Of course. It's a real place, you know.'

She shoved him with her elbow. 'Funny man.'

A red neon sign above the door led the way as they went up the steps. Inside, they chose a slice of cake each, although Scarlett took her own sweet time with so many choices. They sat down by the window looking out at the street and the white lights winding up the bark of one of the trees.

'This is the most exciting city in the world,' Scarlett declared when the waiter delivered a cake he couldn't quite remember the name of with a silky chocolate mousse-like top and curls of choco-late. 'I feel like Meg, although you don't look much like Tom.'

Nathan had never loved movies as much as Scarlett; her appre-ciation of art didn't come from him either – Dawn had been the one responsible for both things. He sometimes needed to remember Scarlett was growing into a fine woman and he wasn't always going to like her choices. Why had nobody warned him that grazed knees, tears, and tantrums would be replaced by parental uncertainty as your child grew up and became independent? What he really wanted now was for her to talk to him, share with him the things she wouldn't have hesitated to tell her mum if she was still alive.

'Well, I'm glad you're having a good time,' he said, 'even if your old man couldn't pass as a movie star.'

'You're not that old at all.' She picked off a chocolate curl with her fingers and let it melt on her tongue. 'Most of my friends' dads are ancient, in their forties, one is in his fifties.'

'Hardly ancient. And remember I was ridiculously young when I became a dad.'

'I'm kind of glad though, it means you can keep up with me.'

'I do my best.'

'What did you think to the street art we saw in Brooklyn?'

'I was surprised how good it was.'

'See, and there you were thinking all art was a waste of time.'

'I never said that,' he protested when he'd swallowed a mouthful of cake.

'Art is my favourite subject at school,' she admitted.

'I know it is.' Her teachers did too and they commented on her talent at every parents' evening. 'And I expect it's a release from the harder subjects.' She'd elected to do art at A level but also business studies and French, the compromise he'd insisted upon so she had some qualifications that might give her more options.

'It's hardly a doddle, I work hard at it.'

'I know, and a range of subjects will help you in the future. I'd hate to see you struggle when it comes to finding a job. It's hard enough as it is.'

'Jobs are ages off, Dad.'

'You'll be looking before you know it.'

'I'll look for something creative, a job where I can use my artistic talents,' she announced with a flourish.

He would've laughed if the topic of conversation wasn't so serious. 'Nice idea, but remember, you'll have to pay the bills. Your mum was good at art too, but she saw that it was a hobby, it wasn't going to give her stability.'

Scarlett's fork clanked against the china plate although the cake was clearly too good for her to let the cutlery go completely. 'That's a very narrow-minded view.'

'Excuse me.'

'I'm not being rude, but don't you see that it is? I thought you might get it after seeing the mural today. Or the 9/11 memorial, which was only built after thousands of submissions to do the design.'

He put his own fork down. Sometimes she was too intelligent for her own good. 'Perhaps it was a narrow-minded comment, but I'm trying to think of you, help you in the long run.' Now if she were to show an interest in building design, it might be something he could get on board with, but when she was talking about painting or murals, throwing her energies into those facets of her education, it felt impossible to accept.

'Did mum regret not pursuing her art?' Scarlett asked. 'Or were you never around long enough to ask her?'

'That's a little unfair.' And the candid question had taken him by surprise. 'Your mum died so young, she never really had a chance for regrets.'

Eyes downcast, Scarlett finished her cake in silence.

When he'd finished his own he said, 'Your artistic ability is all down to Dawn. All her genes, I assure you.'

'I certainly don't get it from you,' she teased, braving looking at him once again. 'What? I saw that map you sketched out on the plane when you couldn't use your phone and were trying to remember where we were staying in relation to some of the biggest landmarks. And I've seen some of your doodles, remember.'

He took out his wallet, fished in the leather pocket behind all his credit cards, took out a small drawing on the back of one of his business cards and turned it over. 'Your mum drew that not long before she died. I thought I'd lost it but I found it in the zip-up pocket of the suitcase before we left to come here.'

'Is that me?' Her eyes glistened. 'And you?'

'She brought you into my work one day, you loved coming to the office. You'd sit on the spinny chair, tap away at my keyboard, you even wrote on the whiteboard once but with a permanent marker.'

'I never.'

'You did. You drew a picture of a seal balancing a ball on the tip of its nose – you'd just been to the zoo.'

'Did I get you in trouble?' She was transfixed by the black-and-white sketch that Dawn had drawn using a biro as she watched her daughter and husband together, heads almost touching as he showed her something on his computer screen.

'No, the boss found it funny from what I recall.'

'Did Mum draw a lot?'

'She did, she loved to draw whatever was around at the time.'

'I don't remember seeing many pictures.'

'I put most of them in the loft.'

'Why? Why didn't you share that part of her with me?'

'I'm sorry.' He gripped her hand across the table. 'I'm afraid I packed everything away years ago because I didn't want it to get damaged, and the more time went on, I suppose I couldn't bear to go through it. I knew it would be painful for me, for you. And my memories are in here.' He patted his heart. 'I don't need pictures when your mum will always be in glorious technicolour for me. I saved everything for you, and I probably should've told you earlier but it never felt like a good time.'

'I'm sixteen, Dad, you need to let me grow up sometime, realise I can handle things.'

'I know, I'll try harder to remember, promise.'

She smiled. 'I like hearing about her.'

'I'm glad.'

'Knowing that my love of art came from her is comforting. Does that make sense?'

'It does.' He'd been in denial, assuming that her artistic flair was something she would ignore in favour of more academic subjects that would set her up better employment-wise. It was one of the top topics for them to clash about at home, had been for a long time. Desperate to keep the moment of bonding going, he suggested, 'When we get back home to England, how about I climb up into the loft and bring everything down for you? You can go through it, chuck whatever you don't want, keep what you do.'

'Dad... tell me more about her.' She sat forwards, all ears, and he revelled in the conversation as they talked more about Dawn when she was Scarlett's age: their similarities, their differences.

'Your mum didn't get on well at school,' he admitted, 'unlike you. I don't deny you're good at art but you're also very able when it comes to all your other subjects. School was always a struggle for Dawn, she didn't enjoy it, but she worked very hard to become a nurse because she knew it was a good career. She had her daydreams but she was a very grounded, realistic person. She never stopped drawing in her spare time though. You'll know what I mean when you see all her sketches.'

'I have a whole heap of my own.'

'I know, strewn over every worktop in your bedroom.' But he was smiling. He'd never once demanded she clear them up – it was a little piece of her that reminded him of Dawn.

When Nathan was Scarlett's age, he also thought he knew exactly which direction he was headed in. He had dreams of a medical career, becoming a top surgeon someday, but right before he was about to start university his then girlfriend, Dawn, fell pregnant and he had no choice but to step up. And that meant rethinking his ambitions, with finances being a top concern. His parents supported them, both him and Dawn moving in with them, and although he wanted to get work straight away, they encouraged him to see the bigger picture, get an education and a better job at the end of it. While not the medical career he'd once dreamed of, his choice of going into business and finance was a worthy one, a path his own father had followed, and with a quicker finish time than medicine would've ever allowed.

After Scarlett was born, Nathan and Dawn got married. Dawn trained as a nurse and excelled in her new career, with Nathan studying until he graduated and then securing a good job in London with an investment bank, and they saved up enough to find a place of their own. But as Nathan's career took off, so did his social life and the theory of being a supportive husband and father who was always there was something he struggled with. He got into the habit of staying out drinking with his colleagues, relishing the camaraderie, the lack of responsibility. He and Dawn had fought many times about his absences but it hadn't stopped him. It was as though at home he had to be this one person, at work he could escape and be another entirely. It was immature and selfish, but at the time he couldn't see it. At least not until he lost Dawn and was forced to pull himself together and parent in a way that Scarlett needed and deserved.

'I know you think I'm wrong.' Scarlett scooped the froth of her coffee from the side of the mug. 'But I figure if I do something that I have a passion for, then maybe it'll lead me to a career I never thought of.'

'I worry you'll narrow your options by only focusing on what you love.' He wanted to encourage her, help her make the right choices, just as his parents had done with him. 'Yours is a good way of thinking about it, but don't deny yourself future opportunities by writing off the subjects you're not as excited about. The other, more academic—'

'Boring, you mean.'

'None of your subject choices will be a waste; they might even help you.'

She must've read the concerned look on his face because she said, 'I'm working hard at all my A levels, not just art, Dad.'

'Good to hear it.' She had an undeniable talent for art, but at GCSE level he'd got her a tutor to ensure she did well in other areas too. Maybe he'd have to do the same again so that business studies and French were as much of a focus as art was for the next couple of years. Then again, if he went on about it too much, he might just push her too far and before he knew it she'd move out and never look back. 'I think it's time we walked off this cake,' he suggested. Enough being paranoid about the future, at least for now.

Scarlett took out the fold-up map. 'I wouldn't mind seeing some

Christmas markets – Darcy told me there are quite a few. There's a new one on Garland Street not far from the inn.'

He peered over at the map. 'You haven't been folding it up properly.' He noted the creases in various places where she'd crumpled it to shove it in her pocket.

'Doesn't matter, still works perfectly fine.'

He resisted arguing the point. Maybe letting go of a bit of control could be good for the both of them. 'I'm happy to check out the Christmas markets, but maybe later. I'd like to take you up the Empire State Building next, then go to Times Square. Both will look spectacular in the dark and if we set off now the sun will probably be starting to disappear by the time we get there. And it's not too far to walk back to the inn afterwards.'

'Deal, as long as we can check out the Winter Village at Bryant Park. It's near there,' she explained, finding it on the map to prove her point. 'It has an ice rink.'

'Nice try, but I'm not up for another stint just yet.' They pulled on their coats, ready for the off.

'Chicken.' The way she smiled told him she'd be testing her powers of persuasion later.

He wouldn't have it any other way.

* * *

Nathan and Scarlett found their way back to the Inglenook Inn after the lights and buzz of Times Square, preceded by a memorable trip up the Empire State Building that gave them a different viewpoint of the city, almost like a model village with its tiny cars dotted on the streets, buildings that looked less imposing now they were dwarfed by their counterpart. They'd passed on visiting Bryant Park on the way back; even Scarlett had seen sense, with their energy levels well and truly ready for a refuel.

They stepped up to the brownstone, the huge wreath on the door made up of different textured leaves, deep-red berries, a bit of sparkle and the tartan bow to finish, a welcoming sight. Miniature pine trees framed the heavy dark-wood door and the second you stepped inside you were drawn in by the garlands winding all the way up the banisters with the delicate lights, the fireplace already going in the communal lounge, and the huge Christmas tree that emitted its scent around the entire space. Nathan was sure they wouldn't have felt anywhere near this comfortable in a hotel.

'I think I need to go lie down upstairs,' he declared, feeling at home, when Scarlett flopped down on the big sofa.

Darcy beckoned him in. 'Nonsense, you can relax here. The fire is for your benefit, not mine,' she smiled. 'Actually, it's for mine too.'

He sat next to Scarlett and Darcy reminded them they could eat here if they couldn't face going out again.

Scarlett kept her voice low so she didn't offend Darcy. 'I've got my heart set on one of those big floppy slices of pizza from a take-away joint.'

'Don't tell me,' he sighed, 'like they do in the movies. They don't look all that appetizing to me.'

Darcy wasn't in the least offended they wanted to venture out again after they'd topped up their energy and as Nathan sat back Darcy asked his daughter all about her favourite movies. They talked location spots in the city, some of which Scarlett had heard of, others she made a mental note to drag him to no doubt.

Darcy adjusted an ornamental fir cone dusted in frost on the tree by the window. 'If you want street food and you're keen to check out the Christmas markets, plus you don't want to walk too far, then I've got the perfect solution.' From the desk she plucked a leaflet, colourful and with 'The Garland Street Markets' emblazoned on the front. 'This is the first year these markets have run and it's a bit of a smaller set-up than some but should have what you're looking for. I have a friend running a knitting stall there this year.' She gave them the gist of the directions and turned the leaflet over to show a map. 'It's not far from here and the market runs along the sidewalk of Garland Street for just over a block.'

'I'm still getting used to words like sidewalk and block,' Scarlett admitted as she got up to nose at the ornaments hanging on the tree.

'How's Myles?' Nathan asked. They'd been texting but he was always so busy.

'He's working hard.'

'He's like his dad,' said Nathan.

'Don't let him hear you say that.'

'I thought things had settled down between them. Not that he told me much, we're men after all, but I got the impression he enjoyed spending time with his family nowadays.'

'He does, but what his dad did in the past was let his relationships suffer because he worked too much.' She gave a tentative smile. 'Myles doesn't want that to happen.'

'I don't blame him. And in our line of work there's a lot of burnout. Neither of you deserves that.'

'Thank you.'

'You seem busy too, and this place is wonderful.'

'Myles and I are both guilty of being very career-driven. I'm so glad you like it here, but I can't take all the credit.'

'I bet you could take quite a bit.'

'Thank you. I do love working here, even when it's crazy busy.'

When her smile didn't quite reach her eyes, he got back to talking markets. 'I think we'll give these a try.' He indicated the leaflet.

'You'll enjoy them; they're only a twenty-five minute stroll away.'

'Sounds good to me. And there's no ice rink by the sounds of it, so I won't be forced to try balancing on ridiculously thin blades again.

'Heard that,' Scarlett called from her position by the window. She was mesmerised by the tree, admiring the decorations. She turned to Darcy. 'Where are all these from?'

'Some are new, some go way back. This one is from Sofia's daughter, who lived in Switzerland for a long time until she came back to New York a few weeks ago.' Beneath her fingers was a cow bell, gold, with the Swiss flag on its front. 'These *Nutcracker* ornaments are from my sister, then there's a ballet shoe somewhere.'

'Here, found it.' Scarlett pointed to one of the upper branches. 'Were you a dancer?'

'Hardly, but I love the *Nutcracker* ballet and try to go every year. It always reminds me of the start of Christmas and I like having ornaments that remind me of places.'

'We're the same, at home we have things I made when I was little – some are a bit embarrassing – and whenever we go somewhere new Dad and I collect another couple if we can.'

'It's true,' Nathan admitted. 'Last year she had a school trip to Edinburgh and came back with a dancing Scotsman playing a pipe, the year before I was at a conference in Miami and brought back a Miami Dolphins snow globe. Hey, I didn't say they were tasteful ornaments,' he added when Darcy pulled a face.

'You know, I worked in London for a time,' she told Scarlett. 'See if you can spot the five London icon tree decorations.' She excused herself to go see to a couple who'd just come in the door and were hanging their coats in the hallway, their banter debating whether it was cold enough to snow yet.

'Whoever finds them first has to eat whatever the other one wants tonight,' Nathan declared.

'You're on.' Scarlett scanned the tree, counting at the same time, and was already at five before he'd even found his second. There was a big red London bus, a Beefeater guard, a London taxi, a Royal Mail post box, and a traditional red telephone box.

Looked like they were having floppy pizza.

* * *

Bundled up against the cold, Nathan found the walk to be a nice way to get the spring back in his step. As lovely as it was back at the Inglenook Inn, he would've fallen asleep if he'd sat in front of the fire much longer.

'I think this is it.' They arrived at the corner of a block and Nathan pointed ahead to the chalets.

'Pizza first, browse after.'

'Never thought I'd hear you say that when shopping was an option.'

'Darcy said there's a pizza vendor right on the end and it's proper New York pizza.'

He followed her, negotiating tourists rushing this way and that as the wind picked up and a light drizzle seemed to turn to crystal and give them the first taste of snow in the city.

'What do you think?' They stood on the pavement attempting to eat the pizza, which was as floppy as they saw on television, as difficult to pick up as he'd imagined but surprisingly tasty with its herbs and stringy cheese. He folded it in half lengthways to stop his toppings sliding off and enable him to eat it much faster. He hadn't realised how hungry he was – their snatched lunch after touring various sites and the amount of walking today had left his appetite wanting.

'Next time we'll try a hot dog,' Scarlett declared. 'And pretzels. And bagels.'

'I'll have to get you out running when we're home if we're going to eat everything in sight.'

'We'll see.'

The potential assent was enough to give him hope. They perused the stalls – an impressive array given the size of the market – with pastries galore, chocolate creations, cheeses laid out tantalisingly ready to tempt, gingerbread enticing youngsters and grown-ups with its rich, buttery aroma, preserves, soaps, roasted chestnuts, and a cider cart.

Scarlett pointed ahead. 'There's the knitting stall Darcy told us about, let's check it out.'

'I might grab some roasted chestnuts first.'

'The pizza wasn't enough?'

'You're about half my size.'

'True.'

While his daughter went to wade through clothing and accessories he waited for a portion of roasted chestnuts, which never failed to remind him of home. His dad had always adored them – they'd been his favourite festive treat and he'd always insisted on using the fire pit they had out back. The first Christmas without Robbie, Nathan hadn't expected the fire pit to get any use, he thought it might bring back too many painful memories, but his dad had been outside doing his thing as though it brought him solace. Which was more than could be said of the Christmas dinner. His mum was still in pieces, Nathan and his dad had cooked it between them and held her up in the absence of the missing member of their family.

His dad had won Dawn over with the roasted chestnuts the year she was heavily pregnant with Scarlett, and right after Dawn died and Nathan had struggled through his and Scarlett's grief and their first Christmas without her, with a sense of déjà vu set fast in his mind from having once before had to deal with a missing person at a key time of the year, they'd gone to his parents. When they arrived, without uttering a word his dad had taken out the cast-iron pan, tarnished from years of use above the flames, looked over at Nathan and he'd followed his dad outside while he lit the coals in the fire pit. Once it was going, Nathan showed Scarlett how to rinse and score the shells of the nuts, then they'd taken the morsels out to her grandad, who'd put them all into the frying pan and held them over glowing coals, the ritual like a balm for their pain. The chestnuts never took long to release the potent yet comforting smell and the family had sat there beneath blankets, thankful for each other, drawing strength from the people in the present, reflecting with sadness on all that they had lost.

'Dad,' Scarlett frowned at him now, at the markets, as she grabbed his sleeve. 'I've been calling you for ages.'

'Sorry, miles away.'

She nicked a chestnut and popped it in her mouth, the heat coming out in puffs when she realised how hot it still was.

'Serves you right for taking it without asking,' he grinned.

She managed to chew it eventually and pointed to the end of the row of chalets. 'What do you say?'

'What are we looking at?'

'You need glasses, I'm telling you.'

'No I don't.' Actually, he probably did. In all their traipsing of New York streets it was Scarlett who spotted the names high up on their signs first; he took longer to focus.

'It's a Christmas tree stall.'

'And...?'

'Why don't we get one for our suite at the inn?'

'Darcy offered us a tree, remember, and we agreed to just appreciate the trees all around the city – we wouldn't have our decorations anyway.'

'I know what I said, but I didn't realise how much I'd miss that smell when I woke up in the morning. I want it so bad.' Her hands were together against her chest in prayer.

'You sound about four years old.'

'It's not Christmas without a tree when I wake up.'

'Go downstairs to the communal lounge in your PJs, Darcy won't mind.'

She nicked another chestnut. 'It's not the same and you know it. Come on, you love a tree as much as I do. And who knows how many Christmases we might have left, what with me growing up and possibly flying the nest?'

He clutched his hand to his heart. 'You know how to get me. Okay then, suppose we get a tree, how are we going to get it back to the inn? It's a twenty-five-minute walk and I can't see you helping to carry it.'

'I'm no weakling.'

'Ask if they deliver. If they do, you're on. If they don't, forget it.'

She clapped her hands together, stole his last roasted chestnut, and skipped off towards the tree chalet. He had to admit, he'd missed having a tree too, but without the ornaments it seemed a bit pointless. Darcy had already told them that she had a whole stash if they changed their mind about a tree and so he fired off a text to check and the reply he got back told him that the man, Mitch, running the stall was actually her supplier when it came to trees anyway, and that she was sure he'd deliver it for them if they were desperate to choose one tonight.

He thought he recognised the girl at the knitting stall as he walked past, carried along in a wave by the crowd, but he was in a city where he knew nobody, it was impossible. When he reached the tree stall, its chalet with a garland on the door, he spotted a young lad with his back to them, taking payment, flanked by two trees bedecked with white lights. There had to be at least twenty trees on display and the debris on the street that a man was sweeping up showed plenty had been here before but were already sold.

'Found anything?' he asked Scarlett, who was admiring a tree in the middle of a big bunch.

'How about this one?' she suggested.

'Can't really tell when it's leaning against all the others.'

She squeezed in closer. 'Looks about the right height, taller than me, probably slightly smaller than you.'

'Is that your accurate method for measuring a tree?' he mused.

'May I help you?' It was the man who'd been sweeping the ground when Nathan arrived. 'You interested in this tree?' When Scarlett nodded he tugged it up tall and held on to the trunk so they could see it in its full glory.

'It's taller than me,' Nathan pointed out to Scarlett.

'Do you deliver?' she asked the man.

'Sorry, afraid I don't.'

Scarlett's face fell. Time for Nathan to come in and save the day. 'I had a sneaky feeling you'd say that, but I messaged the manager, the wife of a friend of mine, at the accommodation where we're staying and she said you might be able to help me out as a special favour.'

'And who is this manager?' His breath came out white on the wintry Manhattan air.

'Darcy, she runs the Inglenook Inn.'

'You should've led with that.' A smile spread across the man's face. He'd looked serious when Nathan first clapped eyes on him but was much friendlier now. He extended a hand for Nathan to shake. 'I'm Mitch, good to meet you. And Darcy is a good friend, she knows my partner well – long story – so I'd be happy to do you a favour. My truck is parked down the street so I can bring the tree to you when I finish up here.'

'Great, how much for this one?'

They dealt with the preliminaries, Scarlett not able to stop herself leaning in to smell the tree, and Mitch asked the lad who'd been lurking earlier to come net the tree to make it easier to transport.

The lad kept his head down and only really looked at Scarlett, a hushed conversation exchanged between them as she watched him operate the netting machine to pull the tree tightly closed, his back still to Nathan. At least the tree wouldn't be like the one he'd bought last year from outside a local pub that had left so many pine needles in his car that it was like the floor of a forest until he'd taken the vacuum to it. He pushed his wallet back in his pocket after he'd paid and looked around for a drinks cart. All that pizza with its salty cheese and then the nuts had made him thirsty. Scarlett was still talking away to her new-found friend and he was about to wave to her to move on when the moonlight caught the lad's face and Nathan saw exactly who it was. He was the boy who'd stolen the money from the ground that evening in Madison Square Park, the same lad who'd stolen his wallet in Cornwall.

He was about to storm over and wrench Scarlett away when a woman came his way holding two steaming cups of hot chocolate and handed one of them to the boy.

It was then he realised he'd been hit with a double whammy. Because she was the girl on the knitting stall he thought he'd recognised when he walked past, but had told himself he was imagining things.

And, by the way they were glaring at him, they knew exactly who he was too.

7

AMELIA

'What is he looking at?' Amelia bristled and muttered the rhetorical question under her breath as she stood with Kyle drinking the hot chocolate she'd found from the artisan stall at the end of the row. She'd been working on the knitting stall for the last two hours, Cleo had sent her to take a break so she could check on Kyle, and she'd go back for an hour or so to finish up. She hadn't expected to find Kyle dealing with this man's scrutiny, again.

Kyle had barely spoken to her ever since she'd found him with the bottle of vodka, apart from asking for the headache tablets the morning after. She'd made some quip about how he wouldn't need them if he'd waited until the right age to have a drink and his body could handle it. And since then he'd been cordial but hadn't entered into much voluntary conversation.

Ignoring the man who was still looking their way and seemed to be with the girl Kyle couldn't take his eyes off, she asked, 'How's it all going over here?'

'I haven't stolen anything, if that's what you're implying.'

'Kyle, for goodness' sake, that wasn't what I meant.'

He locked eyes with her about to retaliate but then thought better of it. 'I know, I'm being a twat.'

He'd made her laugh. 'Hey, your description not mine.'

'I'm sorry I've been such a tosser the last few days.'

'You're getting these descriptions spot on.'

'Okay, no need to go on about it. But I'm sorry, all right? I shouldn't have taken the vodka, or been rude to you.'

She looked around, relieved to find the man had gone. It meant she could focus on Kyle as he finished his hot chocolate, threw the cup in the bin, and took over the task of sweeping up the ground without being asked. She smiled a hello to Mitch as he helped another customer select a tree. Hands warmed with her own hot chocolate, she reached out and gave Kyle a hug and he did well to wait a few seconds before shrugging her off.

As he got back to work she tackled what they hadn't managed to address after the vodka incident. 'I thought your friend had gone to prison? The one you were talking to on the iPad,' she added for clarification.

He stopped for a moment before carrying on, the broom swishing the damp pavement. He bent down to scoop up the debris, which he threw into a box beside the chalet. 'He did, he's out. He's not exactly a mass murderer.'

'He's not someone who's a good influence either.'

'I know, but he's a mate. He called me, not the other way round, I could hardly hang up on him, could I?'

'I don't want to see you led into anything you don't want to do.'

'Stop treating me like one of your hopeless work case studies.'

'They're not hopeless; actually, the kids are a whole lot like you.'

'Well I'm not a project you get to succeed or fail with.'

'I know you're not; you're my nephew.'

She let Kyle work while she finished her drink. At least he was talking, although he'd probably finished his drink so fast so he wouldn't be stuck having to talk to her for too long. 'I'd better get back to the knitting stall.'

'Bye.' He didn't look up.

One last effort. 'What do you say to getting a tree for our apartment?'

That got his attention. 'It would feel more like Christmas.'

'Exactly. And we can buy some ornaments – nothing too fancy, just enough that it's not bare or really sad. I'm sure we could get some bargains if we search hard enough.' She watched him, happy to see him so relaxed when he didn't have his guard up. It showed a hint of his little-boy charm, which she knew was still there deep down, it was just that sometimes you really had to delve to find it.

* * *

The next morning Amelia woke to the smell of Christmas in their apartment even before the heating system kicked in and although it was bare, having been delivered by Mitch only late last night, the tree was still magical to see. She'd messaged Cleo to ask whether she knew the best place for cheap ornaments and she'd told her not to buy too much because Darcy had plenty for her own guests with more to spare.

'I've sorted some ornaments, which I'll pick up later this evening,' she told Kyle as he came out of his room to make a cup of tea. 'But I'm still going out to find some of our own, perhaps a few we could take home to England for souvenirs.'

'I'll come.'

'You don't have to, you go back to bed for a bit if you like.'

'No chance. I want to make sure you don't choose anything too hideous.'

She ruffled his hair before he could escape and she wished Connie could see the way he was when he didn't have everyone on his back, when he was away from the norm. The vodka hadn't been a very good example, but the way Kyle was now, offering his company without having to be begged, was something Amelia knew her sister had forgotten. All this talk of throwing him out of the house if he didn't change was because Connie didn't see how badly he needed help. Connie had let Amelia swoop in to the rescue more and more lately, as though she was tired of parenting, and Amelia hated seeing the way Kyle and his mum's relationship was heading. They'd end up estranged for good at this rate.

Her mind back on the holiday and this magnificent city, Amelia and Kyle set off with a map of the stores they wanted to go to and a budget in mind. Amelia wanted to choose a few extras to make the tree theirs. They'd collect more decorations from Darcy tonight because they'd both been invited over to the Inglenook Inn for drinks. Kyle had said no at first until Amelia assured him it wouldn't just be women. There would be a male cohort including Mitch, Kyle's temporary boss, whom he got on very well with, and Myles, Darcy's husband.

It didn't take long to find what they were looking for and back at the apartment they sifted through their selections. They'd picked up New York baubles in midnight blue with the golden skyline of Manhattan and Santa in his sleigh crossing in front of the moon. Kyle had picked up a box of hundreds of twinkly lights, Amelia had found a set of gingerbread ornaments, each one unique – one held a rolling pin, another had a pinny on, one held a candy cane.

She lay the ornaments out on their tissue paper on the side table in the lounge area as she suspected Kyle would want to do the tree tonight, no matter how late they returned from the Inglenook Inn, and she unwrapped the one he'd chosen of a firefighter uniform, helmet, boots and axe attached. 'What made you choose this one?'

'It's very New York.' He did his best impression of a native accent.

She knew there was more to it than that, but it would take time for him to open up to her, if he ever did. Over the years he'd never quite managed to talk about his dad in the way she knew he needed to. She hoped that unlocking all that grief might be a way to move forwards.

They soon left the apartment and spent the rest of the day sight-seeing rather than shopping. They saw the Flatiron Building, which really did resemble an iron, and Kyle bought another pair of gloves for the temperatures he described as arctic, even managing a smile when she suggested it might snow soon given the frost on the roofs when they'd woken this morning, the wind biting at your cheeks, and the temperatures that were set to plummet in the lead-up to Christmas. They walked for miles, they hopped on and off the subway so they could pose for pictures on the Brooklyn Bridge and outside the Supreme Court. Lower Manhattan was as busy as they'd anticipated but Kyle was keen to visit the 9/11 Memorial Museum and Amelia agreed to go on the condition he ice-skate with her in Central Park tomorrow. She didn't think he'd go for it in a million years but he surprised her when he said yes. The mood then turned sombre with a visit to the museum, contemplative silence enveloping them when they emerged into the Manhattan mayhem once again.

As they walked Amelia said, 'I'm surprised you wanted to go in.' She got a shrug in response. 'I never thought you would. It's quite confronting.'

He said nothing as they headed on towards the apartment to get ready for tonight, just upturned the collar of the coat that probably wasn't enough to tackle a New York winter. She let the silence settle until he eventually admitted, 'I wanted to go in because I knew it would remind me of Dad, in a good way. For his bravery, you know.'

She stopped in the street and apologised to the man behind who'd been walking head down and nearly collided with her. Now she was getting somewhere. It was the most Kyle had said about his dad in years. He usually avoided the subject. How did she not make the connection between the museum and Kyle's own journey? In her job she prided herself on being switched on but now she felt blindsided.

Kyle's dad was a firefighter, had been ever since Amelia met him when her sister introduced her to her "hot firefighter boyfriend". As a little boy, Kyle was into anything to do with his dad's profession. He had his dad play fire drills in the back garden, whereby they'd use the hose pipe and run it along the length of the grass before tackling the fence at the end as though the entire thing was going up in flames. Kyle had loved the game; his dad had turned the hose on him once, soaked him through, leaving Connie rather unimpressed given Kyle had only just got over a cold. Kyle had slept in a fireman costume for weeks until Connie had insisted they finally wash it. It did smell – Amelia had given the little boy a hug when she arrived and it must have been the winced expression on her face that finally sent Connie over the edge. There'd been tears, tantrums, and the second it was dry he'd put it on again. Whenever his dad came home Kyle exhausted him with question after question about his day, things he'd seen, any heroics.

And then one day, Stuart didn't come home. He'd been at the station, it had been an easy day, but out of the blue he had a heart attack in the car as he drove home. No health problems before that, not even a family history to contend with, just one of those things, they'd been told. Connie couldn't make sense of it. She kept talking about how fit he was, how healthy, she'd asked Kyle if he wanted sausages for dinner that night, in shock, business as usual being her coping mechanism. But when Amelia put her arms around her sister, Connie fell apart. Amelia would never forget the wailing, the pain, the tight hold of Kyle and his mother as they huddled in the kitchen until the full moon dared to push its way through the darkened sky.

'I think about him all the time,' Kyle said now, shivering on the side of the street. 'I still dream about him.'

'You never talk about him.'

'Sometimes I open my eyes in the morning and the dreams feel so real that I've leapt out of bed and opened my door because I think I hear his voice.'

They slowly walked on, side by side, all the way back to the apartment. Amelia didn't know what to say to him, this boy who was the closest thing she had to a son. She had so much experience dealing with youths who were angry, grieving, upset, but when it came to her own nephew, why couldn't she process it?

But she knew the answer. If another kid pushed her away, she couldn't do much about it. She hated it when it happened, but that was the end. Failing was horrible but there had never been such high personal stakes as this. If Kyle had kept his grief inside all these years then she'd failed as an auntie and Connie had failed as a mum. Amelia wondered whether her sister had any idea of the damage that had been done.

When they reached their apartment, Kyle stopped her on the stoop before she opened the front door. 'Thank you for taking me away from home for a while.'

'I'm glad you came.' She hugged him. She had no idea what else to say because most kids would've said thank you for bringing them to the most exciting city in the world, to the Big Apple, the city of dreams, yet her nephew seemed to be focused only on the escape it had provided.

And now, Amelia knew, all these years after he lost his dad, Kyle's grief was still there, just as raw. Was it any wonder he had never got his life on track?

* * *

Amelia stood in the shower much longer than usual. It was the only place she could do her thinking, let a tear escape and feel her own emotions bubbling up inside without affecting Kyle. When she eventually emerged from her bedroom dressed in a gold jumper, skinny black jeans and boots, she assumed she'd have to nag her nephew to get him out of the door, but here he was in front of her, ready. She tried not to pass comment on the ironed checked shirt he had on, or the smarter of his pairs of jeans he'd chosen. And if she wasn't mistaken, he'd had a shave and smelt as though he might have used the aftershave his mum bought him last Christmas in an attempt to change him from a grungy, sulky teen into a youth who was well on his way to becoming a man.

'You scrub up pretty nice,' he told her.

'Why thank you, you don't look so bad yourself.' His hair still glistened from the shower water, or maybe it was product. Wonders would never cease. Male grooming, perhaps he'd finally hopped onto the trend.

'Do you promise it won't be just chicks there tonight?'

'Firstly, tweet tweet. And secondly, I told you there'll be other boys for you to talk to.'

'Men, Amelia, if you please.' He lowered his voice and gruffly added, 'Not boys.'

When Kyle was like this he was good company, it was a joy to have him around. 'Don't forget your gloves, it's cold out there. And you really do need a better coat. That one barely has anything to it, it's hardly suitable for winter,' she said as he pulled it on.

'Can't afford to buy a new coat just for a holiday.' He switched the main light off as they headed out. 'This one will do me for years yet.'

'We'll grab a hot drink each to make sure we don't arrive at the party ratty and already wanting to leave.'

'As if,' he protested.

One of the things she really loved about New York was how many good street vendors were dotted about, in almost any direction you turned. And such variety. If you didn't like what was offered on one cart, walk fifty paces and you'd have something different.

They settled on a vendor selling coffees and hot chocolates, went for the former, and making sure to take care on the icy footpaths in the quieter streets, they made their way to the inn chatting away about the city. As they drank, Kyle identified some of the iconic buildings in the distance, debating whether he was right or not, and they marvelled at lights in store windows taking Christmas to a whole new level.

'If I get bored, can I leave?' he whispered as they arrived at the Inglenook Inn and took the steps up to the front door of the brownstone.

'Absolutely not.' She didn't lose her smile because Darcy was already opening the door for them.

They said their hellos, Darcy ushered them in out of the cold, and from behind the desk took out a big box. 'There's plenty in here for you to decorate your tree with.'

'I really appreciate this, thank you.' Amelia wanted to give Kyle a shove because he was looking around the place like he was casing the joint. He looked nervous, uncomfortable. She peeked inside the box of ornaments. 'Look,' she said to Kyle, repeating herself twice and almost at the point of wanting to kick him in the shins if he didn't respond.

'Great,' he said.

'Kyle can help carry it home,' she assured Darcy, who stashed the box back behind the desk for them and launched into hostess mode, offering them drinks. 'Red wine for me please,' said Amelia.

'We do have champagne.'

'Oh go on then, but only if you join me.'

'Of course, probably in a while when I'm less likely to have guests needing me. I've finished organising dinner reservations, called a cab for a couple who wanted to go over to Brooklyn tonight for some Christmas lights, and if any other guests come in, they can join our gathering. The more the merrier. Kyle, what can I get you?'

'A cola please.'

Very polite. Amelia hooked her arm through his when Darcy went to fix the drinks. 'Smile, at least once.'

'Not yet, don't want to use all my smiles up.' But even he couldn't say that with a straight face. 'And does she have to be so cheery?'

'What is up with you tonight?' He'd been fine on the way here but now he was skittish, as though he couldn't settle. And as Rupert brought more canapés out to lay on the coffee table, Amelia hoped her nephew was going to behave himself tonight and at least try not to look like he was waiting for the right moment to either pilfer the family jewels or escape out of the nearest window.

When Mitch turned up, Kyle settled down, relieved to have other males in the room, including Jude, who helped Mitch out from time to time and seemed to get on well with her nephew. Since his dad died, Kyle hadn't had many male role models in his life, but watching him now with Mitch, Amelia could see it was part of what he needed. He had a grandpa on his dad's side but saw very little of him and Connie's choices in men since Stuart died could only be described as diabolical. None of them seemed interested in Kyle, unless you included the guy who'd bullied Kyle and whom Connie had found pinning her son up against the wall. Thankfully

Connie ended that relationship straight away even though she knew he'd likely been antagonised by her son.

Amelia had never been with someone who already had a child from a previous relationship, but she hoped if she ever was she'd be able to factor children in as part of it. Then again, what did she know? Her love life since Paul had been non-existent.

Darcy circulated and chatted with Amelia about the knitting stall, how popular it was already and how busy Cleo had been. Drinks were topped up, canapés brought round, and Mitch had taken Kyle under his wing, introducing him to other people as they talked about his Christmas tree farm in Inglenook Falls and the stall in the city.

Cleo eventually turned up and after grabbing a champagne, sat next to Amelia on the sofa. 'I need this drink more than you know.' She knocked a glug back enthusiastically.

'Trouble in paradise?'

'Ignore me, I'm being a grouch. I'm tired and it's been a long day rather than a particularly bad one. The knitting stall here, along with one in Inglenook Falls, plus the Little Knitting Box, plus the kiddies...'

'I'm tired just hearing that list. Is it good to be back in Manhattan though?'

Cleo smiled, relaxed a bit. 'It is. I don't get to come that often so the market stall is a really good excuse.' She looked over at the men when they laughed at something. 'Kyle seems to be getting on well with Mitch.'

'I'm so relieved.' She relaxed with another sip of her drink. 'I've been thinking, we should come out to Inglenook Falls one day. I'd love to see the Little Knitting Box and I know Kyle would like to visit the Christmas tree farm if Mitch is happy for him to do so.'

'Sounds like a plan to me.' She looked over at him again. 'Getting away seems to have been a real tonic for him.'

Amelia frowned in thought. 'He thanked me earlier, for taking him away.'

'That's a good thing, surely.' Cleo crossed her legs, flicked her dark-blonde hair over a shoulder out of the way. 'I doubt a lot of teenagers would even say thank you.'

'Perhaps I'm reading too much into it, but I thought it would've been a thank you for bringing him to New York, the most exciting thing ever for most kids of his age. But he said it more along the lines of a thank you for the escape. As though I could've taken him anywhere in the world as long as it wasn't near home.'

Cleo put a hand over hers. 'You're a wonderful auntie and an even better sister to step up like this; I hope Connie knows how lucky she is.'

Connie hadn't always taken from Amelia; sometimes she'd given. When Amelia wanted to put herself through university to jump-start a new career direction, Amelia and Stuart had given her free board and lodgings, telling her it was payback for all that child-care over the years. They became equals – Connie wasn't taking advantage, Amelia wasn't a pushover – but since Stuart died, slowly Amelia had slipped back into the role of Connie's sole support system when it came to her son. Amelia had been around when puberty hit Kyle and his hormones raged, when he felt nobody understood him, and she'd been at her sister's side when they found out Kyle had got involved with a gang committing petty theft, lads who had seen nothing wrong with drinking under age and getting wasted. Amelia had been there when Kyle left school, she'd watched him unable to get a focus or direction, drifting along as the mood took him. She'd told him he wasn't the loser he claimed to be, but she could see he was stuck in a place he couldn't see a way out of, and when her sister begged her to talk to him her first thought had been to get him well away from all that was familiar. And here they were.

But Amelia was growing increasingly frustrated with her sister. She hadn't texted many times at all, almost as though with Kyle it was a case of out of sight, out of mind.

Amelia sat up straighter. 'I refuse to be sad tonight.' She shook off the melancholy and clinked glasses with Cleo. 'It's amazing to see you again, and that jumper is gorgeous.'

'Nice change of subject,' Cleo smiled. 'And thank you. I made it myself last year.'

'I wish I had half your talent.' She admired the camel stepped-hem jumper. 'What's the wool? Or should I say yarn?'

'Don't worry, I still forget sometimes and say both. It took me forever to learn to say sweater rather than jumper and I still flit between the two. The yarn is merino and alpaca. Beautiful, isn't it?'

'I loved working in your aunt and uncle's wool shop but I never took to knitting. Mum used to tell me it was weird to be surrounded by beautiful wools and not feel the urge to learn, but I never got the hang of it.'

Amelia accepted a cranberry canapé on a tiny piece of baguette with whipped ricotta when Darcy floated on by as the hostess and stopped with them before taking the food over to the men.

'How's your work going?' Cleo asked. 'You haven't said much about it since you got here.'

'To tell you the truth, it hasn't been great lately.'

'I thought you loved it.'

'I do, but I've had some trouble. This holiday,' she put the word in inverted commas, 'was enforced rather than off my own back. I got too involved with a case, ended up mouthing off to a parent who wasn't doing their kid any favours. Don't tell Kyle – not mouthing off is one lesson I'm always harping on about. It gets you into far more trouble and I've found that out the hard way.'

'Do you have a job to go back to?'

'I do, but I know I need to find some way of separating my work and my personal feelings. It's all well and good getting invested to a certain extent – caring about people is a quality for the job – but I overstepped. I called the mother a bitch.'

Cleo gasped. 'Amelia, that's not like you.'

'No, it's not. But her son has been in a lot of trouble with the police.' She lowered her voice, she didn't want her nephew hearing this. 'I can see Kyle going down the same road if he's not careful, and the mother, well, she reminded me of my sister, always thinking her job and her social life were more important than her son. I know I shouldn't judge, but I saw red, let her have a piece of my mind. The kid thought it was hilarious but nobody else did, and I've had to apologise to her as well.'

'Do you think you did it because you're frustrated with your sister?'

'I didn't realise at the time but, yes, you're probably right. I've been a bit lost lately, since Paul and I ended things, having to move back into the flat and redecorate, all the ups and downs with Kyle.'

'Why don't you talk to Connie?'

'I will, it's finding the right moment.'

'And you'll move on from Paul in time.'

'I hope so.'

'Are you still in love with him?'

'I feel it ended so suddenly. I never saw it coming. I think that's half the problem. If we'd fought a lot or one of us had had an affair, I might have processed the breakup quite differently.'

'And he never really gave you much reason, did he?'

'We wanted different things was all he said. Basically a cop-out. Who knows, maybe he was shagging someone else, perhaps he wanted to spare my feelings in the end.'

'Well, let's hope this holiday is a break for you as well as Kyle. Away from England, the flat, anything that reminds you of Paul.'

Amelia sighed as she watched Kyle again, relaxed, open, different. 'I wish his mum could see him like this rather than the angry, frustrated, sad boy who seems to think the world is against him. You know, she could barely look at me when she dropped him off, it's as though she was passing him on to me. My problem. And it wouldn't have escaped his notice either. It must be hurtful to think your own mum doesn't want you around.'

'I can understand his grief, losing my mum was awful and at times I never thought I'd get over it. At least I had my dad and Teresa, even though I didn't appreciate her at the time. I think she kept him going, gave him the confidence to raise me despite all that we had lost. I don't suppose Connie has had that, so it must be hard for her.' She held up her hands. 'I'm not saying it's right for her to depend on you, but it must be tough doing it all alone and coping with her own grief at the same time. And I never got into trouble the way Kyle has, so my dad was lucky with that too, although he did have the battle with my attitude to contend with.'

'You never liked Teresa, I remember it well.'

'Don't remind me, I was awful to her.'

'You get on well now?'

'We really do. Since the day she showed up in New York and I was forced to face her and deal with my feelings, we've become friends. I never thought that would ever happen.'

'I'm not sure things will be so easy with Kyle. Trying to reason with a boy his age is tough.'

'May I ask why it's you who's come to the rescue and taken him on a holiday?' Cleo probed.

'You remember how I said I always looked after him when he was small?'

'Your sister expected you to, from what I remember. Wasn't it because you worked at home?'

'That's right. But it's my fault, I never said no, and then when Stuart died, how could I turn down anything she asked of me? She was devastated. Like you say, she had nobody to draw strength from.'

When Darcy put on some Christmas music and the sounds of Bing Crosby's 'White Christmas' floated around the room Amelia apologised to Cleo for bringing the mood down more than once tonight.

'Nonsense, that's what friends are for. And now I can moan about my problems to get even.'

'Please do, I'm fed up being the only whinger at a party.'

'I need some advice.'

'Still having trouble with Ruby?'

'She's being a little madam.' Cleo told Amelia all about the cupcakes she was supposed to take into school, those Cleo had bought that had never seen the neatly assembled tables of the bake sale, Prue swooping in and coming to the rescue, Prue feeding Ruby with information that was not only inaccurate but damaging. 'There's no way I don't love Ruby and Jacob, and I'm furious that Prue would even suggest it, let alone to her daughter who is very much a part of my family.'

'Do you think Prue wants to get back with Dylan?'

'Actually, I don't. But it's like she doesn't want him to be happy with anyone else. She was fine for a long while but maybe the permanency is making her uneasy. Not that it was ever temporary, when we've had another two children. Marriage is just a formality so I don't get why she's causing such a stir. It's as though the wedding plans are an official reminder that Dylan chose to be with me rather than give his marriage with her another go.'

'All I can suggest is to keep talking, keep Ruby onside as much as you can, involve her in things, and don't rise to Prue's antics because that's probably exactly what she wants. Why don't you schedule some special Cleo–Ruby time?'

'I don't think Ruby would like that one bit.'

'So make it something she can't refuse. Like a pamper day – she's at the age where girls love all that fuss. Do the pamper day, take her for hot chocolates, maybe to a movie or to see the Christmas lights. But only you and her. Otherwise your focus will be on everything and everyone else. Then, I'd talk to her about your wedding, keep it all in the open. Perhaps search on websites for dresses, get her looking too, say you're giving her responsibility now she's older. It could be anything... choosing flowers, cake tasting, watching you try on dresses.'

'I think you're right. I'm not sure how I'm going to be able to find the time to do it, but I will, and before Christmas,' she said determinedly. 'I can't go into Christmas with things like this, it's really unpleasant. I'm on edge all the time and I'm not sleeping.'

'I didn't realise it had got so bad. Does Dylan know?'

'Some of it, not that I'm struggling to sleep at night. I don't want him forced to take sides. He's seen Ruby playing up so he does know but I don't want to go on and on about the effect it's having on me.'

Amelia put a hand over Cleo's. 'Trust me, he needs to know. You need to manage your stress levels. It's not selfish, it's necessary. Keep him in the loop and it'll make your life easier. And then sit down and schedule a time for you and Ruby.'

Cleo smiled and nodded and when she noticed another guest come to join the party she said, 'That's Holly,' and waved over at her. 'Come on, let me introduce you.'

Holly was as lovely as Cleo had described and she sounded as though she'd found her niche with freelance journalism and photography, and seeing her with Mitch, Amelia felt a pang of sadness that she was single for the first Christmas in a long time. The holiday season seemed to make the loneliness multiply tenfold. And watching Mitch with Holly, Amelia could see the love between them and wondered if she'd ever find that closeness again.

Maybe Paul was her only chance and, for whatever reason, he'd ended it.

When the fire in the grate crackled away too enthusiastically Darcy moved the fireguard across as the last log took hold and Amelia wandered over to the tree to admire the ornaments up close as the lights faded in and out. After the talk with Cleo she was feeling nice and relaxed and wanted nothing more right now than to absorb the holiday atmosphere, merry on the bubbles she'd drunk and pleasantly sated with the canapés that Rupert had treated them all too, each one a perfect-sized portion.

Darcy topped up Amelia's champagne flute before they both looked out of the window and up into the dark skies above the tree-lined street. 'You know, I think it's going to snow soon. When I went to put grit on the stoop earlier the air had that smell about it. You mark my words.'

'I hope so. Kyle isn't keen but maybe he'll change his mind.'

'There's nothing like New York in the snow, you wait. The city falls silent, the park is a sight to behold.' She put a hand against her chest. 'Listen to me, I'm getting far too carried away. Now, let me introduce you to a couple more of my guests.'

She really was a good hostess, giving people space to chat, to have a moment, but not letting anyone miss out. Apparently the Christmas Eve party at the inn was a hit every year – this was just the warm up – and Amelia was already looking forward to being back for another social occasion. When it was just her and a teenager, these occasions were enough to keep her spirits up if things with her nephew were hard.

Amelia turned around ready to be sociable but didn't expect to come face to face with someone she already knew, or at least had met before.

'Amelia, this is Nathan. Nathan, this is Amelia,' Darcy began. 'Nathan is staying here with us. He's a friend of Myles's and missed out on the apartment you and Kyle are in – you got there first.'

'Is that right?' Nathan asked, a twitch in his jaw showing he was either unhappy about that or else he was trying to work out how to treat this woman he'd run into before.

Darcy carried on, oblivious. 'Amelia is new to the city, Nathan, just like you and Scarlett. And you're all from England.'

Nathan extended a hand to Amelia, obviously not wanting to offend Darcy. 'Nice to meet you.'

'Likewise.' The hand shake didn't last long and when Darcy swung off to grab him a drink, she said, 'You're lying.'

'Totally.'

They stood in silence until Darcy came back with his bottle of beer but she was too busy talking to Rupert about more canapés to be brought through to notice the tension.

'Look, this is crazy,' Amelia began. 'Why don't we start again?' She held out a hand but he didn't take it straight away.

'Did you donate the twenty to charity?'

'I gave it to a homeless shelter not far from here, you can go ask them if you need to check. I handed it, plus another thirty bucks of my own money, to a woman called Marion, crazy ginger hair and taller than you.'

He seemed satisfied enough and at last shook her hand. 'Truce?'

She laughed. 'What were we even fighting about anyway?'

'Because your –' He realised she'd been joking. 'You know what, never mind. Cheers.' He chinked his beer bottle against her glass gently.

'Is that your daughter?' Amelia nodded in the direction of the pretty girl in the black sequinned dress and long legs she wished she'd been blessed with herself.

'Yep. That's Scarlett, sixteen going on twenty-one.'

'Must be a handful.' Amelia hadn't missed Kyle already giving the girl the eye. He hadn't been able to take his eyes off her at the markets the other day and it seemed the attraction was reciprocated by the way Scarlett was smiling.

'Hard to manage at times, but then you'd know.' He covered his face with one hand, shook his head. 'Sorry, that wasn't a dig about your son, I was trying to be a parent who gets it, that's all.'

'No worries.' Kyle and Scarlett seemed to have hit it off and from where Amelia was standing she could see their heads locked together in chat away from the other adults in the group. It was then she wondered whether perhaps Scarlett had given away the location of her accommodation when talking to Kyle the other day and that was why he'd made an effort tonight. 'And Kyle isn't my son, he's my nephew.'

'Really? So he's on holiday with you for a while? What happened to his parents?'

'His mum is having a hard time.' He didn't need to know that Kyle *was* the hard time.

'What about his dad?'

'He passed away a few years ago.'

'That sucks.' Wait, was that a modicum of sympathy? 'My brother died when I was younger and then as an adult I lost my wife, Scarlett's mum. Death is a shit thing for anyone to deal with, let alone someone Kyle's age.'

She was almost lost for words at first with how much he'd shared. 'I'm sorry to hear that, it must've been rough. All of it,' she stammered. Perhaps it was the beer making him so open and honest; whatever it was, she kind of liked it. Paul had rarely talked about his feelings – he'd been more of a moody type when something was wrong. Maybe if he'd been more open they could've worked through whatever it was that drove them apart.

'It was.'

'Kyle needs a break,' she explained, 'so I played the auntie card and here we are.'

'It's very generous of you.'

'It's family.'

'You're a natural parent.'

'How so?'

'You stood up for him against me for a start; kids need somebody on their side.'

Conversation lapsed into jobs, his and hers, where they lived in England, the sights they'd already seen in New York, those they wanted to see again. Nathan's visit to the big city had already involved ice-skating and he'd still got the bruising to prove it.

'I'm making Kyle go tomorrow,' she admitted. 'I went to Ground Zero with him, to the museum too, so that was the deal.'

'Fair enough.'

Now it was her turn to talk. She'd never been one to keep things bottled up. 'Kyle's dad was a firefighter. I think the reason Kyle wanted to go to Ground Zero was to remind himself of his dad's bravery, the job he'd done, the lives he'd saved before he lost his own. Rather than remembering losing his dad, he was remembering the man he was before. If that makes sense. Which it doesn't, not now I'm saying it out loud. I don't know, I can't read him, I don't know what he's thinking. What, why are you smiling?'

'You're rambling.'

'I am, aren't I?'

'I get it, you're processing,' he smiled. 'Just out loud, that's all.' Nathan was far removed from the angry man in the park on their first day here in the city as he told her all about the firefighter mural his daughter had shown him and she made a mental note to mention it to Kyle – he might be interested in that or he might hate the idea.

'It's hard to be on holiday and think of things you both like to do when there's a generation gap,' said Nathan.

'It is, but I think it's been good for Kyle and for me.' She wondered, 'What do you think you'd be doing if you were here on your own?'

'Nothing that would involve ice-skating.'

With the tree, the fireplace, and the twinkly lights and garlands sneaking up the banisters, the Inglenook Inn oozed warmth and, helped along by the champagne, Amelia felt the most relaxed she'd been since she arrived in New York.

'How are you doing?' Darcy was offering around more cranberry and ricotta canapés.

Amelia shook her head after Nathan popped one in his mouth. 'No more for me, I'm surprisingly full. Your chef is a star.'

'You're having a good time?'

Nathan put his thumb up, still chewing.

'I am,' said Amelia. 'Thank you for inviting us.'

'My pleasure.'

She couldn't see Kyle; he was probably chatting with Mitch, who had his back to them as he talked with another group. Laughter reverberated around the room; the sense of holiday spirit was right there.

When Nathan moved to talk with the other men in the room, Darcy said to Amelia, 'I hope the box of decorations is enough, just holler if you need more, and send me a picture when it's done, you have my number.'

'You seem to be enjoying tonight as much as anyone else here.'

'I love throwing parties in this place. It's cosy, pretty, I love it.'

'I hear the owner is considering selling up.' She kept her voice low in case Darcy didn't want it broadcasted and when Darcy lowered her voice too Amelia knew it must be a sensitive subject.

'I don't begrudge her.' Darcy looked around as though committing the entire place to memory. 'But I'll miss it.'

'Would you consider buying?'

'The finances might not add up but Myles and I are doing what we can.'

Amelia left it at that. She didn't want to pry, she didn't know Darcy well enough. 'Where is Myles?'

'Still at work, putting in a lot of hours again. He'll stop by if he can. Now, can I get you a top-up?' She indicated Amelia's empty champagne flute.

Amelia nodded and as she waited for Darcy to return with her drink she put a hand out to touch the delicate branches of the tree, prickly, and potent enough that if you pushed them they left a sweet scent on your skin. Outside the street was dark except for the soft glow of streetlamps and the odd passing car. A couple walked past laughing away and it was when Amelia turned back to the group that she saw another couple out of the corner of her eye out on the stoop of the Inglenook Inn.

'Aren't we enough for you?' Nathan brought over her champagne and another beer for himself.

She took the glass. 'Excuse me?'

'You're looking out the window as though you're bored.'

She only had eyes for him now as she didn't want him to see what she'd seen with her own eyes, but too late, he was inquisitive enough to turn and step towards the window and as soon as he did, face like thunder, he slammed his beer bottle down on the coffee table, swore, and stomped off.

Amelia followed quickly, ignoring Darcy's look of what-the-heck-is-going-on? And before she could get there in time to warn Kyle and Scarlett, who'd been locked in a passionate clinch, Nathan had Kyle by the scruff of his neck.

'You,' he jabbed a finger at Kyle when he let go of him, 'stay the hell away from my daughter.'

'Take it easy, mate.' Mitch stepped in – nice that someone did. Amelia wasn't even sure how to handle this level of anger. She didn't have much experience of prising apart a grown man and a teenager.

'Do you have a daughter?' Nathan's question to Mitch was met with silence. 'Then I suggest you stay out of it. And you,' he turned to Amelia, 'keep your boy away from Scarlett.' And even though they were both staying at the inn, Nathan grabbed his coat and Scarlett's, thrust hers at her and led her down the steps without looking back.

'What the hell was all that about?' Darcy, stunned at the hasty departure, stood next to Amelia at the entrance to the Inglenook Inn as snow began to fall lightly, dusting the footpath in white, the steps all the way up, the pine trees at the top on either side of the door.

Amelia shivered. 'It was an overreaction, that was what that was.' And when she looked back at Kyle and put out a hand to touch his arm he shrugged it away. 'If it helps, I don't think that was necessarily about you, Kyle.'

'Who was it about then?'

'Well it was partly you, but I suspect it's also a case of an over-protective father. He probably acts that way with any boy who shows interest.' Kyle harrumphed. 'But you were kissing his daughter right in front of him – talk about waving a red rag to a bull. Given the run-in we had with him in the park, I'd have thought baby steps were needed.'

'It was just a kiss between two consenting parties.'

'You're a fast worker, I'll give you that. You don't even know her. What were you thinking?' Suddenly she was annoyed her evening was ending this way. Couldn't Kyle read a situation enough to do the right thing, ever?

'I met her before at the markets.'

'My mistake, you know each other so well.' Her sarcasm wasn't one of her finest moments, set to rile him more than anything.

Darcy had the party back on track quickly; guest were offered more canapés, conversation returned to normal, drinks were topped up, but when Kyle announced he'd had enough and picked up the box of decorations, Amelia had no choice but to call it a night and follow after him.

8

NATHAN

The lights in New York City were nothing short of stunning, not that Scarlett had any appreciation for them tonight. After Nathan whisked her away from the Inglenook Inn she'd stomped off, totally missing the magic of snow falling all around them – only lightly, but enough to put smiles on the faces of people passing by. She'd marched quite a way too. When Scarlett was in a mood she could genuinely walk faster than most people could run.

'Are you going to keep up the silent treatment?' he asked when they reached Times Square and she finally slowed her pace.

She didn't answer. She stood, mesmerised amidst energetic crowds looking up at the towering digital billboards flashing in a rainbow of colours. He pulled her to one side before they both got knocked to the ground in the melee. 'Scarlett, come on, talk to me. Perhaps get a bit of perspective.'

'Says the man who overreacted!'

'You don't need to yell at me.'

'We were kissing, Dad. I'm sixteen, he's seventeen, I think we're allowed. And then you totally embarrassed me in front of him and everyone else. It was awful.'

'I'm sorry. I guess I did go a bit over the top.'

'You think!'

'You didn't need to storm this far though. My legs are aching from trying to keep up.'

'I wanted to see Times Square at night,' she shrugged.

'Pretty impressive. Where's the ball?' When she pointed up high to the top of a building, he squinted. 'Never mind glasses, I probably need binoculars. I thought it was huge, it was in that movie we saw.'

She gave him a look as though he was a dimwit. 'It probably is close up, but it's a long way from the ground.'

He looked around them. 'So this is where everyone congregates on New Year's Eve. You know, I always thought it would be a proper square, really it's just a junction of roads.'

'It'd be amazing to come here on New Year's. Kyle says...'

'You're allowed to mention his name,' he said when she hesitated. He was trying to be reasonable now his anger had subsided. And since they'd left the inn he hadn't actually thought much about catching Scarlett and Kyle together, but he had thought about Amelia, a brunette with a cute smile and a lot of personality.

'Kyle says he's going to come here and watch the ball drop.'

'With Amelia?'

'His auntie, yes. She looked like she wanted to punch you for upsetting Kyle.'

'I hardly think she's going to do that.'

'Maybe think before you act next time, Dad.'

'Hang on a minute, who's the adult here?'

'You, supposedly. But that means you should be able to control your emotions and your temper.'

'Point taken. Well, I hope he and Amelia enjoy New Year's Eve here with all the crowds.'

'You're probably hoping he gets trampled.'

They agreed to get off the street and enjoy the warmth of the nearest café, where Nathan bought two hot chocolates. He'd had a few beers at the inn but was stone-cold sober now and this talk needed a decadent treat with cream and marshmallows. He wanted his daughter's attention without her getting defensive, if that was at all possible.

Cupping their warm drinks between their palms to take away the chill from walking the streets and seated at a table right near the back with its red Formica top bordered with silver and chairs of the same design, he said, 'I don't want to see the boy trampled. I won't pretend I like him all that much but everyone deserves a second chance. It doesn't mean I want to see his lips on yours particularly.' He stopped her from interrupting. 'No dad would be completely comfortable seeing his little girl stepping into a whole new world of being a grown-up, relationships and all the shit that comes with them.' He didn't even apologise for the explicit language because it pretty much summed it up. 'I'm well aware I won't be able to fight it forever; you'll grow up and have boyfriends. It's just that I didn't expect it to happen on holiday and I definitely wasn't prepared for it to be Kyle.'

'Kyle or someone like Kyle?'

'What does that mean?'

'You probably know he's no longer at school or college. And he isn't working either. I assume you think I can do better.'

'I'm wondering what you two have in common.'

'I don't know much about him, but isn't that what dating is about?'

He couldn't help the laugh he let out. 'You're on holiday, it's hardly dating. And don't you think, apart from an initial attraction, you're both too different? I'm on your side, Scarlett, I promise.' He needed to keep her talking rather than flipping out on him. He'd learnt to read the signs that it was about to happen too. First, she knitted her lips together tightly, then her eyebrows drew in and her nostrils flared a little bit. 'What did you even talk about? How much do you really know about this boy?' Her look gave him his answer. 'I thought as much. He's been in a bit of trouble over the years.'

'That doesn't mean he's a bad person.'

'Did he tell you about it?'

'Yeah, his opening line was, "I'm trouble, don't bother getting to know me or giving me a chance." What do you think?'

'You barely know him.'

She'd used her spoon to scrape all of the cream off the top of her drink. 'I may not have had a serious boyfriend, but I know the drill. You go out with someone and slowly get to know them. If you like them you stay together and gradually the relationship gets better.' He couldn't argue with that. 'I'll bet you didn't know everything about Mum the first time you kissed her.'

'I didn't, no. We got to know each other over time.' But they'd also jumped into bed together pretty quickly and he didn't want that for Scarlett.

'See, you were no different. And you were around my age.'

'And your mum and I were together five minutes before your mum got pregnant.'

She stopped sipping and put down her mug. 'We were kissing, Dad, not sleeping together.'

'Kissing is where it starts.'

She covered her face and peeked through her fingers. 'Is this where you start talking to me about sex, because I'm not sure I can handle it if you do.'

He shrugged. 'I'm not going to go on about it, but I want you to be careful. Careful of getting involved with anyone right now, when you've got school to focus on. And Kyle is on holiday, as are you. Holiday romances rarely go the distance.'

'He's the first boy I've liked in a long while.'

Had there been others? He didn't want to think about it. 'Are you planning on seeing him again?' Her silence confirmed it. But he knew Kyle lived in Cornwall, which was a considerable distance from Hove, so they'd be unlikely to see much of one another back in England. It was just this holiday to get through first. 'And where do I fit in with your plans? This is our holiday, remember.'

'I didn't expect to meet someone. It must be New York, like in the movies, like Tom and Meg or the couple from *Serendipity*.'

He smiled when she did but a frown soon creased his forehead again. 'In those movies the man and woman are adults, not sixteen and getting involved with a seventeen-year-old boy who comes with a whole lot of attitude.'

'You don't even know him, Dad.'

'I know seventeen-year-old boys. I was one, remember.'

'Wait, are you worried about me getting involved with Kyle because you don't like him, or are you trying to suggest I'll get pregnant when he can't keep it in his pants?'

'Maybe we shouldn't talk about this here. Perhaps we should go back to the inn and talk about this tomorrow when we've both calmed down.' She had that look about her that meant she was about to stop taking orders and exercise her right to freedom of speech. She was good at debating at school but she was probably more reasonable in those situations because she rarely seemed willing to listen to him these days.

'Are you going to let me see Kyle again while we're here? I'd really like to. He told me about his dad, you know.'

'Really?'

'He told me he was a firefighter, he told me he died. I think he'd really like to see the mural we found the other day.'

'I'm sure he would.' How had this happened? Kyle was a fast mover by anyone's standards, but Nathan did sympathise with someone who had lost a parent the same as Scarlett had and knew they were probably a comfort to each other, much as he didn't like it.

Her spoon clattered into her empty cup and her frown set in. His lack of an answer about her seeing him again must have pushed her one step too far. 'We're just having fun, maybe you should try it sometime.'

He gulped the last of his hot chocolate and settled the bill. 'Now you're just being rude and I don't appreciate it.'

'What is your problem?' Her voice had gone up so much they were getting stares and, coats on, he bustled her out of the café.

'Don't make a scene. I'm tired, let's go.'

'I'd rather stay out. It's not even eleven.'

'And I'm saying we're going back to the inn.'

Her phone pinged and she read a text before shoving it into her pocket when he tried to see who it was from.

'Was that him?'

She started walking but then turned on the spot. 'I can't remember which way to go.'

He put an arm around her and hugged her. 'I'm sorry if you think I make rules that are unreasonable, it's hard being a single parent sometimes. Hard to know what to do, especially with a girl when her mum isn't around any more.'

'You'll let me see him again?'

'I'll think about it.' He hooked a thumb backwards. 'We need to go this way, head that direction,' he nodded towards the way she'd been going, 'and you'll end up in Central Park. See, you still need your old dad for some things.'

They passed a pretzel cart and Scarlett insisted on waiting in line for one, having not had many of the canapés at the inn tonight. Nathan almost made a comment that perhaps she should've talked to more people other than Kyle, but who was he kidding? Given a choice he could've talked to Amelia all night and ignored everyone else. It's just that the kids' immaturity, or perhaps confidence, had made something happen between them far quicker than it ever would for the adults.

'Not my thing,' he said when he tried a bite of the pretzel at her insistence he eat something so iconic to New York, 'although not as bad as I thought it would be.'

'You're way too fussy.'

They made their way back to the Inglenook Inn, an easy route on foot past the Empire State Building and Madison Square Park, which reminded him of the first time he'd met Amelia. He still had a bad feeling about Kyle's suitability when it came to his daughter but perhaps if he let them meet up a couple more times while they were here, they'd get it out of their systems and then, once they were back in England and Scarlett was at school and geographical distance made it too hard, it would fizzle out.

'That Kyle again?' he asked when Scarlett's phone pinged.

She didn't answer but judging by the look on her face he'd guessed correctly.

'I know you think I'm too strict with you, but you're at an important stage in your life with school. Plenty of time to be distracted by boys later.'

'I'm sixteen, and when Mum was my age she was pregnant so I'd say it's about the age where it's normal to be interested in boys.'

They crossed the street and once they were on the other side walked briskly to get away from the crowd for now. The shivering temperatures couldn't battle through his big down-padded jacket plus scarf and gloves, and it was nice to be outside. It was probably far better than sinking back beers at the inn too.

The snow had stopped but some of the cars still had it clinging to their roofs or bordering windscreens like frames of a painting.

He continued their conversation as they walked on, past shoppers in the festive spirit, another guy collecting for a homeless charity who thanked him for pushing in a donation. 'Having a baby so young changed the course of our lives completely,' he admitted.

'Babies have a way of doing that,' Scarlett replied.

'We both missed out on a lot, we didn't get the freedom that comes when you grow up, and it was harder than I'd ever thought it would be. We struggled financially, I changed career direction altogether.'

She looked at him and nearly walked into a woman coming the other way who wasn't so polite in her rebuke. 'You never told me. I can't imagine you being anything other than an investment banker. You seem to enjoy it. You spend a lot of time at the office.'

He ignored the subtle dig at his absence.

'What did you want to be? Wait, let me guess. An architect?'

'Whatever makes you think that?'

'You got really into it when we redid the house, bossing those builders about, getting everything the way you wanted.'

'They were cutting corners, that's why.'

She thought some more. 'So, if not an architect... plumber?'

'Now I know you're not being serious.' His attempts to fix anything around the house usually ended up making it ten times worse and then having to call in the professionals to fix his bodge job. 'I wanted to be a surgeon.'

'Seriously? Dad, that is way cool.'

'Way cool,' he agreed. 'But it wasn't meant to be.'

'Why didn't you do it? Mum got to be a nurse, why not become a doctor if that's what you wanted?'

'Because it would've involved many, many years of studying, placements, shift work, and I felt with a family to focus on I needed a well-paying job that I could get into a lot sooner.' He'd been sensible and pragmatic when they first found out they were having a baby, but that had only lasted so long before he'd felt the pressures and fought the walls closing in around them, the stress of having to live together under his parents' roof. 'Part of me wonders where I'd be now if I'd kept on the career path I really wanted, even though I have a career I do enjoy.'

They crossed over the next intersection and he came back to the whole point of this trip down memory lane. 'I don't want you to make the same mistakes we did, Scarlett. I want you to have choices while you're young, enjoy your freedom. As I've already said, you're on holiday, so is Kyle. I expect he's looking for a bit of fun.'

'And maybe so am I.'

They'd reached the street where the Inglenook Inn stood proudly in the brownstone on the other side and he did his best not to think too hard about her last comment. 'Holiday romances are usually about one thing, in my opinion.' He didn't even want to think about his daughter wanting the kind of fun he remembered wanting as a seventeen-year-old boy. She wasn't ready. Hell, *he* wasn't ready!

'I know what you're getting at and, for goodness' sake, we've only kissed and we've barely spent much time together – you're being paranoid.' Her face changed, frustration replaced with a scowl. 'I can't believe I never saw it before.'

They'd crossed over and were in front of the inn now. 'Saw what?'

'You wish you'd never had me.'

'Of course not, but I regret we did it so young.'

'Is that why you never spent much time with me?'

'Scarlett... I'm always there for you.'

'You're always around now, but that wasn't always the case, was it? Some of it I remember, the rest I've heard about. I listened to you and Gran once, her telling you that you need to be there for me. Did you think that with this one holiday you could erase all those times I remember as a kid when you weren't there? I'd lie in bed and refuse to go to sleep until you came home. I never lasted of course because half the time you never bothered. Do you know how much I longed for you to be the type of dad to tuck me in and read me a story?'

'God, I'm sorry, Scarlett.' He hadn't realised quite how much she remembered.

'You can't buy my forgiveness with a holiday.'

'It was a long time ago.'

'It wasn't just the stories.' With her boot she scraped at the white dusting of snow on the bottom step of the Inglenook Inn entrance. 'You went away a lot, you worked weekends, and shut yourself away in the study. The time it snowed on Christmas Eve you were down the pub and it was up to mum and I to make a snowman, I don't think you even saw it before it all melted. I cried myself to sleep that night. You rarely made it to my swim lessons, even when I represented the school in a gala once. I was so proud to be there, I searched the crowd for your face but you never came. I know it didn't feel like much, but it was a lot for me.'

'I don't know what to say apart from how sorry I am.'

'After Mum died you were better, you've always been there for me, you had to be, but it doesn't wipe away all that hurt.'

'I know it doesn't. I just freaked out; I felt trapped. I was so young, we both were. The way I reacted, how I distanced myself and stayed away from you and your mum, threw myself into work, it wasn't right. I know that now. But my life as I knew it had been taken away.'

'Because of me,' she concluded with a shake of her head. 'You wish Mum had never got pregnant.'

Exasperated, he said the one thing he probably shouldn't. 'If I'm being honest, yes!' His voice echoed down the tree-lined street. 'I wish I'd been a decade older before I was tied down, I wish I'd followed the career path I planned. There, I've said it.'

'Nice to know, Dad. Nice to know.'

Wishing he hadn't opened his big mouth he added, 'You know I can't imagine life without you now, don't you?'

But she'd already turned and stomped her way up the steps and into the inn, leaving him out in the cold.

9

AMELIA

It had been a week since the run-in with Nathan at the Inglenook Inn. Since then Amelia had tried to talk to Kyle but at the same time she'd given him space. They'd both worked shifts at the markets, they'd both gone off around the city doing their own thing, reconvening in the evenings for dinner.

Amelia suspected Kyle had been seeing quite a bit of Scarlett judging by the way he took longer to get ready before going out, how there was the aroma of whatever body spray he used whenever he was about to leave the apartment, and she'd seen Scarlett lurking by the Christmas tree stall on several occasions when Kyle was working. Tonight she decided it was time to push again, time to talk to him. But first, they needed to decorate the tree, something she'd put off until now, with Kyle being in an unpredictable mood.

She took off her coat, tired from a day at the Garland Street markets but determined to have some time with Kyle this evening to find out more about how he was feeling. In her job she'd been accused of overstepping but this time she'd backed off enough and couldn't do so any longer. 'Did you have a good day?' She'd start with a simple question to gauge his mood.

'Yeah, Mitch is a decent bloke. Don't mind working with him.'

It was a start, he was at least talking in more than grunts or one-word answers.

Amelia had been relieved that the showdown at the inn hadn't caused Mitch to tell Kyle his help was no longer needed at the market stall. The work ethic had to start somewhere and here in another city, without Connie breathing down his neck or undesirables trying to get him roped in with whatever they were up to, it was a start for Kyle. And when he was working and selling those trees he looked happier than he had in a long while.

She eyed the box of decorations still waiting by the curved window that looked out over the street. 'We need to do the tree.'

'Now? I'm knackered.'

'Me too, but look at it. It's not fulfilling its Christmas wish.'

'What a load of...' Her stare stopped him going further.

Standing by the window, she undid the box and when she turned her head as movement caught her eye, she smiled.

'What is it?'

'It's snowing,' she beamed.

Even he managed to haul himself from the sofa to the window. 'Wonder if the ground will be covered in the morning.'

'I hope it is.'

'I suppose we don't have to drive anywhere, just walk to the markets.'

'It's going to be a wonderful Christmas, Kyle, I promise you.'

His smile wasn't quite as big as she would've liked but his enthusiasm was there when he said, 'I'll do the lights, it's a man's job.'

'No argument from me, I hate winding them round. The pine needles get in my hair and I always end up in a tangle.'

With her guidance he soon had the lights on and they tested them, adjusted a few so they were spaced evenly, and tucked the wiring out of sight. Next it was time for the baubles Darcy had given them as part of the collection she was happy to share – silver, ice-blue, and shiny purple. Amelia bossed Kyle about to make sure the colours were evenly spread out.

'What about these next?' He held up a set of twelve red-and-white drums hanging from sparkly white thread.

'Go for it. Evenly spaced, though, and I'll do the pine cones.'

'You're way too bossy. Mum's the same. I thought part of the fun of decorating the tree was letting your kids do it no matter how haphazard it became. Mum likes things to match; last year the theme was tartan. She had ribbons on the ends of branches, ornaments in the right colours.'

'I remember it well, it looked like something out of a catalogue.' Thrilled he was talking more than usual she hung the first of the pine cones on the tree and moved around to do the rest.

Kyle hung the second drum higher than the first and moved round to place the third. 'A couple of years ago she went for minimalistic.'

'I remember.' Scarlett unwrapped a penguin wearing a woollen hat with snow dusting the top. 'I thought she'd forgotten where half her decorations were.'

'Exactly. It was boring.'

'It wasn't her best effort.'

'Dad always did the tree before he died.'

Amelia didn't swallow hard because his voice softened, or because she could remember it vividly, but because he was talking about his dad again. And she knew he needed to.

Stuart had been all about the overindulgence at Christmas, the extravagance. He'd never been the sort of man to sit back and leave it to the women. And he always wanted to shower his family not with gifts but with excitement and the feeling of the season that had never been quite the same after he was gone.

'Your dad loved Christmas.' After she hung the penguin, she picked up the fireman ornament Kyle had bought the other day and that she hadn't probed him about at the time. 'Here, put it somewhere we can see it.'

He lifted the decoration and hung it just above eye level for him, above a light to show it off. 'I made my own fireman decoration once.'

'I remember,' Amelia smiled. 'The silver bauble with the red ribbon. You painted a fire truck onto it.'

'That's the one. Mum must've thrown it out.'

'No way, she wouldn't.'

'Wanna bet? It would've gone around the time she decided to do designer trees. I never saw it again once she got going with those arrangements, saying annoying phrases like "less is more" and "don't forget the theme".'

'Why don't you text her, ask if she still has the decoration?'

He grunted. 'Maybe.'

'Have you spoken to her since we got here?'

'I told her we arrived at the apartment.'

'Since then?'

'I texted her to tell her I worked at the market. Thought it might make her happy to know I wasn't being too annoying for you.'

'I'm glad you're keeping in touch while we're here.' As soon as communication dwindled, it would only get worse. Some kids needed distance from their parent or parents to get some perspective, to order things in their mind, but not Kyle. He needed people in his corner, he needed to be reminded he still mattered to them. And quite why Connie wasn't doing that right now was anyone's guess.

'Looking good,' Kyle declared as he stood back to admire their handiwork. 'But you're too much of a short arse to put the angel on top.'

'Cheek! I'm not that short.'

'Go on then, put the angel up there.' He nodded to the top of the tree.

Even standing on tiptoes she had no hope but she gave it her best shot until an amused Kyle stood as tall as he could and popped the angel, sparkling peach skirt and all, at the top so she could look over the room.

'Now it feels like Christmas,' Amelia smiled.

They ordered Chinese takeaway and, over noodles and a sensational beef dish with rich red peppers, Amelia decided to tackle what had happened at the inn the night of the party.

'Nathan was out of order,' she said to Kyle and by his reaction he knew exactly what she meant.

'I'm used to it, don't stress.' He gave up using the chopsticks and picked up a fork.

'I don't blame you for being angry.' At least they'd come back to the apartment that night and he hadn't stomped off into the city without her. She was relieved licensing laws were so strict too; he'd have no hope of getting into a bar because given past performance, it wasn't completely outside the realms of possibility he'd turn to a bottle to drown his sorrows. Like many kids, he'd learnt a way to escape reality, fast.

'I'm not angry.'

'You are.'

'Are you trying to make it worse?' He was agitated; maybe she'd pushed it too far.

'Don't shout, you'll have the neighbours complaining at us, you and I will get thrown out, and we'll have to sleep in Central Park in sleeping bags.'

A hint of a smile tugged at his mouth. 'Don't joke, if Mum gets her way that's what I'll be doing sooner than you think.'

'She won't throw you out, she just wants to see you sorted.'

Although Amelia had an uneasy feeling coursing through her because Connie had been vacant lately, as though she was disinterested, as though she had finally decided she'd had enough and she couldn't handle Kyle any longer. She may as well have shouted "Your turn!" to Amelia when she'd dropped her own son off for this trip.

'And don't change the subject,' Amelia went on. 'We're focusing on Nathan and Scarlett and what happened at the inn.' And she wondered whether Nathan had any idea Kyle had been seeing Scarlett ever since.

'The guy's an arsehole.'

'Call him that when you're in your room on your own, but don't use that language with me please.'

'Shame he's not more like Mitch. He's a good guy. He wanted to know if I'd like to go see his Christmas tree farm in Inglenook Falls.'

'I was thinking the same thing. We can do that if you'd like.'

'You don't need to hold my hand.'

'I know you're perfectly capable of getting the train there but I've been talking to Cleo about it already and I'd like to come. I can catch up with her, see the Little Knitting Box, and I can check out the local markets too. I'm sure I can amuse myself for the day without coming anywhere near you.'

'You don't need to go that far,' he smiled. 'I know you'll want to see the Christmas tree farm, you'll want to know where I'm spending my time, suss it out before you leave me to it.'

'Am I really that transparent?'

'Yes.'

She sat back on the sofa and eventually Kyle leaned back too.

'Scarlett's a very pretty girl.'

A slight colour appeared on his cheeks but she couldn't see much beneath his dark hair that hung enough to hide it. 'She's nice.

Clever too. She goes to one of those really posh schools and got grades that blow mine out of the water.'

'You two must've talked more than I thought.'

'I've been seeing a bit of her.'

'I know.' He seemed to be bracing himself for a rebuke. 'What's she going to do when she leaves school?'

'She wants to go to university. She's really good at art, but her dad says that isn't a proper subject.'

'Now why doesn't that surprise me?'

Kyle appreciated the remark. 'I told her it's her own life, she can't study something she isn't interested in. But she says she also needs to think about what job she can get afterwards, so it isn't always about your passion.'

'It sounds as though she's giving it serious thought.'

'More thought than I ever gave my future.'

'You've still got time, you're young,' she smiled.

'She gave me something.' He went over to his jacket and out of the pocket pulled a rolled-up picture.

When he handed it to her Amelia opened it out to see a pencil sketch. 'This is you. Wow, she drew this? She really is talented.'

'She admitted she took a photograph of me at the Christmas tree stall when I was working, and drew it from that.'

The details she'd captured in soft grey, a deeper shade for the contours of his face and his hair, were powerful. 'You should frame it. If someone drew such a nice picture of me I'd want to treasure it. And it's a wonderful keepsake.'

'I probably won't see her after this holiday.'

'That's the attitude,' she added sarcastically.

'Be serious. She lives in Hove, I live in Cornwall. Neither of us has a car. Makes it pretty difficult. Not to mention her dad hates me. Even if she fell head over heels in love with me, her dad would set up roadblocks to stop us ever seeing each other.'

'You're probably right. Hey, at least you can take your aggression out on those trees at the Christmas tree farm soon. Until then, try to keep a cool head.'

They were in a good place, for now, and when Amelia called it a night she fell straight to sleep, but when she woke in the early hours and couldn't settle, she decided to try to catch Connie on the phone before she left for work.

'It's me. Amelia,' she clarified again to the groggy voice at the end of the line. Had she totally got the time difference wrong? She double-checked on her phone but she hadn't. 'What's up? I thought you'd be about to leave for work.'

'I'm not going in today, I'm not feeling great.'

'Ah, your work Christmas party by any chance? Hangover from hell?'

'Busted,' Connie replied, still half asleep.

Over the years Amelia had enjoyed seeing Connie let her hair down after everything she'd been through with Stuart and Kyle. But right now, when she was tired, Amelia didn't seem able to summon the same forgiveness. 'Aren't you going to ask about Kyle?' Her voice demanded an answer, she was ratty because she cared.

'How is he?' Woozy still, most likely dry-mouthed from alcohol, Connie sounded more asleep than Amelia was and it only served to wind her up all the more.

'He's fine. Bit of attitude, accused of stealing, in trouble because of a girl, the usual thing.'

Connie cleared her throat and Amelia could imagine her sitting up in bed. At least that was something. 'Start from the beginning.'

So Amelia did. She relayed everything that had gone down since they arrived, starting with the accusation of theft in Madison Square Park, finishing with Kyle and Scarlett and Nathan's manhandling of Kyle at the inn.

'I'm sorry he's not behaving better.' Connie sounded shattered. 'How's the work at the market stall?'

'That's going well.'

'I'm glad.'

'I wish you'd talk to him more, try to help him.'

'I never seem able to get through to him,' Connie replied, coughing before she even got to the end of her sentence.

'Have you really tried though?'

'Of course I have.'

'He's still grieving about his dad and having me to talk to isn't the same as you.'

'Ease up, Amelia, I can't deal with this right now. I feel really bad.'

She resisted the urge to yell about her partying and her carefree life with Kyle out of the picture. If Connie had a man in bed beside her then Amelia would truly lose the plot. 'You need to deal with it, it's not going to magically go away.'

'I know.'

Amelia softened at the hopelessness in Connie's voice. 'He's hurting, Connie.'

'He's so angry most of the time. At me, at the world.'

'I expect the anger is bundled up with his grief and he hasn't separated the two, but the more you back off, the worse he's going to get. He needs you.' She was about to snap and demand a reply when she realised Connie was crying. 'I'm doing my best, but I'm not his mum.'

'I know.' Connie sniffed her tears away. 'I tried to tell him to work harder at school but at the same time I didn't want to nag. Then he got in with a bad crowd and I just didn't know what to do.'

'He doesn't want to hang out with them, you know. I can tell. Coming here has really helped him to see how things could be if he turned his life around. He hasn't said as much but it's obvious.'

'I really appreciate you doing this, Amelia. You're a good sister.' Exasperated, her voice rising with frustration, she said, 'I bet you see this all the time at work – I'm another hopeless parent who needs to get it together.'

She didn't argue otherwise. 'Just promise me you'll take steps to work on this when we come back to England.'

Coughing on the other end of the phone gave away that Connie had likely succumbed to a cold, most probably the result of too many shenanigans with her new-found freedom. 'I'm sorry I'm so hopeless. I really am grateful for everything you do, and I know I don't tell you enough.'

Amelia was drained from the heavy conversation and she lay back against her pillows as they moved on to safer topics for some semblance of normality. 'We got a tree at the apartment.'

'I'm impressed. Did you make Kyle help you decorate it?'

'Make him? I couldn't have stopped him.' When Connie went quiet she tried not to sound so cutting. 'You know boys, they like to take over. And we'd left it far too long. Bet you put yours up ages ago.'

'It's been up a while.'

'And what's the theme this year?'

'No theme.'

'Really?'

'I decided I'd go back to basics.'

'Any plans for the big day?'

'My friend Jill is coming over from Wales.'

'She's the chef, right?'

'I'll be well looked after but I'll be helping her. She's already made a timetable of preparation and cooking.' She sounded brighter now, perhaps the thought of Christmas keeping her going. 'She's making her famous sticky figgy pudding with caramel sauce.'

'Well, don't you two have too many Irish cream liqueurs this time, I know what you're like when you get together.'

'I'll do my best.'

'Jill usually heads off somewhere hot, doesn't she? How come you're getting the special treatment this year?'

'I think she fancied a change.'

'Good for you, eh?' When an awkward silence overtook the sisterly banter she asked, 'I was wondering, do you still have the bauble Kyle made?' If he wasn't going to mention it then she would. 'The special one with the fire truck.' God, please don't let her have thrown it away. He'd be devastated. 'Connie, you still there?'

'Still here.'

'Have you got it?' If she'd thrown it out Amelia would have to break it to Kyle and she already knew the kind of reaction he'd have.

'I still have it.'

'Kyle says you don't put it on the tree any more, since you went all designer.'

'Is this call a chance to chat and tell me about your holiday or is it all about me and what I've managed to get wrong with my son?'

'Connie...'

'I need to go, Amelia. I should get up and go into work.'

Her voice softened. 'I think we both know you're not going anywhere. You sound like shit.'

'Thanks, love you too, sis.'

'Don't worry, I get it. I'm a ratty cow too when I'm not well,' Amelia smiled. Hangover or just a cold, her sister really did sound terrible.

'I haven't forgotten Kyle, you know, even though he's away with you.'

'I know you haven't.' Her heart warmed at the admission.

'I think about him all the time, every day. I think about his future – what if…?'

'What if what?'

'Nothing.' Her voice trembled before she asked whether he was awake. 'I'd love to chat with him.'

'I expect he's sound asleep, but I can check if you like.'

'No, don't disturb him. I'll talk with him next time, ask him all about his trip.'

'Scarlett's nice.' She was suddenly desperate to keep the conversation going on a bit longer and she didn't really know why. Sometimes she just got a feeling when she spoke with Connie. Call it a sisterly bond, whatever, but now she didn't want the call to end. 'You'd like her. She's talented too, can draw like nobody's business. Even drew a picture of Kyle I've told him he has to get framed.'

'It doesn't sound as though the dad likes the idea of Kyle much.'

'He's not so bad, maybe he'll come round.'

'I see right through you! You like this man.'

'I do not, I just sympathise with him, that's all. He's looking out for his daughter. Remember what Dad was like when either of us brought a boy home?'

'Don't remind me. It was like the Spanish Inquisition if a male acquaintance dared to knock on the door for either of us. Talking of boys and men, have you heard anything from Paul?'

'No, why would I?'

'It's Christmas, I wondered if he'd changed his mind about ending things with you.'

She'd thought the same thing, but as time went on it became less and less likely. 'He's probably met someone else by now. I hope they're very happy.'

'Liar,' Connie giggled. 'You always were too good for him anyway. I really do have to go,' she coughed.

'You'd better rest up and I hope you're better soon. Love you.'

'Love you too, sis. And thank you again, from the bottom of my heart.'

For all that Amelia felt put upon over the years and had resented this trip a couple of times when she felt Kyle was a problem her sister wanted to wash her hands of, the emotion in Connie's voice brought Amelia back down to earth. They'd talk about it more when she was home, but this wasn't the sound of a woman who wanted to disown her son, only a woman who seemed stuck for which way to turn.

Amelia hung up and crept out of her room to Kyle's room to check on him. She knew how happy he'd be that his mum still had that Christmas ornament. But he was sound asleep, snoring lightly as he lay on his front, one arm at a right angle on his pillow, the same way he'd slept as a toddler. And beside his bed was the picture Scarlett had drawn of him, a boy with the weight of the world on his shoulders yet with so much possibility.

She'd tell him about the ornament in the morning but for now she sent Connie three photographs she'd taken of him. One at the Christmas tree stall as he laughed with a customer, another of him chowing down on a triple burger they'd found in a diner, and a third of him with a wool hat on, his hair flicking out from the bottom, the same smile he'd always had. And he looked happy.

If she could, she'd get one of him with Scarlett and perhaps it would all help Connie to see that her son was just a little lost and needed help to find his way to a better place, like they all did from time to time.

10

CLEO

Amelia was due to come to the Garland Street markets any minute now, which meant Cleo could finally act on her advice and have some time with Ruby. She'd been putting it off, work and dread getting in the way, but today, Prue was bringing Ruby to meet her and they were going to have one-on-one time.

'Business is going well here.' Kaisha put out a few more men's sweaters on the display tables in the chalet. She was helping out today along with Amelia and so Cleo wouldn't have any need to worry. She could focus solely on Ruby. 'Do you think you'll do this again next year?'

Cleo put her gloves back on now she'd finished serving the customer who bought the bottle-green cashmere sweater that had been hanging at the open door of the chalet. Some days they wouldn't put much stock on the doors if the weather was more brutal but today there didn't seem any hint of rain or the snow they'd been treated to yesterday. 'I think a store, the Inglenook Falls markets, and a wedding to organise might just be enough for us all.'

'I know you too well; you might not be able to resist it.'

'True. And we are making more money here than in

Inglenook Falls. It's not a whole lot more, but I expect it will be a tidy sum by the time we finish. We get more exposure here too and I'm hoping it might draw people to Inglenook Falls and the Little Knitting Box. It's been delightful to have a few of my old regulars from the store I had in the West Village stop by and say hello.'

'I heard a woman asking about your workshops earlier. She wanted to bring a group of friends along.'

Cleo smiled. 'There you go. Coming here has drummed up more business.' Now she needed to make sure she didn't take on too much and ignore her other commitments. Cleo never once thought she'd end up married with a blended family when she arrived in New York for the first time, and now she wouldn't want it any other way, but her headache this morning was a sure sign things were getting to her. And she was always careful to stay on top of her emotions given the family history with depression. Recognising the signs that she was overdoing it was key and was difficult to do when she was so busy all the time.

Cleo waved to Amelia, who'd just said goodbye to her nephew before he made his way to Mitch's stall. She did a quick handover before she spotted Prue's blonde, immaculately styled bob approaching over the heads of a couple of teenagers. 'Prue, good to see you. Hey, Ruby.' She smiled down at Dylan's eldest and her soon-to-be stepdaughter.

Ruby smiled but was soon talking to Kaisha, the trendy assistant at the Little Knitting Box who was almost a surrogate auntie in many respects. Ruby had often come to the store and sat out back waiting for Cleo and during those times Kaisha had taught her some basic knitting skills and they got on well.

'Thanks for bringing her to the city, Prue.' *And you can go now*, Cleo thought, although Prue was picking up garments already, which Cleo found surprising because these items didn't come with a designer label. 'That one would suit you.' She had hold of a burgundy roll-neck sweater.

Prue put it down. 'I'd better go.'

'Before you do...' She made sure Ruby was well occupied with Kaisha. 'I wanted to talk to you about Ruby.' She took another step away so they wouldn't be overheard. 'She's been a bit...' She wasn't sure how best to phrase it. Bolshy? Rude? Off? 'She's been a bit out of sorts lately.'

'She seems happy enough to me.'

'I mean she's been strange with me, not anyone else.'

'And you want me to talk to her, is that it?'

Actually it was the opposite. It was most likely Prue being in Ruby's ear that had caused half the problems in the first place. 'I just wanted to make sure we were on the same page.'

Prue looked at her watch impatiently. 'Get to the point, Cleo.'

'Ruby and I got on well for a long time, but lately she seems to be pushing me away.'

'I'm sure it'll all blow over.'

'Maybe.'

'I was terrible at that age,' Prue laughed, and Cleo could see there'd be no talking to her today, especially when her laugh had already caught Ruby's attention. Kaisha was showing her the multi-coloured scarf she'd been knitting and Ruby was wrapping it around her own neck, parading up and down the back of the chalet like a model on a catwalk.

'I have to go,' Prue said again, fingers waggling in the air in her daughter's direction. 'Bye, Ruby,' she called out. 'And stop worrying, it's not good for the face,' she told Cleo before she breezed off.

'I heard that.' Amelia was right by her side. 'Talk about catty.'

'That's Prue.'

'How was Dylan ever married to her?'

'I think he was wowed by the blonde hair, the long legs, and the glamour.'

Amelia put an arm around her friend. 'Well, it's a good job reality finally set in for him.'

Cleo emptied out the last two boxes of stock that they had and reiterated to keep an eye on the items hanging on the open doors in case a light-fingered shopper came along. The woman two chalets down had had jewellery stolen and had taken to having her husband man the doors. Shame: Cleo wasn't sure anyone would be keen to browse the earrings and necklaces if they first had to get past a man who sported a Forrest Gump-like beard, was well over six feet tall and didn't seem to have many smiles to offer around.

'I have my phone if you need me,' she told both Amelia and Kaisha.

'Go!' they both urged.

'Don't worry, we've got this,' said Amelia.

Ruby followed Cleo out of the chalet. 'Where are we going?' She at least had on sensible boots today and not the pair Prue had bought her with a little heel, and she was wrapped up nice and warm too.

'Somewhere very special.'

Ruby perked up when the Magnolia Bakery came into view but it wasn't cupcake time and they kept walking until they reached a quaint boutique with a curved window at the front.

'Mind the step,' said Cleo, trying not to look too pleased that Ruby's face exuded pure enrapture at seeing the wedding gowns on display behind the glass. This was where Darcy had found her dream dress and Cleo knew then that she'd come here if she and Dylan ever tied the knot.

They stepped down into the store where Serenity and Alexis, the jolly sisters who owned the boutique, were busy at the till with another customer. 'I thought you could help me out today,' she told

Ruby, trying to act as though she didn't already know Ruby was excited. 'Maybe with my dress and bridesmaid dresses too.'

She felt a bit like Prue, trying to buy Ruby's affections, but she wasn't attempting to do anything of the sort – it was more an effort to soften Ruby's feelings and let her in on the planning stages, which might help her come around to the idea. Perhaps her barriers would gradually come down a little.

Serenity came over to say hello, recognising Cleo but not remembering her name, and Cleo gave her the brief of what was going on – a wedding next December, a wedding gown as well as bridesmaid dresses to find, this being the initial stage of their research.

Ruby brightened even more as they went through a rack of wedding gowns, each one heavy to move aside. They talked colour themes. They looked through A-line dresses, ballgown style – the ultimate fairy-tale dress with the full floaty skirt – they looked at the more bouffant styles, those with a bustle, some with box pleats. The store had so much, it was quite overwhelming.

Serenity gave them their space but when she sensed they needed help she was there, adjusting the tape measure that had slipped slightly from its position hanging around her neck. 'May I ask where the wedding is going to be?'

'I haven't sorted that yet,' said Cleo. 'Having it next December is as far as we got.'

Serenity blew out from between her lips. 'You sort this one out,' she told Ruby. 'She wants a December wedding and hasn't booked it yet? Good luck.'

Ruby giggled.

'Do you think I'll get somewhere?' Suddenly Cleo felt the urgency.

'If you're flexible with days you might, but don't leave it much longer.'

'Can I help you choose somewhere?' Ruby asked.

'You know what?' She touched a hand to Ruby's long hair, almost the same shade as her own. 'I'd really love that. We could make this our project. I'm going to need a lot of help as I've got way too much to do as usual. My fault: I keep saying yes to things.'

'Like the market.'

'Do you mind me doing it?' Cleo asked when she got the feeling the reminder had jolted something for Ruby.

Ruby shook her head and got straight back to dress discussions with Serenity as though she was a mini wedding planner. They looked at gowns with beading, lace, tulle, those for a fuller figure, others for the petite bride, some for women who were an hourglass shape. They waded through white, cream, blush-pink, and champagne dresses and Cleo was none the wiser as to what she wanted to go for.

Serenity swooped in with the offer of a glass of fizz but Cleo turned it down in favour of treats at a café very soon.' She tried to gauge whether Ruby was getting fed up or not but she seemed more animated than she'd been in a long while. Cleo would have to thank Amelia for the very simple suggestion of making a day for her and Ruby, just the two of them. It was obvious when you thought about it, but Cleo had needed someone else who wasn't involved to point her in the right direction.'

'Okay, Ruby, I think it's time to move on and look at bridesmaid dresses.' Ruby's smile warmed Cleo's heart.

They went through the bridesmaid dresses on display, Serenity explaining that plenty were hired or they could be specially made if needs be. There were so many colours, some gorgeous, others hideous, although Cleo was thankful Ruby didn't voice her opinions of those too loudly but instead shared a little smile and moved on to the next.

Ruby's enthusiasm grew when they saw the midnight-blue dress hanging at the end of a collection. It had a scoop neck, lace, tulle, beading, and Cleo knew from the little girl's reaction that it was exactly what she was looking for.

'How about we go buy some bridal magazines from the kiosk we just walked past?' Cleo suggested to Ruby. 'We'll buy a big notebook too, and then we can sit in a nice café, drink hot chocolate, and make more plans.'

'Mum said I wasn't to badger you all afternoon, what with the market stall.' Ruby's gaze dropped from the dress to the floor. 'She told me to call her if you had to get back.'

'The market stall is in good hands,' Cleo assured her. She thought Prue knew the deal but she clearly hadn't listened to Dylan properly. 'You're stuck with me for the rest of the day, Amelia and Kaisha have the Garland Street markets covered, and we'll go home on the train together. But only when we're ready.'

Before they left the boutique, Cleo booked another appointment for January, on a Saturday so Ruby could definitely come along too, and Serenity told her, 'Promise me you'll book your venue before I next see you.'

'I'll make sure she does,' said Ruby, making Cleo share a smile with Serenity at how beyond her years the little girl sounded. The Ruby who'd always been so amenable and had loved Cleo from the start was still in there somewhere, she just knew it.

They picked up four bridal magazines, plenty to leaf through in the café, and Ruby found a pretty A4-sized notebook plus a pen with a big fluffy pink topper on the end for them to use to make their plans.

Ruby had already scribbled plenty in the notebook by the time Cleo brought over their order of hot chocolates topped with a swirl of fresh cream and a bowl of marshmallows on the side.

'This magazine is all about themes,' Ruby told her as she flipped through the pages pausing when something caught her eye.

'Colours, you mean?'

'No, themes,' she said with exaggerated impatience. 'There's something called rustic, what's that?'

'Darcy's wedding was rustic, casual too, and very beautiful.'

'You could have a garden wedding.'

'In winter?'

'Or romantic, or vintage. Why don't we brainstorm venues?'

Cleo's laugh nearly blew the cream from the top of her drink as she lifted it to her mouth. 'Since when do you use the word brainstorm?'

'I heard Dad talking with someone on the phone the other day.'

That explained it. 'Right, then let's brainstorm.' She tried to turn serious but Ruby sounded way beyond her years with this discussion, something Cleo felt sure was an influence from Prue, who thought a ten-year-old needed to eat out at classy restaurants and have their nails and hair done rather than run around in the woods or kick through great piles of leaves in the fall like Dylan and Cleo would let her do. 'Where do you suggest?'

'There's the new hotel with the spa,' Ruby began. 'Mom took us for pedicures and manicures.'

'The Corbridge Hotel might be a bit too fancy for what your dad and I are looking for, but write it down.' It could be an option and the foyer was indeed beautiful, especially with the roaring fire and ornate surround.

'What about Central Park?'

She smiled at her little organiser. 'I'd love to have it somewhere so beautiful, but it's a little far out for our local guests to go. But jot it down anyway,' she encouraged, 'you're on a roll.'

Ruby seemed pleased with how this was going too.

'There's a manor in Bampton,' Cleo suggested, 'smaller than the hotel, but it could work. I think they do weddings on the veranda.'

Ruby scribbled it down. 'What about the same place as Darcy?'

'It's an option, it was a stunning venue, but I think I'd rather have something different to my friend.'

Ruby didn't write it down. 'I didn't like having my party at the same place as a girl in my class. She had her party first so everyone had already been when it was my turn.'

'That sucks.' They carried on brainstorming. Cleo thought hard. 'Write down Country Club. There's a club about twenty miles out of Inglenook Falls and I know they do amazing functions including weddings, large and small, so that might be an option.'

'What about the Plaza?' Ruby's eyes widened.

Cleo stopped drinking her hot chocolate. "I think it's way out of my budget.'

'Can I write it down anyway?' Ruby's pen was poised.

'Sure. That's what you do when you brainstorm. You write down whatever comes to mind, then go back to the ideas and work out if they're feasible or not.' And as they carried on talking , it was more about this, the bonding between them both rather than the choice of venue that had Cleo wanting to make the moment last.

'Would you get married in England? Like in a big castle or something.'

'It didn't really cross my mind. Our lives are here, and with your grandad and Teresa coming over next winter it seemed a good time to do it here.'

Ruby flipped the page of the notebook. 'Can we talk about dresses?'

'We're done with location?'

'For now.'

Cleo smiled. 'Fair enough. So are we talking your dress or mine?'

'Yours first.' She turned serious as they ploughed through various styles, colours, cuts and photographs of accessories. 'What colour if you can't wear white?'

'And why wouldn't I wear white?' Cleo quizzed.

Ruby shrugged. 'Mum says if you've been married before, then you can't. And you're not allowed a veil either.'

Prue. Again. Bonding like this, she'd almost forgotten Ruby wasn't her own daughter, but facts were facts, and Prue would always be there butting in when it wasn't wanted.

'I think once upon a time that might have been the case, but nowadays you can do anything.'

'Like getting married under water, or in a windmill, or on a beach.'

'Exactly. Although it might be a bit cold to head to the beach in December,' she smiled.

They carried on planning, flipping through the pages together, Ruby totally on board. But Cleo wasn't daft. She knew that as time went on and the wedding approached, Prue would be doing her best to come between them in whatever way she could. Jealousy had reared its ugly head and while Dylan thought his ex-wife had moved on and wasn't interested in what he did any more, Cleo could tell that she still harboured some resentment and seemed intent on doing what she could to upset the equilibrium they'd managed to achieve with their blended family.

Maybe Amelia had some advice about ex-wives as well as the psychology of kids. Because she could really use some pointers right now.

11

NATHAN

If he could turn back the clock he would've kept his big mouth shut with Scarlett the night he admitted his true feelings, how being a dad had come at totally the wrong time and if he could've done it differently he would have. But his biggest regret in life wasn't that they'd had a baby; it was that he'd been too immature to handle it properly and had been absent at times when he really should have been around. And being pulled up on that particular failure by his own daughter hurt more than anything.

Breakfast at the Inglenook Inn was a quiet affair this morning, as it had been for the last week since he and Scarlett had had the confrontation, and it wasn't making for a pleasant holiday.

'I'm sorry about what I said,' he told Scarlett, again. He'd tried so many times to apologise but she was stubborn, something he knew she got from him.

'About not wanting me, you mean.'

'You're sixteen, not six, I know you don't believe that.'

'I suppose not.'

He hated to admit it but maybe it was time with Kyle and without her dad that had calmed Scarlett down. She hadn't said that was who she was seeing, how she was filling her free time, but it was kind of obvious. 'Not being there for you when you were little will always be my biggest regret.'

'Is that why you're so overbearing now?'

'I wouldn't say I was overbearing, but I guess it's why I'm so obsessed with trying extra hard to help you make good decisions.'

'And not make the same mistakes,' she added for good measure.

'I want what's best for you.'

'And what about school? Do you think I'm making a mistake wanting to take my passion for art further? I've been looking at universities, you know.'

'I know, I've seen you googling them. I'd love to be involved if you'll let me.' He scraped together the last mouthful of toast and egg sunny side up, its yolk smeared across the plate. 'We could go look at some. I can take some days off work, make sure you're making an informed choice.'

'Sounds good, unless it's all a ploy to make me choose something I don't really want to do.'

'I'll do my best to embrace what it is that you want, and how about we make the choice together?'

She didn't seem keen. 'This is why we never talk about it. It always comes down to what you think I should do. You say we'll choose together, but together really means I get an opinion, but your word will be final.'

He didn't have a chance to deny it before she stropped away from the dining room, past the Christmas tree decorated just as beautifully as the one in the lounge. He put his cutlery together on his plate as Darcy appeared with a coffee.

'I didn't order that,' he told her.

'You didn't but I'm bringing it anyway. And my company if you need it, though happy if you don't.'

He gestured for her to sit down. 'What is it with teens? One minute you feel like you're making headway, the next...' He looked towards the empty hallway his daughter had just stomped along to get to the stairs that would take her up to their suite. 'This holiday seems to be pushing us further apart rather than closer together.'

'From my experience, daughters and fathers will always fall out when it comes to boys. I can't say my dad was ever that happy when I brought someone home. Even when I introduced Myles to the family, Dad took a while to warm to him. It's a dad thing.'

'It's hard, that's what it is.'

'It must be hard being a single parent,' she said.

He added cream to his coffee but no sugar. 'It is.'

'Girls need their mom. Myles told me about your wife, I'm sorry.'

'Thank you. It's not been the easiest of roads for Scarlett. I know I haven't helped matters but since Dawn died, I've been doing my best.'

'Are you worried about her interest in Kyle?'

'I don't want Scarlett to make the same mistakes as her mum and I did.'

'And you think she might with Kyle? Have you told her?'

'Yes, and I shouldn't have done because she twisted it around to mean I didn't want her.'

'She surely doesn't believe that.'

'No, of course she doesn't. But she did use the conversation to point out how crap a dad I was to her when she was little. I was young and I didn't handle the responsibility all that well. I went out a lot, I partied, I did as many extra hours at work as I could.'

'A career can be a great escape, take it from someone who knows. But for what it's worth, Kyle doesn't seem a bad kid and he seems to really like Scarlett. And Mitch is impressed with the job he's doing helping at the Garland Street markets. He's even invited Kyle out to Inglenook Falls to help at his farm and see what it's all about. I think the kid needs a focus. I'm not here to sell him to you, but maybe give him a chance. I'm pretty sure he won't be kissing Scarlett again without checking where you are first.'

'I'm really sorry, again, that I made such a scene at the party.' He cringed, thinking of all their faces when he lost his temper.

'Don't be silly, you did no such thing.' A smile began to form.

'What's that look for?'

'The Inglenook Inn actually has a bit of a history.'

'In fist fights?'

'No, in romantic liaisons. Myles and I hated each other when we first met – long story – but he proposed on the stoop on Christmas Day. Mitch and Holly took a while to get to where they are now and they made it up here at the inn when he surprised her at one of our parties. A couple here for Thanksgiving got engaged by the Christmas tree. Maybe this place is a good omen for Kyle and Scarlett.'

'You're saying I should let this thing between them run its course?'

'Why not? They're young, they're having fun.'

'You might be right.'

'Don't forget to make time for yourself too.'

'I'm seeing plenty while I'm here.'

'That's not quite what I meant. A certain woman, also from England, seemed taken with you at the party.'

'Amelia? No, we were just talking.'

'Trust me, the look she gave you told me it could be more than that. Don't shut yourself off to possibilities, that's all I'm saying.'

When Darcy got on with the task of talking with Rupert about the menu for that evening, Nathan headed up to the suite. Scarlett had pulled on sparkly socks and was sitting by the tree using her phone. He wondered what would happen if he was brutally honest about what really frightened him about Kyle. But how could he? He may have wronged Scarlett by not being there for her when she was little, but how could he explain the extent of his fuck ups? How could he tell her that what really worried him about Kyle was that he saw a lot of himself in the boy and he didn't want her dragged into any kind of mess? Nathan had been luck; his parents had stuck by him and bailed him out countless times, they'd set him on a path to sort his life out. If they hadn't, he may have ended up living a totally different life; he could've got himself into so much trouble he would've ended up in prison, not university. And Scarlett wouldn't have wanted to have known him then.

* * *

The tension between Nathan and Scarlett didn't ease much when they headed to the Guggenheim Museum. He tried to make conversation when they arrived in the foyer with its spiralled layers going up and up and people looking down at them as they made the adventure all the way towards the top.

He did his best to make semi-intelligent remarks as they looked at painting after painting, sculptures he was indifferent to. But what the visit did do, as he watched his daughter talking with someone who worked there about a particular artist she admired, was bring it home to him how fast she was becoming her own person. She always had been independent-minded but now he was starting to see that it was time to embrace her opinions more, respect them even, and, while guiding her, let her make her own decisions. He needed to work out the magical balance between laying down the law and backing off enough to let her find her way.

When they emerged from the building and the bite of the New York winter got them both straight away, Scarlett suggested they go to see Carrie's brownstone, from *Sex and the City*. She'd gone from art lover to television devotee in an instant. 'Let's do it before the rain starts again,' she urged.

An hour ago the heavens had opened and it had been lashing down as they took refuge in the café area of the Guggenheim and wondered how long they would have to hover to avoid getting a soaking when they left. 'Why don't we walk round the Central Park Reservoir first? I need a breather before we go full-on into tacky girls' television mode.'

'Fair enough. You gave me art, I'll give you a scenic walk. But can we at least eat something before we go on a trek?'

They found a hot-dog vendor and ordered one each with the lot: onions, mustard, sauce. Their fingers enduring the cold without gloves until it was time to screw up the napkins and drop them in the nearest bin.

They headed into Central Park and even the dreary day couldn't detract from the beauty of the green space in the middle of Manhattan.

'Come on,' he said, 'this way.' Everyone seemed to be walking or running in one direction around the lake so they followed on and talked about the park some more, what it would look like beneath a foot of snow or when it was icy, they discussed movies they'd seen it in, they talked about snow back in England, school closures when the country came to a halt, how different it was taking a holiday in winter compared to summer.

They completed the loop of the reservoir, found the exit, and he ushered them towards the nearest subway station on 86th Street on the Upper East Side.

Once the train had whisked them all the way to 14th Street, Scarlett began to wonder where they were going. 'It's not much farther,' he told her. 'Follow me.'

He led her into the Chelsea Market, the building that housed eateries and small businesses. The smell was wonderful, the atmosphere electric. Behind glass partitions, pizza slices were lined up ready for selection, a bakery sold loaves in all shapes and sizes, they were tempted by gelato despite the season, brownies, cupcakes, in this modified building that retained its industrial structure. An Italian eatery offered a range of pasta, different sauces, an abundant choice of cheeses. The markets had pictures on the walls, a signpost for businesses in dark wood with touches of colour, a delicatessen selling things they'd never even heard of and a waterfall unique in its tranquillity. And then they saw it: the sign for the Lobster Place, Seafood Market.

Scarlett was forever pestering him at home to cook more seafood. She was a much bigger lover of the cuisine than he was, but as they stood at the tables at the back taking apart their lobster and dipping pieces into garlic butter, Nathan was sold. It was hands down the best he'd ever tasted.

When Scarlett checked her watch for the fourth time – he'd been counting because despite their chatter she was visibly distracted – he asked, 'Somewhere you need to be?'

'I said I might stop by the Garland Street markets and see Kyle,' she admitted, eyes not leaving his, most likely waiting for a reaction.

'Fine, let's go.'

'Seriously?'

'Yep, wouldn't mind going there myself.'

'Dad, no way. Not if you're going to start on him again. Just forget it.' She got back to devouring the remaining pieces of lobster.

'I'm not going to start on him. There's something I want to do, that's all.'

He checked his maps on his phone to make sure they knew which direction to go but when they set off, she didn't delve into his reasons for wanting to go there. He knew he'd made a fool of himself at the party that night and he was embarrassed, particularly because it had happened in front of Amelia, who he'd been enjoying getting to know. Darcy's comments about a connection between them had been something he dismissed but deep down wondered if she'd read the situation just right. Because the fact was, he couldn't stop thinking about her.

They reached the knitting stall first and it didn't take long to spot Amelia pushing a knitted item into a bag to hand to a customer. Her dark hair poked out from beneath a burgundy hat and he could see puffs of white air coming from her mouth as she spoke from inside the Swiss-style hut. He didn't know how these traders managed to stay out in the elements for hours on end, although surely it was good business for nearby cafés and coffee carts.

'I don't need an audience,' he whispered to Scarlett before Amelia saw them. 'You wander and I'll meet you at the far end by the Christmas tree stall in twenty minutes.'

'What are you going to do?'

'Never you mind.'

Amelia spotted him as soon as Scarlett left him to it and she waited until her customer bustled off happy with their purchases. 'I hope you haven't come to yell at me again.'

'I've come to apologise actually.'

She couldn't have looked more surprised. 'So you admit you overreacted and made a bit of a fool of yourself.'

'Steady on. I'll apologise, but I'm not going to grovel.'

A rebuke was on the tip of her tongue, he could tell, but she pressed her lips together firmly for a few seconds and then told him, 'Fair enough. Apology accepted. But it's not really me who needs to hear it. He's at the Christmas tree stall.'

'That's my next stop. Scarlett's already headed down that way so she's probably warning him.' He picked up some ruby-red gloves with sparkly silver thread running through them. 'While I'm here, can I take these? For Scarlett's stocking,' he explained.

Amelia softened a little, her green eyes less on the alert for trouble. 'I miss those days as a kid. The excitement, the anticipation. What else are you putting in there for her?'

'So far I've got chocolate, earrings, a keyring of a yellow New York taxi, and a miniature manicure set.'

'I'm impressed.'

'You should be.'

She looked away when another customer cleared his throat as he waited to pay for a sweater. 'I'd better get on, see you later.'

He hoped he would. He could've stayed chatting to her for much longer.

When he finally reached the cluster of Christmas trees surrounding the hut and spilling out onto most of the sidewalk, he hung back again. Kyle and Scarlett were talking, laughing about something, and she looked happy, relaxed in his company. Scarlett leaned in to smell the tree Kyle was about to put into the netting machine and it tugged at Nathan's heartstrings as he remembered how Scarlett had always done the same thing as a kid. She'd toddle up to the tree, right close so her hair got caught on the spiky pine needles, she'd close her eyes and inhale the scent of Christmas. And then she'd turn and smile, the biggest grin across her face. When she was really little it had been a moment that solidified how glad he was she'd come along, despite being unplanned, regardless of whether he and Dawn were ready. And when her mum died it had been the little moments like that that had kept him going.

From here, Kyle didn't look like a bad kid as he sipped on the hot drink Scarlett must have taken him. Perspective: that was what his current train of thought called for. It was a shame he hadn't had any that night at the inn.

The second Scarlett saw him she came over and hooked her arm through his. 'Ready.'

'I need to have a word with Kyle.'

She was trying to pull him away. 'What? No, you talked to Amelia, that was enough wasn't it?'

'I'm afraid not.'

'Dad...'

'Don't worry, he'll be in one piece when you get back.'

'Fine. I'll go get us a mulled cider each.' But she didn't look at all sure when she walked away.

Nathan waited for the customer to take the tree Kyle had netted and when Kyle saw him waiting with no Scarlett around to leap to his rescue, he looked as though he was preparing to stick up for himself, standing tall, chest pushed out like a pufferfish doubling in size when it felt threatened.

'Can I have a word?'

Immediately defensive, Kyle's only response was, 'Why?'

'I wanted to apologise. I was out of order at the party.'

Kyle lined up Christmas trees to cover the gap that had just been made by the sale, feigning nonchalance the best he could now instead of looking ready for a fight.

'Scarlett seems to like you,' Nathan tried again even though Kyle had his back to him. 'I think we got off on the wrong foot.'

'You accused me of stealing when you saw me in the park.' He was fiddling with the bottom branches of a tree Nathan suspected didn't need attention at all.

'Kind of understandable given our history, though, don't you think?' He got no response. 'I'm sorry if I got it wrong this time.'

When Kyle stood up to full height he wasn't far off Nathan's six foot two. '*If* you got it wrong?' Pufferfish was back.

'Look, I'm trying to apologise. I made assumptions at the park, and I really shouldn't have gone off at you at the party. But I do worry about my daughter. And that's the part I won't apologise for.'

Kyle backed down. 'She's a nice girl.'

'I know she is.' And he wanted her to stay that way. She was good at school, she worked hard, she was carving out a future. Kyle on the other hand had a past that had left him angry and, from what Nathan knew already, it was enough to give him cause to worry. He never wanted Scarlett to be collateral damage in whatever was going on in Kyle's life.

Scarlett appeared and thrust a cup of hot mulled cider into his hand, probably in case he was tempted to manhandle Kyle. Which he wouldn't. He was just a kid.

'Everything okay?' Scarlett looked from boyfriend to dad and back again.

'We're good, aren't we, Kyle?' said Nathan.

Kyle shrugged but it must've been Scarlett's influence when he held out a hand to Nathan. 'No hard feelings,' he said.

Not yet there weren't. But Nathan shook his hand anyway.

* * *

Nathan did his own thing for the next hour. He wandered along to Union Square Park. Although wandered probably wasn't the right word. With Christmas less than a week away the crowds in Manhattan seemed to have doubled. The streets were full of colour, life, excitement, but he wasn't brave enough to tackle these holiday markets. Instead, he was content to absorb the atmosphere from the perimeter. A tree with coloured lights illuminated the velvet sky interspersed with towering blocks that made up the city. He watched a street entertainer, a one-man band playing a bright-red guitar, blowing into a harmonica, using feet attached to strings to play the drums fastened to his back. And when he'd had enough of sightseeing, Nathan eventually made his way back to the Garland Street markets, where he'd agreed to meet Scarlett at the Christmas tree chalet.

When Amelia beckoned him as he sneaked a glance at the knitting stall when he walked by, he couldn't say he was sorry. She handed her customer some change and turned to him. 'Did you catch up with Kyle?' She was a good auntie and her commitment to family was something to admire. He'd had his parents in his corner his whole life; it was good that Kyle had someone to look out for him too.

'I did.'

'And...' Her impatience was amusing.

'Are you worried things got heated?'

She battled a smile. 'A little.'

'Don't worry, we're cool.'

'Cool? Just like that, you're fine with him, with him and Scarlett?'

'I wouldn't go that far, but they're on holiday, I'm going to do my best to appreciate the location and the time away from work and stop worrying so much.'

'Liar.'

His laughter echoed around the inside of the chalet, mingled with puffs of cool white air against Manhattan's chill. 'I'm doing my best here, all right?' He was about to ask her how business was going, settle into a conversation like the one they'd had at the inn when they were relaxed and getting to know each other, when his phone pinged with a message from Scarlett. 'She wants to head out to Connecticut tomorrow,' he related. 'Although I'm not sure why when she's in New York City. Seems like the dull option to me.'

Amelia pulled a face. 'That's possibly my fault.' She straightened a purple sweater at the front so it sat comfortably next to a smooth, mint-green one. She tucked in the sleeve beneath a sky-blue woollen cardigan that a customer must've unravelled. 'Scarlett and Kyle came by a minute ago on their way back from grabbing hot chocolates and she heard us talking about going to Inglenook Falls.'

He took a deep breath as he made the connection to something Darcy had mentioned to him once. 'Kyle is going to the Christmas tree farm,' he concluded, adding Darcy's name to the mix to explain how he already knew.

'I think it'll be good for Kyle to spend the day at the farm. Mitch said he'll let him use the axe to chop up logs they sell there too.'

'Does he realise how hard that is?'

'You've chopped wood?'

'Tried it once.' He flexed his muscles but his jacket was zipped up tight, which didn't make it easy. 'You're right, though, a bit of grafting will probably do him good. Although you're not really selling the idea to me, sending Scarlett off with a boy I'm unsure about and one who will soon be wielding an axe.'

'Give him a chance.'

'I think he might've refused my apology had Scarlett not been standing there.'

'He takes a while to warm to people, especially those who might have prejudged him.'

'Can you blame me when we've crossed paths before?'

'I guess not.' She broke the conversation to sell a fawn scarf with matching gloves to a customer and when the transaction was made said, 'He'll move on soon enough; he's not one to hold a grudge. And he and Scarlett might think they're all grown up but really they're still kids, and vulnerable at that.'

'They have all the confidence, not always all of the common sense.'

'Totally agree,' she smiled.

'There's a first time for everything.'

Amelia was a beautiful woman when she wasn't scowling or when his vision wasn't clouded by a teen about to get his own teen in trouble. Her wavy dark hair was held in place beneath her woolly hat and every now and then she swished a bit away from where it was making her chin itch. She wore deep-red lipstick he'd noticed at the party but here it seemed brighter, glossier beneath the light globes dotted at intervals up one side of the pointed chalet roof and down the other.

'I'd be happy to watch out for Scarlett tomorrow,' Amelia assured him. 'I'll be in Inglenook Falls checking out their markets, catching up with my friend Cleo at her knitting stall. Scarlett can spend time with Kyle or with me and it's only a small town, she'll be very safe.' She served another couple of customers and when he told her he should go to meet Scarlett, she stepped out of the chalet after him. 'Why don't you join us tomorrow? Come to Connecticut.'

'Scarlett would love that,' he laughed.

'Don't make out you're only going to keep an eye on her. Tell her you want to see Inglenook Falls for yourself after you heard so many good things about it at the party.'

'Which I did. It sounds like a slice of America that's a little different to the big city.'

'Exactly. And this way you get to spend time with your daughter, you see a new place, and you won't be pacing the sidewalk here, wondering what she's doing and whether Kyle has mastered the use of an axe.'

'Okay, you're on.'

'Great,' she smiled. 'Then we'll meet you both in Inglenook Falls. Kyle and Scarlett can text the exact arrangements.'

'Or we can too, if you give me your number.' He was pretty sure he noticed a contented smile as she took out her phone and texted him when he told her his own number. 'Sorted, see you tomorrow.'

And when he walked away, he felt as though he'd just arranged a date. Only it wasn't an official date, and they'd have a couple of teenagers on the periphery.

* * *

Scarlett took his suggestion of going with her to Inglenook Falls well. And now here they were. It was ridiculously early, a few days before Christmas Eve, and the journey here had granted them icy scenery, glistening frost, and the promise of snow on the air. Inglenook Falls was as quaint as it had sounded from the descriptions, and as they walked from the station and saw the green sign welcoming them to town, he could see a green space dusted in white ahead of them, a bandstand with lights and garlands wound around it. They had a brief check-out of Main Street and its café, a handful of shops, and got their bearings before they found the track that they needed to follow to reach Mitch's Christmas tree farm.

Mitch was already standing on the porch of the little log cabin, leaning against one of the posts and sipping a cup of steaming coffee. 'Welcome!' He raised his other hand as he stepped down to greet them. 'You found the place okay?'

'Easy enough.' Nathan shook his hand in greeting. 'It's pretty wonderful out here.'

'Bit different to the city, eh?' Mitch held up his cup. 'Coffee?'

'No, don't want to put you to any trouble. I'll head off to the café. I saw one on Main Street.' He had plans to meet up with Amelia, not that he'd let it slip to Scarlett. On the train this morning he'd gazed out of the window wondering how he could've gone for years in England never finding anyone to get serious about, yet here in another country entirely he'd found a woman he was interested in getting to know better. Maybe that was why holiday romances were a thing. Your guard was down, you were more open to possibilities.

'Enid at the café will sort you out,' Mitch advised, 'but don't go for a brownie, they're addictive.'

'I appreciate the warning.'

The pretty auburn-haired woman, Holly, who he'd met at the party emerged from one of the sheds next to the log cabin holding a big painting.

'What's it a painting of?' Scarlett asked Holly, her interest piqued.

'It's Main Street, Inglenook Falls.'

'We saw the bandstand on our way here,' Scarlett smiled. 'Although it was dusted in frost, not like this painting where it's bathed in sunlight. I love the contrast.'

Holly pointed out the bakery on the painting, Marlo's café, and the gap leading to a guesthouse that was set back enough that they hadn't noticed it earlier when they were on Main Street itself.

'Did you paint this?' Scarlett asked.

Holly grinned and looked to Mitch. 'I didn't.'

'Guilty.' Mitch lifted the coffee cup into the air by way of acknowledgement. 'Bit of a hobby of mine. It needs work but Holly thinks it's finished so she's insisting we put it up inside.'

'He's far too modest,' Holly reprimanded, but landed a kiss on Mitch's cheek. 'He's a brilliant artist, and he made this frame too.'

Nathan was even more impressed as he looked at the cedar wood surrounding the work of art. 'Painting, frames, and a Christmas tree business.' He whistled through his teeth. 'You've got your work cut out.'

'Good job I enjoy what I do.' Mitch knocked back the rest of his coffee, did up his jacket, and pulled on gloves before the winter chill could get to him. 'And as a side business, the painting and the frames do quite well.' He told Nathan all about a couple of exhibitions he'd had in the city, how he sold frames in a few stores in

Connecticut now business was picking up, as well as at holiday markets.

'And what about this place?' Nathan asked. 'Is it a year-round job?'

'It sure is. I sold off a bit of the land but the rest takes a lot of work. Lucky for me my son comes up regularly and Jude, a kid I've known a while, helps out. I recently opened up to the public to come choose a tree from here, so it's been a bit of a change, especially with the markets in Manhattan to deal with too.'

Holly had emerged from the cabin minus the painting but with a camera strap hooked around her neck. 'I'm off to take some pictures of the Inglenook Falls markets. Scarlett, you're welcome to join me if your dad doesn't mind.'

'Another time?' Scarlett ventured.

'I'll hold you to that,' Holly smiled.

'Kyle is already out in the fields.' Mitch picked up on the reason she didn't want to go with Holly. 'I'll take you to him.'

Nathan didn't want to hang around like a spare part so he followed Holly up a different, much steeper, track to the one they'd come down to get here. She told him how she'd tumbled down it once before, which was how she'd met Mitch.

'I literally fell into his life,' she laughed, leading the way, avoiding any patches of ground between trees that had iced over. 'It's our little joke.' She stopped and they turned so the little log cabin could just about be seen down below. 'He's a good man. I didn't think so at first but he really is kind. He'll look after Scarlett, so please don't worry.'

'Is it that obvious?'

'Yes,' she smiled. 'Come on, this way is much quicker, Main Street is just up there.' She pointed towards where a sunbeam highlighted a long path.

They parted ways at the top and Nathan took in the beauty of

Main Street, the roofs glistening in the wintry air, people huddled up against the season's chill and chattering away to one another as they went about their business. There was none of the urgency of Manhattan, no battling a hectic city in a biting wind, and somehow the cold here still managed to coax a smile. He hadn't thought places like Inglenook Falls existed any more, but the charm of a small town was strongly present with its old-fashioned shops and creaking awnings, the little green where a group of kids chased each other, the vehicles that passed through Main Street with an apologetic politeness compared to the bullying traffic of Manhattan.

He wasn't meeting Amelia for another forty minutes so he walked towards the markets he could see in the distance and passed beneath the arched entrance sign, some of Mitch's trees for sale on either side. It was early enough for the ground to still have the crunch of frost beneath his feet but the market was beginning to bustle with stallholders lining up their wares, greeting customers, making the most of the last few days before Christmas.

When he saw Amelia, Nathan hung back and watched her perusing the chocolate stall. He couldn't deny how much he'd been looking forward to seeing her today, how it felt a bit like a date. On holiday or not, he'd found a woman he wanted to get to know much better. And he wondered whether she possibly felt the same way.

12

AMELIA

Amelia waved over at Nathan when she noticed him hovering near the roast-chestnut cart. She let a laugh escape when he stumbled on the less-than-even grass beneath, looking as though he'd had one too many at this early hour.

'I'm glad my clumsiness amuses you.' He quickly righted himself and made his way over.

'You were a bit comical, I'm afraid, arms waving everywhere.'

'Not quite the impression I was going for.'

'You've got to watch the ground here; it's uneven and you can't see when it's frosty. I stumbled about ten minutes before you did.' She looked around them, stallholders embracing the season, visitors milling and moving excitedly from one stall to the next. 'What do you think to Inglenook Falls? Bit different to the city, isn't it?'

'Completely different, and in a good way. I'm glad I came.'

She stood on tiptoes and pointed back towards the entrance, where across the street there was a small row of shops and you could just about make out signage for Cleo's store. 'That's the Little Knitting Box, where I've been helping out as well as bringing boxes of stock over here from. Did you and Scarlett find the Christmas tree farm all right?'

'We did, and I'm sure Scarlett is in good hands.'

'You're not worrying too much?'

'Not right now, no.'

The way he was looking at her suggested she was as much of a distraction for him as he was for her. His company would stop her worrying about Kyle so much. 'Kyle said he'd be finished with Mitch around four o'clock.'

'He'll be exhausted after a full day. I wonder if Scarlett will attempt any lifting or chopping.'

'You never know.'

He seemed a lot calmer about them spending time together, which was a relief. She gestured towards the market stalls. 'Were you looking for anything in particular today?'

'I'm just killing time really.'

'Come on, I've done the rounds already. Do you like cheese?'

'As a matter of fact I do.'

'Then I've just the place.'

Over the next hour they savoured many of the tastes on offer at the winter markets, their first stop spent sampling cheeses, the stronger the better, although one variety nearly knocked his head off with the chilli hit he hadn't expected. Amelia had done her best not to laugh too hard and cautiously took a bite of the same variety. They enjoyed a mulled cider each, tasted chocolates in all shapes and sizes, one so rich Nathan drew the line at having any more.

'This is starting to become an eating holiday,' he declared when they passed the knitting stall and waved a hello to Cleo.

'They have the most amazing doughnuts at the end.'

'No way, I'm done. And please tell me it's almost time to warm up at the café, I can hardly feel my toes.'

'Drama queen.'

She loved how he was open to trying new things. Paul had always been what he declared a traditionalist. He liked fancy restaurants but kept his choices conservative; when he enjoyed wine he stuck to blends and varieties he knew. But Nathan seemed to go with the flow. Paul had never been able to handle spicy food so wouldn't have tried a crumb of the hot cheese. Mind you, perhaps Nathan was regretting it given how quickly he'd downed the cider straight afterwards.

They moved on to a stall with picture frames and Amelia told him this was Mitch's work.

'He's a talented man,' said Nathan.

'It was once a secret hobby, according to Cleo – I've been with her all morning, she's updated me on so much local gossip that I feel as though I could slot right in here as one of them.'

They walked back to the entrance, where Mitch's Christmas trees were being snapped up and Nathan was able to direct someone to the Christmas tree farm as they wanted to select their own. And when both admitted they'd put a tree in their accommodation in the city, Amelia laughed. 'I had no intention of doing so. I figured there would be so many to admire around Manhattan.'

'Same here. I was going to make do with enjoying the tree in the communal lounge and the other in the dining room, but Scarlett was having none of it.'

'Kyle hasn't always had the best Christmases and I thought perhaps we both needed it.'

'Why do you need it?'

'Long story.' She looked away as they walked across the street. 'Why don't we go to the café? Never mind your feet, my fingers are cold even through these gloves.'

'New York winters are a shock to the system,' he agreed. 'I've heard February is worse.'

'Still hoping for snow though,' she smiled.

Seated in Marlo's and welcomed by a woman called Enid who wanted to know their connection with the town, they ordered a couple of coffees and passed on any food when she offered and so she left them to it. 'I'm hoping to take Scarlett for an Italian meal tonight, if it's not too dull for her to go out with her old man. She might get a better offer.'

Amelia sipped her coffee tentatively but it was way too hot yet. 'Are you asking me if Kyle already has plans?'

'I suppose I am.'

'Don't worry, I'll keep him busy and I think he'll be knackered anyway after working at the farm. I'm pretty tired myself after the early start, so I'm planning on Chinese takeaway from the place Cleo recommended. I'm going to eat it out of those quintessentially New York white cardboard boxes with the little metal handles.'

'Sounds better than my idea. Maybe sitting in a swanky restaurant with my teen could be a step too far.'

'Are you inviting yourself?'

'I promise I wasn't. And as much as Scarlett wants to see Kyle, she wouldn't want me hanging around.'

'Maybe another time.' She was disappointed. Having adult company was nice. She hadn't realised how taxing it would be emotionally to spend a lot of time not only with a teen but worrying about him too. Having Nathan there as a buffer and Kyle distracted with Scarlett would be a complete break from it all. Plus, Nathan was good company. And not bad to look at either. Cleo had been teasing her this morning about how long she'd chatted with him at the inn, but she had so much to focus on right now; getting involved would only complicate things.

He relaxed against the back of his chair. 'Tell me then, why do you need to get away from it all?'

'A couple of reasons.' Her coffee was still too hot to hide behind so she settled for clasping her hands around it instead.

'I'm a good listener, promise.' He held up a hand to stop her listing all the examples of this not being the case at all. 'Try me.'

'I went through a breakup six months ago. Since then I've been a bit all over the place.'

'You don't seem the type of person to fall apart.'

'I wouldn't say I fell apart, but I'd been with Paul for five years and I really thought he was the one. He's a few years older than me, he was more settled than anyone else I'd ever been out with; he had his own place, he wasn't a lad who was going to cheat. I'd had that experience once before.'

'What went wrong?'

'I still don't know. He said we wanted different things. To me, we wanted the same, but clearly somewhere along the line I got my wires crossed. He also thought I put everyone else first, before him.'

'And did you?'

'Sometimes, yes.'

'Have you seen him since?'

'No. I moved out of his place, back to my flat after I gave my tenants notice, and slowly I've been getting back to normal. But it was what you might call an abrupt breakup. Usually there's a more specific reason or there's an affair. I still don't feel as though I fully understand why he ended it.' She grinned and shook her head. 'Would you listen to me? You'd think I was the only person who'd ever been dumped. He gave me his reasons, perhaps I'm just choosing not to see them properly.'

'You need to talk to him again, find out for sure. Then you can move on.'

'I don't know, maybe it's better to be ignorant.'

'Give me your phone, I'll message him.'

Giggling, she pushed his hand away and lowered her voice when Enid looked interested at the change in atmosphere. 'You will not.'

'But you still have his number, right?'

'Yes.'

'So ask him. Text and demand an answer. What's the worst he could do? Ignore you?'

'He could reply and I might not like it.'

'Then I'll meet you in the city, get you horribly drunk, and you can take it from there.'

Her insides did a loop-the-loop at his suggestion of taking her out.

'Come on, Amelia, get the closure you deserve.' He nodded towards the phone she'd left on the table in case Kyle called.

With a deep breath she picked up the phone, tapped out a quick message asking for an explanation, and pressed send before she could change her mind. With a nervous laugh she put it face down on the table again as though by hiding the display she could avoid his reply when, or indeed if, it came.

'Well done. Feel better?'

'In a weird way I really do. I should've done that a long time ago.'

'No, wouldn't have worked, you weren't ready. But now you are.'

'What makes you so sure?'

'Whoever you were when you were with him, I get the feeling it wasn't the same woman as the one sitting opposite me now. Am I right?'

'I suppose you are.' He barely knew her yet he was spot on. Connie had said something similar to her when she and Paul first broke up. She'd said that he was always trying to turn her into the person he wanted, the type of girlfriend who complemented him, rather than let her be a person in her own right. At the time Amelia thought her sister was being dramatic and she was too devastated to really consider what she meant. But now Amelia saw that perhaps Connie had made a really astute point. And it had taken Amelia thousands of miles and a stranger to point it out for her to really get it.

'So what's the other reason?'

'Excuse me?'

'You said there were a couple of reasons for you needing this break.'

Sitting opposite him this close made her nervous, but she'd shared so much already, she may as well confide everything now. 'I got into a bit of trouble at work.'

'And what is it you do?'

'I'm a youth worker.' She waited for Enid to wipe the table next to them, wondering whether she was attempting to eavesdrop and feed the local gossip mill.

'I'm not surprised; you're a bit of a natural.'

'I wouldn't go that far, especially these days. My problem lately is that I get too involved in my cases.'

'I would've thought that was a prerequisite.'

'Calling a kid's mother unsavoury names wasn't exactly in the job description.'

'What did you call her?' The corners of his mouth twitched in amusement when she reiterated what she'd said. 'I can see why she and your boss may have taken exception.'

'I shouldn't have shot my mouth off but I was frustrated. I guess that's one of the drawbacks of the job. So much is out of your hands and even if a kid shows all the signs of reordering their life and turning themselves around, all it takes is a parent to start calling the shots and ruin all the hard work. I'm not saying it's all parents, but a few don't seem to understand that their kid has potential, they can have a better life. And when I see them deliberately sabotaging a kid's efforts and making them feel awful about themselves, well, I get pretty annoyed.' She took a deep breath when she realised she was getting agitated all over again.

He smiled. 'You do ramble when you're nervous.'

'What makes you think I'm nervous?' But she already knew her cheeks had coloured inside out of the cold in front of this man who was a pleasure to be with.

'Your job sounds tough.' His eyes never left hers when she braved looking up.

This man seemed far removed from the one who'd confronted Kyle in the park on their first night here or the man who'd flipped out at the Inglenook Inn when he'd seen Kyle kissing Scarlett. 'This holiday was an enforced break by my boss,' she explained. 'He told me to take time off, get some perspective. I'll have to apologise to the parent I was brutally honest with, but getting a warning in my job wasn't something I saw ever happening. I usually know when to back off before I overstep.'

'What was different this time?'

'I don't really know, I guess I'm tired of it all. Paul ending things, Kyle getting into trouble, my sister relying on me. I think everything got a bit much.'

'When you talk about Kyle, you sound like *you're* the parent rather than your sister.'

'Over the years it sometimes felt as though I was. Part of it was Connie's doing, the rest most likely mine for never forcing her to be more accountable.' It was a novelty to have a man take such an interest. Paul had never wanted to listen about Connie or Kyle, but then again, he'd seen enough over their time together to know the situation. 'I don't think Connie ever realised quite how much she's relied on me, and talking on the phone to her helped. I think when we get back to England she and I need to sort a few things out. She knows she needs to step up for Kyle. I just don't think she knows the right way to go about it.' She let out a breath she didn't realise she'd been holding.

'You and Kyle seem really close.' He pushed his cup of half-drunk coffee far enough away that he could rest his elbows on the table and steeple his fingers beneath his chin, bringing him even closer and sending a zing of electricity through her body. 'Surely being an auntie is like being a grandparent – you should get all the best bits and none of the crap.'

'I guess I volunteered a lot of the time, or I never said no, so she's always relied on me and it kind of gained momentum as Kyle got older. I think Connie sees my work experience as another reason to turn to me. I know she worries she's doing a rubbish job at parenting.'

'Ironic, given she's putting the responsibility onto you.'

'I should've said no a long time ago. But then I got attached and, to be honest, I like having Kyle in my life.' Paul had never wanted kids and she'd thought she was fine with that – she had Kyle in her life and he was more than enough, plus the kids at work. She'd agreed, at least on the surface, that handling another tiny human might have been too much for them both. 'When Kyle was sick I'd look after him so Connie could go into the office. She had a horrible boss who'd berated her for time off more than once and I knew she couldn't afford to lose her job, being a single mum.'

'But it meant your sister went about her day as normal and you didn't. You worked at home, and I'll bet your output was nowhere near as productive. No way can you look after a baby or a toddler and get a good day's work done. Believe me, I've tried it when Scarlett was little, never bloody worked.'

'You're right. It wasn't particularly fair. I'm glad Kyle and I are close though, something I think happened without really trying because I spent so much time with him. It means that now he's older he knows he can depend on me.'

'He's lucky to have you. When did you work, if you were looking after him during the day?'

'If Kyle slept, then I'd work. Or I'd wait for Connie to pick him up in the evening.' She rubbed her hands across her face. 'Why am I such a pushover?'

'You're not. You care, that's all. You stepped up when your sister was having a hard time and devoted all your attention to looking after her and her son rather than yourself. That's admirable.'

'Admirable, really? Or do you mean pathetic?'

He shrugged. 'We can go with your description if you really want to.'

'I like yours better. And Connie isn't a bad person, you know.' Sitting here going on about her sister made her feel guilty.

'I'm sure she isn't. I don't think you'd put up with her if she was.'

'You know, sometimes I think life would've been easier if I'd kept on doing telesales from home. The job worked for me for a while – I earned good money, I had no travel expenses or commute, which meant I put in longer hours. My parents worry about the career I've chosen now. Paul did too. Nobody wanted me getting involved with families and kids in crisis.'

'Do they have much need to worry?'

'Sometimes.' She didn't give away the specifics, but gave him an overview of some of the more difficult projects they'd implemented where she'd spend time with a street team working in rougher areas, often finding opposition to the positivity they were trying to instil. 'The way I see it is that all jobs come with a risk. If I'd become a teacher a student could've turned on me, if I was an electrician I could electrocute myself—'

'If you'd stayed as a telesales executive you could've died of boredom.'

'I wouldn't go quite that far,' she laughed, 'but I'm glad I made the change.'

Enid gave them a knowing smile when they left the café and Amelia hoped Nathan hadn't noticed, although she was buzzing inside at spending time with this man, way across the miles and away from everything familiar.

Outside, they buttoned their coats up straight away. Darkness had descended and there was a hint of snow still on the air. 'Thank you,' she told him, her fingers scooping her hair away from her mouth as the breeze insisted on blowing it there. 'For listening to me, I mean. Letting me moan about my troublesome life, which really isn't all that bad.'

'For what it's worth, I admire you. Kyle seems a nice lad deep down and I reckon a lot of that is down to you.'

She nudged him and grinned. 'You like him, you're happy he's with Scarlett because you know he's good. Admit it.'

'Never.' But he smiled at her and only broke eye contact when he looked up and said, 'Talking of the teens, here they come.'

Wary of Nathan at first, it took Kyle a bit of coaxing to talk about what they'd got up to all day. Scarlett too. Kyle had chopped log after log, bagged them up, carried them to customers' cars, he'd helped fell several trees, he and Scarlett had taken photographs of some of the most amazing trees that bordered the edges of Mitch's land. Holly had made them all lunch – soup with crusty bread and Kyle had had two helpings, he was so hungry – and both of them looked the better for the fresh air and space.

Amelia watched Nathan's reaction when the kids walked ahead of them and Scarlett slipped her hand into Kyle's. He seemed reluctant to take it but when he did, Nathan didn't say a word.

Maybe Nathan was managing to see the Kyle she knew, the boy who was kind and considerate, polite and dependable. And today, she'd got to see a man who was very much the same.

And when she looked at him as they boarded the train and she got a waft of fresh aftershave, she wondered whether the kids were the only ones who'd found a bit of holiday romance.

13

NATHAN

With Christmas Eve fast approaching, Scarlett begged her dad, yet again, to go ice-skating and when they investigated the Bryant Park winter village he found himself agreeing. He was in such a good mood after his time with Amelia in Inglenook Falls that if Scarlett wanted him to walk a tightrope across Central Park when it was thunder and lightning outside, he'd probably do it.

After Amelia's company yesterday, she and Kyle had headed back to their apartment while Nathan and Scarlett had found a charming Italian bistro last night not too far from the Inglenook Inn. They'd dined on lobster ravioli, mains of wild mushroom and cream risotto, and a dessert of the silkiest panna cotta he'd ever eaten. But amazing as their meal had been, Nathan had found himself thinking of chatter and laughter over little cardboard take-away boxes with chopsticks poking out of the top. After dinner they'd trawled the city for light displays, and his mind kept going to Amelia, wondering what she was up to, what she would think of the giant evergreen that had become tradition at the Rockefeller Center, the floating displays of Christmas trees on one of the lakes in Central Park, the stunning decorations on Fifth Avenue. His good mood even survived Scarlett shopping in stores she'd only ever seen in the movies, her excitement mounting, spending six months' worth of allowance in one hit. Amelia was an unexpected and very welcome distraction on his holiday and more than once he'd been tempted to text her and see whether she wanted to meet up again.

'You're getting better,' Scarlett told him after they'd handed back their skates at the winter village.

'I wouldn't go that far.'

'Mind if I go meet Kyle?'

'As long as you're back at the inn by eleven o'clock at the latest.'

She did her best to hide her surprise at his willingness to let her go. 'What are you going to do?' She had him hold her bobble hat while she ran her fingers through her long hair before plaiting it to the side and popping her hat back on. It brought back a memory of putting her hair into plaits one morning for school. He'd felt so accomplished dropping her at the gates. He bet none of the other dads had such skill. But he'd only done it once or twice before she announced she was old enough to do her own hair now, thank you very much.

'Don't you worry, you go have fun without your old man. I'll just have an early night.'

'No way, that's dull. It's three more sleeps until Christmas Eve, you're in New York.'

'Okay, maybe I'll go back up the Empire State Building. You weren't interested in reading all the placards, the history. I wouldn't mind seeing it all again.'

'I wish you'd told me at the time.'

He hugged her. 'Have a good time tonight. I'm making a fuss of you now so I don't embarrass you in front of Kyle.'

They made their way towards the Garland Street markets, where Kyle had finished working the tree stall.

'She won't be late,' Kyle assured him.

'I appreciate that.'

Nathan sneaked a look at the knitting stall but Amelia was busy, customers forming a line at the chalet, so he walked to the Empire State Building, taking in the skyline, the sense of fun and festivity in the air, the feel of the cold on his cheeks and the freedom of only having himself to think about for once. The building loomed in the distance, its lit-up spire in the centre of midtown Manhattan twinkling with the rest of the city's lights.

He passed in through the Fifth Avenue Lobby, taking in the art-deco-inspired ceiling murals in gold and aluminium leaf. He went to the *Dare To Dream* exhibit that chronicled the planning and construction of the building; there were period photographs, architectural sketches, and reproductions of the mementos from the thousands of workers who'd helped create a piece of history in the city. Up on the Main Deck he felt the bite against his cheeks when he went outside. He needed another layer but it was hard to resist staying out here for the three-hundred-and-sixty-degree views of New York City, the high-powered binoculars that were dotted strategically affording him a better view of the lights of Times Square and the Statue of Liberty. The city sparkled beneath, he soaked up the New York atmosphere, the feeling of Christmas. He and Scarlett usually went to his parents' for the day itself but already he was looking forward to the change, to eating their Christmas dinner in the company of other guests at the inn. He'd booked it with Darcy soon after they arrived and he'd seen a framed magazine article on the wall titled 'Christmas at The Inglenook Inn', the write-up accompanied by a photograph of the dining room dressed for Christmas with a huge platter in the middle, a turkey so big it could feed half of Manhattan.

Without Scarlett moaning about him taking his time, he read as much as he wanted in half the time he expected and was soon walking out of the foyer back onto the street. He took off his gloves so he could scroll through the map on his phone and see where else he could kill time with Scarlett out until eleven. He walked farther towards the Chrysler Building, snapping photos as he went. The thing about New York was that you needed to remember to look up, no matter how much you were hunched against the cold, or you'd miss too much.

When he reached Grand Central Terminal, with its row of New York cabs lined up out front and the Tiffany clock up high above the station's famous name plaque, he could see the guide books weren't wrong. This place was huge. It was a shopping and dining destination as well as a transport hub, all under one roof. Inside, the vast concourse with its information desk and brass clock teemed with people, warm golden walls encased the chaos, the American flag hung on one wall, departures boards told passengers what platform to head for and when, and there were plenty of people like him who were here to admire the architecture and the building itself. The vaulted, celestial ceiling loomed above and a golden luminosity fell across the entire space with chandelier lights, lamps dotted around the border, and archways leading to platforms emitting a welcoming glow.

But Nathan had had enough of being a tourist for one night and, unable to stop thinking of Amelia, he headed back to the winter markets, where, armed with two hot chocolates, he went straight for the knitting stall, queue or no queue. The holiday was almost at an end and if he ever wanted to make anything happen he needed to stop being such a wimp about it and let her know.

'Hello, Nathan.' It was Cleo he saw first as she arrived at the chalet. 'Quick stop for some food and now I'm taking over from Amelia.' He didn't know her well but she looked stressed out. Then again, she was a mum of four, ran her own business, and took on extras like the Garland Street winter markets.

Happy it sounded like Amelia was free to go, and clasping a

steaming cup in each hand, he was pleased to be greeted by a big smile from Amelia when she caught sight of him hovering.

'For me?' She eyed the hot chocolates and grinned when he gave one to her. 'You read my mind; I need this. It's been a long shift until Cleo got here. I was tempted to stay, though – she's exhausted, and she has trouble brewing at home again.'

'You're too kind.'

Cleo stepped onto the street out of the way of the lines forming at the chalets. 'So what brings you here?'

'I was hoping I'd catch you before you left. I'm at a bit of a loose end with Scarlett out and thought you might be too, without Kyle to look out for.'

'Hardly, I've been busy here.'

'Should I take that back?' he nodded to the hot chocolate.

'No chance, I know which cart you got this from.' She read the familiar purple writing on the takeaway cup. 'You'd have to wrestle me to the ground to get this back.' She seemed awkward with her comment, which left him amused, and she suggested, 'You could walk me home while we drink these.'

'Sounds good to me. And we probably need the exercise. These are full-fat, extra cream, real chocolate flakes on top. I saw them being made, and kind of wish I hadn't.'

They set off past the market stalls, some beginning to pack up, others making the most of trading time, and he recounted his tour of the city. 'It's a luxury to be out so much. At home it's all work, parenting, and the daily routine.'

'I couldn't agree more. It's really nice to be away.'

'Do you mind working while you're here?'

'It really doesn't feel like work and when free accommodation was up for grabs, I leapt at the chance. Cleo made it very hard to say no.' They walked on in the direction of the East Village and Amelia and Kyle's apartment. 'How's Scarlett?'

'Talking to me a lot more since I eased up over her and Kyle.'

'Kyle will keep her safe.'

'I believe he will.' His own hot chocolate was going down a treat and sipping it filled any silences, not that there were many of those. 'Have you heard back from your ex?' He pulled her out of the way when a taxi drove so close to the kerb they would've got splashed with the puddled water.

She thanked him and they stuck closer to the building fronts to avoid a repeat. 'Not yet. But I didn't expect to. Maybe it's for the best.'

'Well, give me a shout when you need someone to go and get drunk with; I'm a willing volunteer.'

'I'll try to remember that if I need to drown my sorrows.' They waited for the pedestrian lights to change and she looked across at him. 'Kyle told me how interested Scarlett is in art, how good she is.'

'I've always been reluctant to encourage it,' he admitted. 'I know, not very supportive. I was trying to do what's best.'

'You're a good dad.'

'You want to say something else, I can tell.'

She smiled at his astuteness. 'I don't know your history, but imagine if you really wanted something so bad and someone stopped you doing it. What would you do? Accept it and move on or put up a fight?'

'You think she'll end up resenting me if I push her into something she doesn't want?'

'I'm interfering, sorry.'

He put a hand on her arm. 'Don't apologise, I like talking to you.' He took both their empty cups and dropped them into the nearest bin before they crossed to walk through Madison Square Park, pausing to admire the decorated Christmas tree once more. 'I wanted to have an entirely different career, once upon a time.'

'Why did you change your mind?'

'Scarlett came along, it was time to accept my responsibilities. Dawn and I were both so young, I'm afraid I didn't handle it very well. But in some ways it was the making of me.' Standing by the tree he told her, 'I wasn't always as together and sensible as I am now.'

'You had a rebellious side?'

'My brother's death hit the family like a head-on collision. We were all lost for a while. I watched the pain my parents were in. As far as they knew, I was coping and holding it together. I was doing well at school but outside of that institution I was a mess. I got into fights most weeks, came home with a black eye once and a split lip. I told my parents I'd been mugged on my way home from school but I refused to let them call the police. I could see I was adding to their grief so I backed away from the trouble the best I could. But then I started to drink. I got in with a bad crowd who hung around the local park in the evenings. I'd smuggle out what I could from home – gin, vodka – and everyone brought something. We'd sit there all night and get wasted; I told Mum and Dad I was studying at a friend's house and they bought it.'

'How did you keep up with school work?'

'It was some kind of fluke that my school work didn't completely fall apart. I guess in some ways it was another source of distraction. I'd throw everything into my days at school, I'd do homework right after, I never put on the television, and I'd only sneak out once I had caught up on everything.'

'Doesn't sound like the usual story I hear in my job. Usually school work is one of the biggest casualties.'

'I figured if I could keep getting good school reports and grades, my parents never needed to know what else I was doing. I couldn't stand seeing them fall apart, I never wanted to make it worse, and now I've got Scarlett I can't ever imagine what it was like for them.'

'What about what it was like for you?'

Staring at the lights on the tree was a balm that helped him tell her all of this. 'It was hell.'

'You must be clever for your brain to handle the academic side with everything else going on.'

'Could've been a surgeon,' he added with sadness.

'Is that the career you missed out on?'

'I guess it wasn't meant to be. I was a wild child, got Dawn pregnant, and then I realised I couldn't do that to her as well. I couldn't go off and study for years on end, do my residencies, end up elsewhere for long periods of time, add in the shift work along with her own as a nurse. My parents never really knew the extent of my drinking and cavorting around the neighbourhood, and thankfully I never got in trouble with the police, it ended before it could get that far and it saved them the embarrassment and heartbreak to add to what they'd already gone through. I think I made my parents really proud the night I told them I'd changed my plans, I'd be getting a good career and a job to support my family. I wanted to give them stability and show I hadn't thrown my life away with one mistake. And giving them Scarlett brought a joy that helped ease a small part of the pain of losing Robbie.'

They moved out of the way for a couple who posed for a selfie with the Christmas tree behind them, and they carried on walking through to the other side of the park on the path that would lead them out and towards Amelia's apartment.

'We're similar, you and I,' she said. 'I always wanted to make other people happy, as though somehow I needed their approval. I know I don't really, but with approval comes acceptance and it makes me happy with myself, if that makes sense. I've been doing it for so long I don't know how to switch it off, which is why it's so hard to tell Connie how I really feel.'

'I get that. I kept the truth from Mum and Dad, thought it was for the best. But it only made me all the more confused, and resentful even. Maybe if I'd put myself first then it could've all turned out very differently.' He watched her, read the signs of a smile almost there but not quite. 'What is it?'

'It's just that the way you describe your younger self...' She looked up at him, her eyes twinkling beneath the moonlight. '...you sound a lot like Kyle.'

'I know,' he admitted and when he started grinning it was her turn to ask why. 'I'm reluctant to tell you this, but when I got caught up with the wrong crowd, we may have pick-pocketed a few innocent people.'

'You did not!'

He covered his cold cheeks with gloved hands and shook his head. 'I've never been so ashamed in my life, even at the time. The other lads laughed, counted cash, spent it on fags and booze, but all I kept thinking about was those poor people who'd been the victims of our stupidity. What if we'd taken a woman's last bit of cash for a safe taxi home? What if the person we took money from didn't have enough food? What if it was their bus fare to get to the hospital and see a sick relative? I felt so awful that when I came to my senses and steered clear of the gang I'd hung out with, I'd use my pocket money and drop it into charity collection pots every week until I'd covered the fifty quid I'd pilfered and used for myself.'

'It shows you have a conscience.'

'Doesn't make it right, though.' And what was he doing? He wanted to make a good impression with this woman, not make her want to run for the hills.

They walked on, down a street, past a group of buskers belting out Christmas carols on a saxophone, an accordion, a singer pelting out the tunes with onlookers joining in. They crossed the next street and were soon outside Amelia's brownstone apartment building.

'This is me.' She took off her hat and ran a hand through dark hair that looked silky to the touch. 'Do you want to come up? I can't promise to make such a nice hot chocolate as we just had but I've got ingredients to make a mulled wine. If you're interested.'

Oh, he was definitely interested. 'I can stay a bit longer. I'll text Scarlett, check she's okay.'

Amelia put a hand on his before he could take out his phone. 'Leave them, I'm sure everything is fine. We'd hear if not.'

Inside the apartment she turned up the heater before grabbing a pan to get started with the mulled wine. 'Kyle turns his nose up at this every time I suggest it.'

'Not really a seventeen-year-old's drink.' He put his gloves on the radiator so they'd be warm for when he left, hung his coat on the hook near the kitchenette. He watched her pour an entire bottle of red into the pan. She added orange, sugar, a bay leaf, and spices and stirred as they chatted about spending Christmas in a different country, each with a teenager in tow.

He took over the stirring of the liquid while she put some Michael Bublé on the docking station, guaranteed to put even the biggest grinch in a Christmas mood. He'd bought Scarlett the album last year and she played it over and over for the entire school holidays and while it had irritated him with its repetition, the memory made him smile now.

Amelia opened cupboards until she found a sieve to strain the mulled wine through. She looked in a couple of cupboards up high this time until she found two mugs. 'Not sure the glasses will be heatproof so don't want to risk it,' she told him, and he did the honours, straining the wine and pouring out two generous measures.

With a mug each they sat on the sofa stretching along the exposed-brick interior wall.

Amelia took a deep inhale of the steaming liquid. 'It smells like Christmas.'

He gently tapped her mug with his. 'Cheers. To a great holiday, a wonderful Christmas, and a very happy new year.'

'I'll drink to that.'

Talk moved to some of the highlights of the city, the kids' favourite things and theirs. They touched on what their lives could've been like had he become a surgeon and if she'd stuck with telesales.

'We'd be very different people,' she concluded. 'For what it's worth, I think Scarlett has a good head on her shoulders, she'll make the right decisions about her own studies.'

'You're trying to coerce me into letting her follow her dreams of art again, aren't you?'

'I'm only trying to help.'

He almost reached out and touched her knee when he said, 'I know you are and I appreciate it.' But he didn't want to scare her off by making her think he was after a quick fling on holiday, and besides, he was way out of practice. He'd dated since Dawn died, but with his responsibilities as a dad, he'd never really wanted to get seriously involved with anyone before now. 'I think you've probably got a better insight into the way teens' minds work than I do,' he said. 'I thought I might suggest sitting down with her when we're home and going through some of the information on art degree courses, look at the employment opportunities it could lead to.'

Amelia's smile was well worth it. 'She'll see what the right path is. You both will.'

'I have to admit, I find this stage really hard.'

'The teen years?'

'The breaking away, the independence kids inevitably learn. I spent so long being the only adult in Scarlett's everyday life that it's hard to let her go, difficult to accept she needs to make her own mistakes.'

'Half the battle is recognising what you find difficult, and you just nailed it. Maybe tell Scarlett how you feel – it might help.'

After a sip of the warm wine brimming with Christmassy spice he said, 'I'm making you put your work hat on.'

'I don't think I take it off very often.'

'This is good,' he said of the wine, suddenly nervous in her company, wondering how she'd react if he leaned across to kiss her right now.

'There's more in the pan.'

'I'd better not.' Time was marching on, he kept losing his nerve. If he kissed her and it wasn't what she wanted, he'd be gutted for the rest of the holiday. 'I'll head back to the inn next, make sure I'm there for when Scarlett arrives home or I'll be the one in trouble.'

'Kyle is pretty good with curfews; he won't keep her out.'

He rinsed his mug and set it in the sink. 'Thanks for the mulled wine.'

'Thank you, too. It was nice to have another adult to talk to.'

He pulled on all his layers yet again and the toasty warm gloves from the radiator. Impulsively he reached out and held her cheeks so she could feel the warmth for herself and she looked as surprised as he was. He moved closer, his hands still on her cheeks. He bent his head a little and when she didn't move, he watched her lips, slightly parted as though she knew what was coming. He was going to do this, take the leap, hope her reaction was a good one. And why wouldn't it be? She wasn't backing away.

A knock at the door interrupted them before he got a chance to feel what it would be like to kiss her, this incredible, unexpected woman who'd stepped into his life on holiday.

'That might be Kyle. I'd better get it.' His hands still cradling her face, she took a moment to step away and answer the door.

The delivery man holding a clipboard ready for Amelia to sign ruined the moment and it was time to go. Maybe it was a sign, that he had New York romance on his mind, too much potent mulled wine and a sense of longing he hadn't realised he had until he met Amelia.

'I'll leave you to it.' He left her signing for a parcel and made his way back to the Inglenook Inn still thinking about the kiss that never was.

* * *

'Good evening, Darcy.' He greeted the hotelier the moment he stepped inside the communal lounge, where she was humming away to Christmas carols softly playing as she swept the tiles in front of the grate.

'Someone's chirpy tonight,' she beamed.

''Tis the season!' He grinned, and took the stairs two at a time up to their suite.

Inside, he hung his coat on the peg and was about to kick off his shoes when he heard giggling from Scarlett's bedroom. She was either home and watching television or she'd be facetiming her friends in England, telling them all about the holiday.

He went into her room with a huge smile that might have given the game away had it not faded so fast when he saw Kyle in there too.

They both sat bolt upright, guilty as charged, tugging clothes back to their rightful places, and his mood plummeted to a new low.

14

CLEO

Cleo tugged a hand through her hair and came back into the kitchen after Ruby stormed up the stairs.

'Dare I come in?' Dylan asked. He'd been in his study on a work call and Cleo had tried to keep the noise to a minimum.

She squirted surface spray on the countertop and used a cloth to take out her frustration, rubbing at marks that had already begun to set. Ruby was getting lazier and lazier, and this household only worked if they all did their bit.

'What happened this time?' Dylan ventured.

Cleo scrubbed at another mark. 'She had waffles for breakfast and left a trail of syrup on the countertop and more dripping all over the floor. I stood in it barefoot. For all I know she did too and has walked it all over the house, which will make even more work for me later.'

Dylan called Ruby downstairs and repeated much the same lecture as Cleo had just given her. And from the glare Ruby was directing Cleo's way, she didn't appreciate it.

So much for their day of bonding bringing them closer together. Whatever good that day had done had soon been forgotten and

Cleo could only put it down to her and Dylan talking at length about the wedding last night. That, or the fact Ruby had come home from her mum's with even more negative thoughts on board.

'You need to apologise to Cleo, please.' Dylan told Ruby.

'I wiped up the mess.'

'Clearly not.' He indicated Cleo still with a cloth in her hand, still cleaning up syrup. Ruby had made a token effort with a dry cloth that had done nothing more than smear the mess even farther.

'Sorry,' she said reluctantly, barely looking at Cleo now.

When Ruby went back upstairs Dylan wrapped Cleo in a hug. 'I thought she was settling down a bit.'

'So did I.' At least she felt a hundred times better in his arms right now. 'I thought I'd made some headway at last.' Defeated, she said, 'We can't ignore her behaviour and assume it will go away.'

When they heard Emily crying on the monitor, Dylan stopped Cleo before she could leap into action. 'I'll go, you have a shower.' Tabitha came toddling through from the playroom but he whisked her up before Cleo could. 'Go, or you might never get the chance again.'

She kissed Tabitha's chubby cheek and felt herself melt at the sweet smell of her daughter, at an age you thought was challenging until you were faced with a ten-year-old who had a whole new agenda. She headed upstairs for a shower and tried to wash away the rising stress.

The shower worked, or at least it did until after drying her hair she walked past Ruby's room and saw what she'd been doing. Over the time Cleo had been living with Dylan, she and Ruby had put together photo collections of the entire family. It had been their thing, their bonding project. It was easy to neglect photographs nowadays and keep them all on devices, but they'd printed some of their leaf-peeping outing in the fall, others of the summer months

when they'd gone hiking in Stratton Brook State Park and holi-
daying on the island of Nantucket. Those were times Cleo had
never thought her family would feel strain like this, at least not
until they hit the tumultuous teenage years.

And now, here were all the photographs, ripped into shreds,
scattered over Ruby's bedroom floor. And by the sounds of it Ruby
was downstairs ready to go to school. Had she left all this on
purpose, for Cleo to see, to upset her?

Cleo called Dylan upstairs and when he saw what she'd done
he yelled at Ruby to come up here now. 'What the hell have you
done?' Ruby's bottom lip quivered; she wouldn't make eye contact
with Cleo. 'I asked you a question.'

Cleo had never seen Dylan so angry, furious with his eldest
daughter but helpless to know what to do. Still fuming, he told his
daughter, 'We'll talk after school. Go get your bag, I'm taking you
today.'

When she did what she was told, Dylan crouched down next to
Cleo. She was on her hands and knees sifting through the pictures,
tears streaming down her cheeks. Ruby had cut her out of each and
every photograph. He pulled her to him and she leaned in to his
muscly chest; she felt safe, loved, but still distraught that Ruby
could do this.

Dylan held her tight. 'We'll sort this out, I promise you.' But the
sobs didn't stop and they only pulled apart when a voice behind
them said sorry.

Cleo, tear-stained face, looked to Ruby but rushed past her to
the bathroom. She couldn't face a ten-year-old kid right now. There
was something about hacking her out of the pictures, all those
special memories, that was brutal. Did Ruby hate her this much?

When Dylan called through the door that they were leaving for
the school run and he was taking Tabitha and Emily with him too,
she managed to get out an 'okay' but she didn't come out of the

bathroom until she heard the car doors shutting outside on the driveway and she knew it was safe to do so.

Cleo stood at the bedroom window at the front of the house watching the car head into the distance, the end of the street where predictably it turned right, and she was left completely alone.

And then she found herself doing something she never thought she would. She picked up the phone to call Prue.

* * *

'I don't know why this couldn't wait,' Prue huffed as she stepped through the front door into Cleo's home, 'this is my only day off work and I was on my way to get my nails done.'

Jeez. Nails? Really! 'I apologise but, no, this can't wait.' She hoped this would be easier with just the two of them. Cleo had fully intended to have Dylan sort this out but maybe it would be better coming from her. And besides, she couldn't bear the thought of stewing all day without taking some kind of action, and with the market stalls and the store manned for now, this was her chance. 'Coffee?' she offered.

'No thanks.' Prue looked at her watch as if to make a point.

Cleo sat at the table and emptied out the box in the centre, the photograph pieces scattering all over the surface.

'What are these?' Prue asked.

'Take a look.'

She sifted through. 'They all seem to be photographs of you.'

'Cut from photographs of all of us together. I found them in Ruby's bedroom this morning.'

'She wouldn't.'

'She did.'

'But why?' Prue looked genuinely shocked.

'I was wondering if you'd be able to help answer that.'

'How would I know?'

'You and Ruby are close, as you should be.' How could she phrase this lightly, without it sounding accusatory? 'I think she's struggling with the idea of Dylan and me together.'

'You've been together long enough. She's had plenty of time to get used to the idea.'

'But now there's talk of a wedding. It changes things. I know. I had a stepmother to deal with too and I'm ashamed to say I didn't handle it all that well.'

Prue looked at a pretty perfect nail, inspecting it, before she looked at Cleo again. 'She did hope Dylan and I would get back together.'

'That's natural, you're both her parents.' Although she wanted to remind Prue that it was a long time ago that that particular scenario had ever been on the cards. 'Has Ruby said anything to you? About me? The wedding?' Or had Prue said something to her?

'She really hasn't. As far as I knew she was happy with it.'

'And *you* haven't said anything?'

'You're blaming me?' Okay, here came the Prue she knew so well. 'You think this is my fault?'

'No, not at all. It's just, I know you're never going to be my biggest fan.' *Because I ended up with Dylan and you didn't.* 'I wondered if Ruby picked up on that.'

Prue looked about to launch into a tirade but then she settled back into her chair. 'I won't lie to you, I hated you when you first got together with Dylan.'

'Great.'

'But that was then. I've moved on, I've had other men in my life. Dylan and I would never work together; he's changed a lot since I first knew him.'

Cleo let that comment go. He had, and for the better in her opinion.

Prue stood up, hooked her bag over her shoulder. 'I'm sorry I can't help you but I don't poison Ruby's mind, I don't want Dylan back, and I wish you well with your wedding.'

'You're leaving? Just like that?'

She checked her watch. 'If the traffic is kind I'll make the next nail appointment.'

'Right.'

'Ruby will come round. She's a kid, they have mood swings, it's all normal.'

'I wondered if it would be a good idea for you to talk to her.' One last attempt to get help from a woman who seemed determined to cause friction.

'What, and ask her why she cut you out of all the photographs?' She swished her immaculate blonde, bobbed hair out from under the strap of her bag and it obediently settled back to how it was before. 'You and Dylan can deal with this one. This is what you signed up for, Cleo – the family, all the kids.' And with a smile she added, 'I'll see myself out.'

* * *

'There's no need to call her that,' said Cleo after she told Dylan how the conversation with Prue had gone and he had a few choice words about the woman. Cleo had been at the store, followed by the Inglenook Falls markets, and he'd been out all day with Tabitha and Emily. She'd replied to his texts assuring him everything was fine, she was okay, and she'd waited until they were both home before she told him about her encounter with his ex-wife.

'Ruby!' he called up the stairs. 'Ruby!' he bellowed again when she didn't come running. 'Believe me,' he told Cleo, 'I said plenty to Ruby in the car on the way to school but she hasn't been anywhere near you since she got home, she certainly hasn't apologised properly.'

'Can you keep Jacob, Emily, and Tabitha amused in the kitchen and let me have the lounge?' she asked him.

'You don't need to do this on your own. It's time I said something and stopped trying to play the nice guy.'

He was looking out for her, Cleo knew. He was stuck between his fiancée and his daughter, much like Cleo's dad had once been trying to please Cleo and Teresa. And she'd never gone easy on either of them. 'I do need to do this on my own, Dylan. Ruby will be expecting you to tell her off, me to cry, and then Prue to pick her up to take her for dinner.' Dylan had already called it off with Prue and she'd been more than happy to postpone, citing Christmas drinks with friends – most likely to let Dylan know she had a social life of her own. She'd always been in some weird kind of competition, childish but completely Prue.

When Ruby eventually braved coming downstairs, Cleo asked her to come into the lounge and shut the door behind them. 'You and I need to talk.' Silence. 'Why did you do it, Ruby?' More silence. 'Come on, you're not leaving this room until we've had this out.' She was no longer angry, just sad.

Cleo moved Ruby's hand that was tugging at the loose thread on the bottom of her favourite multicoloured sweater, which Cleo had knitted for her last year, thankful it had escaped the chop this morning unlike the photographs.

When Ruby began to cry Cleo could tell she wasn't doing it for attention or because she thought it would save her from having to divulge what was going on. The little girl was genuinely upset, confused, and Cleo waited for the tears to flow, handed her a tissue, and stayed by her side. 'I thought you and I were friends,' she said when Ruby's sobs had faded to a subtle sniff. 'I don't think friends cut each other out of photographs, do you?'

'No.' Ruby looked younger than her ten years now, forlorn, nose snotty, hair falling across her cheeks so Cleo couldn't see her.

'Why, Ruby?' She hooked Ruby's hair over her ears so she could see her face. 'I'm going to let you in on a bit of a secret.' Red eyes looked up at her. 'Nanny Teresa is, as you know, my stepmother. But what you never knew was that once upon a time I didn't get on with her.'

Her sniffling stalled as she looked up at Cleo. 'But you love Nanny Teresa.'

'Now I do. But back then I was rude, mean, or I just didn't talk to her.' Ruby took a shuddering breath, verging on the point of tears that threatened to come again, but Cleo ploughed on. 'I didn't like her at all when my dad first met her. I thought she was trying to replace my mum. I suppose in some ways I also thought she'd take my dad away from me, and I'd already lost one parent.' Cleo smiled. 'Since I got to know Teresa and stopped seeing her as the enemy, we get on really well. She's kind, loyal, fun, she loves me and, what's more, she makes my dad very happy. But it took me many years to be able to see that. And my dad was too nice to me, Teresa too, because they backed off and let me work my way through it. I'm not sure if I wish they hadn't, or whether it was all for the best.'

She led Ruby over to the sofa and sat them both down. 'Nanny Teresa came to see me here in New York when I had my store in the city. Before that I'd been civil to her but not much else. But when she came, we really talked and I got to know her, how insecure she'd been feeling, how much she longed for my approval.' She clasped Ruby's hand. 'You see, losing a parent is really hard, whether it's the way I lost my mum or the way you lost yours.'

'But I still have my mom.'

'But she's not with your dad any more, and I think that sometimes makes you sad.'

'It does.'

'Do you wish they'd get back together?'

This time Ruby shook her head. 'Dad says they used to fight a lot. Mom says it too. I don't think they'd be very good together any more.'

'But you've still lost something, Ruby, that's what I'm trying to say. Maybe you've lost the idea of your mum and dad being together. I understand, I really do. But I'll never try to replace your mum, and I'll never take your dad away from you. He has a whole lot of love to give, for all of us.'

'That's not it.'

'No?'

Ruby's tears started again and this time Cleo pulled her to her. 'Talk to me, Ruby, please. I can't help if you don't.'

It took her a while but eventually Ruby got the words out. 'You ran away.'

'From England? Well, yes, I suppose I did.'

'Not that time.'

'Then what time are you talking about?'

'You ran off once, you went missing, before your friend's wedding.'

'How did you know about that?' She and Dylan had always been careful not to frighten the kids with too much adult stuff, but her doing a runner that one and only time had been something they'd likely talked about thinking they weren't overheard, not realising little ears always had a surprising ability to pick up the things you really didn't want them to hear rather than those you did.

'I heard you and Dad talking.'

Cleo thought how best to word this. 'I did disappear but not for long, I needed space. I never said anything because we didn't want you kids to worry.'

'You ran away from us.'

'Oh no, is that what you think?' She pulled Ruby in tighter and planted a kiss on the top of her head. 'Is that what's got you so upset and worried? I love you all, I promise you that.'

'Jacob and I aren't your children.'

This again, and no doubt some of it came from Prue. 'I've told you this before, but I'll tell you again because I really want you to see it the way I do, Ruby. You *are* my children, you and Jacob. I might not be your mum but you're very much my children. From the moment I moved in here with your dad, we became another version of family.' She looked at Ruby now. 'Is that what started all of this doubt? Why you've been misbehaving? Is it because you think I don't love you two enough?'

'You might run away and leave us again. Mum left. You might not have come back if Dad hadn't found you.'

She kept Ruby close to her side. 'I ran for reasons that had nothing to do with your dad or you kids.' She took a deep breath, remembering the time as though it were only yesterday not more than a year ago. 'I was very sad at the time about losing my own mum. I was sad that she would never get to meet her grandchildren, and by that I mean all of you. I was sad that she'd left my life when I was so young, that I never got the chance to know her more. The problem with sadness and grief is that you don't have a timeslot in which it's all dealt with, it creeps up when you least expect. It comes in waves.'

'Like the waves in the ocean, you mean.'

'Exactly. Think of the ocean, how calm it is sometimes.'

'Not when there was the storm in Nantucket.'

'No, not then, those waves were big, dark, and angry. I guess that's how my emotions go sometimes. The wave got bigger and that time it managed to topple me over and I ran away.'

'Where did you go?' Ruby turned to face her, her legs tucked up on the sofa between them, her expression inquisitive.

'I went to a place that had very good memories for me. I went to

Litchfield, where we've all been before, leaf peeping, do you remember?'

A guilty look crossed her face. 'The place in the photos.'

'We can print them all out again.'

'Can we?'

'Of course.'

'I'm sorry I ruined them. It was mean.'

'You were knocked over by a wave, Ruby, that's all.' She pulled her into her arms again.

'You promise you won't leave us?'

'I promise. Not even when you're a teenager and telling me you hate me.'

'I'd never say that.'

Cleo smiled and didn't say out loud that of course she would, and she'd take it, every single thing Ruby threw at her, and Jacob for that matter. 'You need to promise me something too, Ruby.'

'Anything.'

'Promise me you'll be the best bridesmaid ever and help me plan this wedding. I'm going to need all the help I can get.'

And with a smile Ruby flung her arms around her and told her she'd never let her down again. And Cleo wouldn't let any of the kids down because she'd take it all, every single bump in the road of parenthood, because they were finally beginning to find their way to happiness in their peculiar patchwork family pulled together in a mishmash of colours.

15

AMELIA

Amelia had been thinking about Nathan for the last twenty-four hours, since he'd almost kissed her. Good-looking, sophisticated, with a hint of trouble, a man she hadn't liked at first but who she was very much attracted to. She'd thought about him all evening as she enjoyed another mulled wine, all this morning and the entire time helping out at the market stall, wondering whether he'd show up. He didn't, and she found she was disappointed.

As she walked back to the apartment alone after Kyle stayed back to work, flat out serving people who'd left buying a tree ridiculously close to the big day, there was still no sign of the snow they'd been promised, the kind that would settle and blanket the city. It was still freezing, however, and the second Amelia got inside she ran a bath. She added in the lavender oil she'd bought herself from the chalet next to hers at the market. Today the cold seemed to have seeped through all her layers with no regard for how many there were, but it was time to relax. She didn't manage it when Kyle was around but tonight he'd offered to hang back and help Mitch clear up after the rush died down. Mitch was paying him cash in hand, perhaps that was his incentive, and it would go towards a lovely gift for Scarlett this Christmas if that's where his mind was heading.

She sank into the fragranced water for a bit of well-deserved relaxation and to carry on her daydream about Nathan, who she wished had come by to see her today or at least sent her a text. But he was probably busy with Scarlett, who'd be missing Kyle with the extra hours he was putting in. Kyle must be so wrapped up in Scarlett that he'd been in late last night and out first thing this morning. He'd even forgotten to open his parcel.

Blissful in the warm water, she only stirred twenty minutes later when a knock at the door had her attention. She climbed out of the bath, wrapped herself in a towel, and tiptoed towards the door, hoping it was Nathan. Clutching her towel, she went right close to the peephole. But when she saw who it was, her heart plummeted.

Another knock.

Amelia gasped. 'Just a minute,' she called. There was no time to get dressed, no time to think about what to say. When she'd sent that text she hadn't expected a reply, let alone a visit in person.

She opened the door and Paul, the other side, beaming one of his smiles her way, looked as though the past six months of separation hadn't happened at all.

'What are you doing here?'

'What kind of a welcome is that?' He stepped forward and wrapped his arms around her. 'I've flown thousands of miles to see you.'

His familiar smell enveloped her and she hugged him back, the moment surreal.

'I got your text.' He'd closed the door behind them and Amelia was aware of him taking in the fact she was dressed in very little.

'You could've replied rather than fly all the way here. I don't mean... I don't mean I'm not pleased to see you.' Her voice softened and he pulled her in closer. But when he pressed his body against hers a funny sensation zipped right through her. It wasn't the same excitement as the first time they'd been intimate, but rather a feeling of unease most likely brought on by the fact that this was out of the blue. 'How did you even know where I was?' she asked, scrambling for answers as she tried to make sense of this.

'I called your sister's number – figured she'd ignore a text – lied and said I wanted to send you a Christmas card. She sounded terrible actually, if you don't mind me saying, drunk maybe, that or really sick, couldn't get me off the phone quick enough.'

Connie had never been his biggest fan so no wonder she'd kept the conversation short when he called. But it wasn't like Connie to party quite so much even if they were coming up for Christmas and it wasn't like her to give out Amelia's address without asking questions. Maybe she had come down with the flu rather than a mere cold, but Amelia couldn't worry about it right now, she had to shake it off, because Paul was here, standing in front of her. A few months ago she would've fallen into his arms and not let go but, now, she wasn't so sure what to do.

'I got a flight easy enough,' Paul rambled on, 'although I had to fly cattle class.' He shuddered. 'That wasn't pleasant, but I'm sure I can book us both into business for the way home. My treat.' He took in the apartment. 'This is a nice place, bit shabby but it's true New York, and nice and cosy for one. My hotel cost a lot this close to Christmas, but it's huge, great view, you'd love it.'

'I'm sure I would.' Did he ever take a breath? And judging by what he'd said about this apartment being cosy for one, he had no idea she was here with Kyle. Connie must have really wanted to get him off the phone.

He stepped forwards, smiling, and cupped her cheek with one hand before he ran it down her neck and across her collarbones. 'I've missed you.'

'Really?'

'Don't sound so surprised. When I got your text...'

'But you ended it between us, I don't understand.'

'Your text said as much.' He sighed. 'I guess I didn't explain myself very well.'

She gripped her towel tighter. 'Explain it now.'

Taken aback with her serious tone, he said, 'May I sit down?'

'I'll get dressed.'

'Don't, the towel suits you.'

'I'm being serious, Paul.' Maybe she'd forget getting dressed; she wanted him to talk, now. 'Why did you end it between us? You said we wanted different things. That I always put everyone else first.' Why couldn't he have turned up in England and done all this? Perhaps then she'd have some idea how she felt. Why couldn't he have talked before she'd moved all her things out of his place, before she'd been so emotionally confused that it had begun to impact her work life too?

'I told you the way I felt at the time. I was being honest.'

'So it was about me putting my family first all the time.'

'Family, and work.'

'It's my job, you must get that.'

'Kind of, but I always worried about you too, some of the families you were involved with...'

'Families who've had a tough time.' Who weren't born into money, with two parents who stayed the course, without family in their corner. She'd never told him about the black eye she'd got trying to restrain a teen who was out of control and taking his anger out on chairs and tables in the community centre, throwing them around as though they were confetti. A chair had clocked her high on the cheekbone and the bruise had come up a treat. Paul had been away on a work conference for a fortnight and so by the time he returned the swelling had decreased and the discolouration was easily covered with a good dose of foundation.

'You put everyone else before us,' he claimed again.

She shivered in just a towel, but now he was here, she wanted to process the reasons behind the breakup. 'So you didn't think you got enough attention?'

'You make me sound like a petulant child, Amelia.'

'I didn't mean it to sound that way. But I've always been the same person ever since we first got together.'

'Not true. You were a telesales exec when we got together.'

His attempt to lighten the mood didn't work. 'Deep down I'm still me. Are you saying my choice of job drove us apart?'

'I'm saying I found it hard. I felt as though you and I were always on the back burner. Behind your family, behind your work. Remember our plans to go walking in the Lake District last year and how excited we were?'

'I do. And I know you went to a lot of effort to arrange the surprise.' They'd booked to go to a remote area and camp, walk all week, and eat out at restaurants. Kyle had pushed the boundaries yet again, Connie was freaking out, and instead of the Lakes, Amelia had driven to Cornwall to sort it out. The thing was, as far as Amelia knew, all they'd sacrificed was a campsite booking they could revisit any time. Paul had been so angry. He'd actually booked a luxury cottage with a roll-top bath, a log burner, an idyllic hideaway where they could get away from it all, walk all day, cook together in the evenings and cosy up with each other and enjoy fine wines.

'It wasn't the only time either. You cancelled dinner on your birthday because of trouble at work and that time I'd arranged a room at the Shard no less. And you didn't come to Christmas with my family, who were all excited to have you there, because Kyle had done a runner and you were scouring the streets of Cornwall.'

'He's—'

'Family, I know.' But his mood simmered. 'I felt as though I always came second, that's all. I started to resent all the plans that were cancelled because of your sister and your nephew.'

'It didn't happen that many times. Work took over occasionally, but no more than your work.'

'But at least those trips were scheduled, I wasn't dropping everything just like that.'

'I suppose not.'

'Do you get where I'm coming from?'

'I guess so.' He'd always been a good debater, able to convince people round to his point of view, and she kind of got it, but weren't relationships supposed to be deeper than that? Surely he should've seen how pained she was to mess him around, how much she had going on, how difficult it was to be stuck between responsibilities for family and career and the man she loved?

'I love that you give projects and family your all, I just wish that sometimes your all would come my way.'

She gripped his hand that was resting on his knee. 'I didn't realise how strongly you'd felt. You should've talked to me rather than ending it the way you did.'

'I'm here now to do just that. Your text came a couple of days after the office Christmas party, which was a miserable affair if I'm honest. I didn't have a date, most other people did, I ended up talking to the boss most of the night and went home early.'

He'd always loved having her at his side at work functions. 'Sounds dire.'

'It was, without you.'

She shivered again. 'I should get dressed.'

'I can help.'

He was looking at her like she was a Christmas present to unwrap and she really wanted her PJs now. Not seeing him for months had been agony, not hearing anything from him even worse, but seeing him now was disconcerting and she didn't know quite what to make of it. She was out of her comfort zone, New York was making her confused, and at the forefront of her mind was Nathan's company and the near-kiss.

'I'm sorry I was such a dickhead.' He took hold of her hand when she stood up and leaned his head against her towel-covered thigh as he remained seated on the sofa.

'You were a dickhead.' At least he still made her laugh, and seeing how sorry he was made her wonder if they really could try again.

'I'm trying to see the bigger picture, the picture where you and I are together with a family of our own.'

His words had her frozen to the spot. He wanted a future with her, he had plans, he was talking about family when he'd never wanted to go down that road before.

'If you'll let me,' he said, standing up, not letting go of her hand, their bodies pressed together, 'I'll make it up to you.' Her heart was pounding against his chest as he spoke. 'Show you how sorry I am. I want you in my life, in my house, at my side, Amelia.'

'You never wanted to settle down and have a family.' His breath against her neck was tantalising, made it difficult to think. 'What's changed?'

'Like I said, I see the bigger picture. I don't want to mess around any more. I want you, Amelia.'

'I don't understand.' His touch made her dizzy with confusion.

A smile crept across his face. 'I wasn't going to tell you yet, but there's something else. I've been doing well, got promoted twice already, but now I've been offered a position in Edinburgh. It's more money than I ever thought I'd earn, it's the job of a lifetime. It'll be a solid future for us.'

'You're taking the job?'

'I'd be crazy to turn it down.' His eyes dazzled with excitement and she remembered how passionate he was about his career. 'I'm hoping you'll come with me. Say you will, Amelia.'

'What about my work, my flat?'

'You've got the qualifications and experience to take it to the next level, if that's what you want, and you could rent your flat out again. It was a good investment before.'

'You've thought this through.' He'd never seen her career as important, not like his. He earned four times as much as her and although he had never come out and said it, he saw his own work as taking priority. And if he was thinking that way already, what would happen if they did end up together and having a family? She'd be stuck at home, single-parenting, while his life would carry on regardless. He'd be putting his all into a career when he'd criticised her for doing the very same thing.

He ran his hand through the length of her hair before resting his fingers against her face. 'I've thought of nothing else in the last couple of months. I was scared to try again with you, I thought you'd tell me to get lost. But when I got your text I had to go for it, I had to come and get you. What do you say?'

'It's what I wanted for a long time,' she admitted, but she didn't have a chance to add that she had no idea what she felt any more because he took her pause as acceptance and kissed her hard on the lips. She pulled back and another knock at the door rescued her from anything more.

'Who do you know in this city? Ignore it.' Paul tried to kiss her again but she pulled away.

'It might be Kyle.'

'He's here?' The familiar muscle in his jaw twitched the way it always did when something irritated him or when someone crossed him. 'Why is he with you?'

'Long story.' Another knock. 'I need to get that.'

'Go,' he said, gesturing to the door. 'Jump to it, you usually do.'

'Paul...' She didn't have time to talk him down from his mood right now, so she opened the door but didn't expect both Kyle and Nathan to be on the other side.

'What's going on?' She looked from one to the other. 'Kyle?'

Both of them clocked Paul but Nathan soon refocused. 'Ask him!' He pointed a finger towards Kyle and his eyes only betrayed him once by dipping towards the towel that she was doing her best to keep a tight hold of.

'You're crazy!' Kyle yelled back at Nathan.

Amelia shut the door behind them to keep the noise inside rather than out in the corridor. 'You'll have the neighbours calling the police in a minute. Nathan, please calm down,' she pleaded as he grabbed Kyle by the scruff of his neck.

'Not a chance,' he fumed, but at least he let go of Kyle and Kyle seized his opportunity to take a few steps back.

Paul piped up at the least convenient time. 'Do you two mind?' He looked from Kyle to Nathan. 'Me and Amelia... we're kind of in the middle of something here.'

Amelia, Nathan and Kyle all turned in his direction. All of them lost for words. All of them ignoring his request.

Amelia turned back to Nathan. 'What's he supposed to have done this time?' So much for the truce, the acceptance of Kyle and Scarlett.

'I found them in bed together last night,' Nathan snapped. 'I told Kyle to leave, which he did. But I also told him to leave Scarlett alone and this evening I found them both together again.'

'You found them in bed?' Amelia wasn't sure she was ready for this particular showdown. Her auntie role only went so far. 'Were they...?'

'Not quite, but I've been a seventeen-year-old boy, remember.'

'Don't judge me by your crappy standards,' Kyle hollered across the room, although Amelia was thankful he was at least keeping his

distance and that she, far too vulnerable in just a towel, could step
between them.

Paul piped up again. 'Typical.'

'What did you say?' Kyle's head whipped around to confront
him, the man standing there in a suit as though he'd just been to
the office not travelled across the miles to surprise his ex-girlfriend
and tell her he'd made a mistake. But then Paul had never let
himself be seen looking anything other than pristine, much like
women who didn't let their partners see them without make-up,
hiding their true selves behind a disguise.

'You always were trouble,' Paul went on, 'and Amelia doesn't
deserve it.'

'He's right.' Kyle addressed Amelia now. 'You don't deserve the
shit I give you, but this time I didn't do anything. I swear. Apart
from ignore him asking me to keep away, which I don't see is necessary when I did nothing wrong!' He finished his spiel, yelling the
last few words in Nathan's direction.

When Paul went to say something else, Amelia's hand in the air
silenced him because whatever remark he was about to come out
with, even if he was defending her, which she didn't fully appreciate
right now, was only going to make it worse. She turned to Nathan. 'I
could understand your anger if he'd forced himself on Scarlett, but
unless I'm mistaken, he didn't.' She didn't even need to ask that
question because she knew Kyle more than this man did.

'How do you know?'

'Did you ask him? Did you ask her?'

Her harrumphed. 'He may not have forced himself on her, but
I've no doubt it would've been his idea.' He wasn't waiting for an
answer. Instead he slung something into the apartment across the
floor. 'You left these behind last night, mate. Don't you ever come
near my daughter again.' And he didn't even look at Amelia when
he left this time.

She shut the door, leaned against it, her heart still pounding. But her eyes fell on whatever Nathan had thrown inside and she went to pick it up. She handed the packet to Kyle and her heart sank a little. 'Yours, I believe.' Condoms.

'Notice it's unopened,' Kyle said defensively. 'And also take note, they're not mine!'

'Pull the other one.' This time Paul's comment incited such a rage that Kyle nearly flew at him.

'Into your bedroom, now, Kyle!' Amelia instructed. 'Now!'

The thing about Kyle was that no matter what trouble he got into, no matter the arguments, he did respect her. She knew it and he knew it. And he retreated into his own space, away from trouble.

'Wait here,' she told Paul. 'I'm getting dressed.'

'You can order me into the bedroom like that too if you like,' he teased, his eyebrows raised suggestively, but her look kept him rooted to the spot.

She was back in lightning time so Paul and Kyle would have no time to start their war again. The navy-and-white snowman pyjamas she was now wearing were ones she'd bought at the markets earlier and they were snuggly and warm. Just a shame the atmosphere wasn't.

'Cute PJs,' said Paul, but she went behind the kitchen counter to avoid him reaching for her. 'You're angry.'

'I wish people would give Kyle a chance, not assume the worst.'

'Who's the bloke?' he asked.

'Nathan.'

'Who is he? And who's Scarlett?'

Amelia filled him in on the goings on since they'd arrived and Paul concluded, 'Wow, never thought Kyle had it in him.'

'Had what in him?'

'To be a fast worker with the girls.' He seemed impressed for some reason. 'But he's bringing trouble to your door again and I don't like what it does to you. I always hated the way your sister took advantage.'

'I know, you told me once or twice.' Or was it a million times?

'I know all about the trouble Kyle got into and I hate that it was impacting your life, our lives too.'

'He's family and I love him as if he were my son.'

Paul reached a hand out and covered hers with his. 'It's one of the reasons I fell in love with you, your willingness to put others first. You were always thinking of your family and how to make it better all round.'

'I thought that was one of the things you hated about me.'

'I never hated a single thing. I found it a lot to handle, that's all.'

Sitting on the sofa again she said, 'You and I weren't together when I came on this holiday, so you can't be angry that Kyle's here.'

He tried to kiss her but she turned away. 'You know, my hotel in Times Square has a great view, it's the penthouse suite, own bar and a freestanding bathtub in the bathroom. I know how much you enjoy a bath at the end of a long day.' He did, he knew her well, they had a history and now he was coming back to her asking for another chance. 'Why don't you sort Kyle out and tomorrow you and I can have some time together.'

'I'll be working at my friend's market stall during the day.'

'We'll meet up in the evening then.'

'We can get takeaway and eat here.'

'Let me treat you to a proper meal at the hotel, or out in the city somewhere.'

'Fine,' she conceded, having no energy to argue. 'Text me the full address so I don't get lost.'

'Of course I will.' He kissed her gently on the lips and this time she let him, although Nathan's face was right there again. 'I'll leave you to it. See you tomorrow. A nice meal, fine wine, overlooking Manhattan. You'll love it.'

Once Paul left she turned her attention back to Kyle, trying to ignore the fact that once again her sister only had a backseat view of her son's life. That had to stop and Nathan's visit tonight proved it. Finding Kyle and Scarlett together, discovering the packet of condoms – it all showed that this was beyond what Amelia could do as an auntie. Kyle needed his one remaining parent and Connie would have to step up whether she liked it or not. No wonder Paul had walked away. It must've been frustrating to watch the woman he was with give in to her sister's demands over and over again.

She knocked on Kyle's bedroom door. 'Can we talk?'

The door swung open. 'Is Paul still here?'

'He's gone to his hotel.'

'Thank God for that.'

'Kyle.'

'He never liked me.' She didn't deny it. 'What's he doing here anyway? Come to ruin the fun? I thought you two split up ages ago.'

'We did, but right now it's not about me. Care to tell me exactly what's been going on with Scarlett?'

But his attention turned to the parcel on the countertop he'd neglected to see earlier. Perhaps it would be a good way to calm him before they talked further. 'That came for you yesterday but you've barely been here.'

'I've been avoiding you.'

'Wonder why.' At least he was talking.

He sat down next to her with the small box in his hands and tore off the thick brown tape before opening the flaps at the top.

'What is it?' She peered inside when he said nothing, just stared. 'Is that…?'

'My Christmas ornament.'

'Connie must've sent it straight over.' She briefly recapped her recent conversation with his mum before she noticed a letter lurking in the bottom of the box. Kyle picked it up and as he read she filled a glass of water from the tap.

'What does it say?' she asked when she'd given him enough time and space to get through it.

'You can read it for yourself.'

She took the letter and sat on the sofa next to him. Judging by his face it was going to be an emotional and unexpected outpouring of Connie's feelings, but something Amelia couldn't avoid. Slowly she began to read...

Merry Christmas to my wonderful son. I hope you're having an amazing time in New York with Auntie Amelia, who is the best sister I could ever have asked for. I don't think she knows that; I've neglected to tell her things I should've done over the years, but I know you get on with her so well that I've no doubt the two of you will be having a fabulous Christmas.

I hope you're pleased to see this decoration after so many years. I never put this on the tree after your dad died, and you never asked me to but I suspect it was because you were afraid to upset me. I'm sorry I wasn't better able to help you through your grief; my own overwhelmed me so much. I watched you and your dad paint this Christmas ornament and with him gone I couldn't look at it. I had to change the habits we'd formed, which meant new decorations that didn't have memories attached. I know now that I was wrong to do it. It was selfish of me and there have been many times I've thought of giving it back to you.

I will be thinking of you at Christmas. My friend Jill is coming over from Wales and you might remember how good a cook she is. I won't go hungry! She's already given me a schedule of what has to be done and when so I suspect she'll have me putting my apron on the second I get out of bed.

I'm looking forward to you coming home in the new year and if you like, we could spend a couple of days at Jill's farmhouse on the edge of the Brecon Beacons, as long as it doesn't snow here and stop us from driving anywhere. She would love to have us both there and it would be good to spend some time with you.

Have a think about it, and wishing both you and Amelia a very merry Christmas.

Much love,

Mum xx

Amelia bet Connie had no clue as to the extent of Kyle's feelings, how it made him feel when she'd pushed him away, how it made him doubt himself. Perhaps this was a start, a way to mend things between them. 'It's a nice letter,' she said when Kyle said nothing, just stared at his decoration, in his hands again after all this time, no doubt bringing the memories with it. 'Do you think you'll take her up on her offer?'

'Wales? With Mum?'

'I know, it's not very exciting.'

'Are you kidding?' A tentative smile began. 'She's never suggested going away before, not since I was really little, when Dad was around.' There were tears in his eyes but Amelia didn't point it out. 'Either she had a partner who she went away with, or she was working, or she was pushing me off to your place to sort me out. I was angry at her, you know. I thought she should be the one to help me when Dad died, I felt it was wrong for her to struggle when she's the adult.'

'She's had a tough time, you both have.'

'Scarlett told me she must have her reasons for how she acts.'

'Scarlett?'

'I talk to her about things. And she's really clever, Amelia. She's amazing in fact.'

'I don't doubt it. But tell me the truth, what really happened last night?'

'Nathan's a total freak.' He put the ornament down on the side table.

'That's not an answer. Tell me straight.'

'We had a great time in the city, just me and Scarlett. We wanted to eat at Ellen's Stardust Diner but the queue was huge so we grabbed takeaway noodles from a café I can't remember the name of. We were close to the Inglenook Inn and Scarlett invited me back there. She said her dad wouldn't mind, I said not a chance, but she told me we'd eat in the dining room. Darcy doesn't mind if you grab takeaway and do that.

'When we got there she had a message from her dad to say he'd been to the Empire State Building and was out wandering but he promised he'd be back by eleven at the latest; he joked about not missing his curfew. Scarlett persuaded me we should go eat upstairs seeing as he wouldn't be back for a while. We could have a bit of privacy and get away from the other family in the dining room who had a crying baby with them. When we got up there I kept checking my watch and Scarlett told me not to be so jittery. So I tried to relax, we ate, we hung out, we were messing around. But then...'

'You need to tell me. I can't stick up for you unless I know the truth.'

'We were kissing, then Scarlett suggested we go to her bedroom. I didn't exactly protest.'

'Were you going to have sex?'

He covered his face with his hands. 'This is so embarrassing.'

'I'm sure it is, but you need to tell me.'

'We were fooling around, Scarlett took off her top, then she took out a packet of condoms, said she'd bought them that afternoon just in case.'

'*She* bought them?'

'Yes, but don't be angry with her.'

'I'm not. Although you've only known each other five minutes. It's a bit quick. But then again, at least she was thinking about safety, the risk of pregnancy, not to mention STDs.' She was spilling her thoughts out loud now, trying to process the events of tonight. 'Would you have gone through with it if Nathan hadn't caught you?'

'I've never... you know.'

'Has she?'

'No.'

'But you took the wrap for Scarlett. You didn't deny the condoms were yours, at least not when Nathan found them.'

'How could I? She's his little girl, he's overprotective as it is, I didn't want to make it worse for her.'

'I'm proud of you for having that attitude. Because it would've really put him in his place to tell him it was her and not you, but you didn't.'

'I told you, I really like her. I know we're on holiday and nobody ever thinks holiday flings go anywhere, but it feels as though this one will.'

'I need to talk to Nathan, clear the air.'

'You can't tell him, Scarlett will be mortified.'

'But it's the truth.'

'Do you think it matters who the condoms belonged to? Do you think if he knows she bought them then he'd say, oh well kids, go on then, go off and enjoy yourselves?' When Amelia started to laugh, he joined in. 'Okay, that wasn't a very good impression of him, he sounds way more anal than that.'

'Hey, watch your mouth.'

'Sorry.'

'I think we both need some sleep. We'll deal with this in the morning.'

'What's going on with Paul? What's he even doing here?'

Now it was her turn to feel uncomfortable. 'He's here to see me, says he made a mistake.'

'He's got a nerve.'

'Yeah.' She asked, 'Would you mind if I had dinner with him tomorrow night?'

'I think I'll be able to cope without you for the evening.' He seemed glad the topic of conversation had shifted from him. 'But don't let him talk you into anything, like getting back with him, not if it's not what you want.' When she smiled he said, 'I'm still wide awake, I might call Mum and say thank you for the decoration.'

'That sounds like a good idea.'

He left her to it and she tugged the band from her hair before shaking it out. She sat by the window in the lounge, the sounds of the city carrying on around them. From here there was a view of the street, the brownstones opposite much like the one they were in now. Fire escape routes zigzagged up some of the frontages like an elaborate game of snakes and ladders, shouting came from below but soon passed. She wondered whether Nathan had managed to calm down yet, whether he was sorry for bursting in like that, whether Scarlett had told him the truth over at the Inglenook Inn.

She used the time alone to reflect on everything that had gone on in the last couple of days, everything from the near-kiss with Nathan, to Paul's arrival, Kyle and Nathan's latest run-in, and now Connie's letter. She thought life was complicated before they left for this holiday but somehow it still was, just in different ways.

'Did you have a good talk with your mum?' she asked when Kyle eventually emerged. 'You were on the phone a while.'

'She never usually chats that long.'

'She never was as talkative as me.' She beckoned him to come and sit with her. 'Her school reports would urge her to participate more in class, mine only said Must Stop Chatting.'

'She asked if I'd send her a photo of the decoration hung on the tree.' He'd taken the fireman ornament with him, maybe he'd held it as they talked, not wanting to let go of that piece of him and his dad. Now, he went over to the tree and hooked it onto a branch at the front, wiggling the white light behind it around so it was illuminated rather than shielded. He stood back and took the picture, his fingers nimbly operating his phone to send it across the miles to his mum.

'Did you talk about your dad?'

'A bit. She didn't say much, she only apologised for not talking to me more.'

'It's a start.'

'I guess. But it's as though she wants to forget him when I want to remember.'

'She probably wants to forget the pain of losing him, which isn't the same.'

'She was a bit weird on the phone.'

'But you were talking for ages.'

'That's the weird thing. I kind of got the feeling something's up, she was gearing up to tell me something. Do you think she's going to suggest I move out? Stand on my own two feet? She threatened it before. She said either I get my act together or I could find somewhere else to live.'

'In the heat of the moment we often say things that we don't mean.' Amelia had heard Connie talking about it a few times, wondering whether tough love was the way to go, but so far she hadn't followed through.

'She told me one of the good things about being here is I can't hang out with my friends.'

'The bad influences?' she asked.

'That's Mum's official name for them,' he clarified.

'Why do you hang out with them?'

He shrugged, then his shoulders slumped back to the same

hopeless position. 'They're not all bad. We have a bit of a laugh. But when they do stupid things I know it's not good to be around them, I just don't seem able to break the habit. Only one of them has a job you know, the others sponge off their parents, one is on the dole and boasts about living off the state. It's easy to think I won't end up the same as the rest of them, but I worry all the time.'

'Then don't let it happen.'

'Derek, the one who was in prison, has already done another break-in. He asked me to drive the car for him, park it down the lane out back of the house so he could pass stuff over, then jump the fence.'

'I'll throttle him.'

'He made me feel bad for saying no. They all took the piss out of me, although I could tell Warren didn't want to get involved either.' He sat back against the sofa. 'This trip to New York couldn't have come at a better time. Derek's been talking about pilfering kids' presents from round the tree, he's got all these photos on his phone of houses with amazing trees in the window, says there'll be Xboxes, iPhones, gadgets, parcels of money, we can all share it between us.'

'He sounds charming.'

'Dad once went on a shout after a burglary where whoever did the robbery set fire to a Christmas tree for a laugh. Half the house was destroyed. Dad was really upset, I saw Mum with her arms around him as he cried. I overheard him telling Mum the family had lost their son the year before and it was their first Christmas without him. Dad went to see the family and took presents around to their temporary house, anything to help.'

'Your dad was a good man.'

'And he'd be ashamed of me right now.'

Kyle was a seventeen-year-old boy who'd never admit he needed a hug but right now he fell apart, his shoulders heaved, tears spilled down his cheeks. He was wallowing in self-pity, some of it his own doing, some of it life's way of changing rapidly and unfairly until it brought you to your knees.

'Aside from the blubbing now,' Kyle managed to say, roughly swiping away his tears with the heels of his hands. 'I haven't felt this happy in a long time.'

'And why do you think that might be?'

'Being somewhere totally different where nobody knows me. Some of our neighbours at home give me a wide berth when they see me coming. They never used to but since I got in with Derek, Dale, Warren, and the others, they keep their distance.'

From her line of work she knew how hard it was for kids like Kyle to break away from people like that. 'I need to talk to Connie. Between the three of us we can make some changes. You're not on your own, remember.'

'I want to work, I really do. I want to sort myself out.'

'I know you do. You're a good boy.'

He looked at the ornament on the tree, then at Amelia. 'I never told Mum but I've always wanted to join the fire brigade.'

Amelia smiled. 'I once suspected that was the case but I figured when you didn't do anything about it, perhaps you'd changed your mind.'

'I didn't do anything because of Mum.'

'You think she'll hate the idea?'

'I know she will. And it's all I've ever wanted to do. I felt like I was betraying her, going after a career the same as Dad where she was on edge half the time waiting for him to come home. I went to a careers talk on it last year and I floated the idea with Mum by telling her another boy in my class was joining up as soon as he was the right age. She made a comment about how glad she was that it wasn't her son. She touched my cheek, gave me that same look she saved for when I'd go off on school camp and she was going to worry the entire time.'

'She never told me. And she doesn't really talk much to me about your dad either.'

'But you two talk all the time. Bet it's usually about me.'

'You're not wrong there. She's a worrier, your mum. And I think she's a bit lost.' Connie had been all over the place, more so lately now Amelia came to think about it. She'd been trundling on with her life since Stuart died with a few false hopes of happiness when she met other men but she'd definitely been worse over the last six months. And Amelia couldn't say with one hundred per cent certainty that she wouldn't make Kyle move out if he didn't get his act together. Perhaps the letter, the suggestion of a trip away, was all preparation for telling him it was time to fend for himself. Maybe it was make-or-break time for both of them.

When Kyle yawned it set Amelia off too. 'It's late, and I may not be due at the markets until lunchtime tomorrow but at this rate I'll be too tired to get up until well into the afternoon.' She switched off the lamp in the corner, Kyle grabbed the phone charger from the plug in the kitchen to take to his room, and Amelia didn't miss him checking his phone again.

'Have you heard from Scarlett?' she asked and when he shook his head she suggested, 'Maybe give Nathan a chance to calm down.'

'Scarlett's part of the reason I've felt happier here.'

'I know.'

'I've never met a girl like her. She listens to me.'

'Hey, what am I then?'

He grinned, gave her a playful shove. 'You're an oldie.'

'Cheek!' She pushed him back. 'But I'm glad you have her to talk to.' She only hoped Nathan would stop being such an arse about it, maybe remember how he'd been once upon a time, and give Kyle a break.

* * *

It was all systems go at the winter markets the next day and it had the power to take Amelia's mind off Kyle and Scarlett, Nathan, and Paul. She must've been exhausted last night with everything that had gone on because she'd had the best night's sleep since arriving in the city.

Amelia watched her footing on the icy pavement in front of the chalet when she returned with a sandwich for lunch. They were so busy, the lack of a big tree or an ice rink like the bigger, more established markets not affecting footfall in the slightest. People were here in droves, flocking to the Swiss-style chalets with their lights strung around the roofs, and the knitting stall was doing a roaring trade.

'I hope you've got more supplies,' Amelia told Cleo as she demolished her sandwich quickly enough that she could multitask and serve a customer. 'Today is the busiest I've seen it. You'll have no stock left at this rate.'

'Don't worry, I've got a couple more boxes in the corner, then I'll bring even more tomorrow.'

They carried on, replenishing stock, advising customers, taking payment, pushing garments into paper bags, and when there was a lull Amelia and Cleo talked about Ruby and everything that had happened before it came to a head. 'It must be a real weight off your mind to have her back on side.' Amelia was glad to see Cleo looking far less stressed.

'All I ever wanted all along was for the kids to be as happy about the wedding as us, and now I think they really are. All I need to do now is find time to plan the big day.'

'Is that all?' Amelia teased.

'I hope you'll be there.'

'Another visit to New York at Christmas time? It'll be hard, but someone has to do it,' she joked. She hadn't confided her own problems. They'd been too busy and with Ruby and Cleo finally able to move forwards; she didn't want to burden her friend with the crap going on in her life. At least not yet, not when she had no idea in her own mind what the next step should be. She'd woken this morning and her first thought had been Nathan but it was very soon replaced with thoughts about Paul and the fact he was here. He'd come to tell her he'd made a mistake and it was a big gesture that left her confused. Once upon a time they'd had a relationship that others envied; he spoiled her, he was always there for her. And if he'd done the same thing a few months back it would've been easy, she'd have leapt at the chance. But now she'd begun to get used to making her own decisions and settling into life without him. Nathan was in the picture too – at least she thought he might be, although he hadn't looked too friendly when he'd come to the apartment with Kyle and seen Paul, and her in just a towel. He must've put two and two together and come up with an answer that was completely incorrect.

'Did Mitch say anything about Kyle this morning on your way here?' She helped Cleo straighten the sweaters on display and positioned the small cardboard price sign in front of them when they were done.

'You have nothing to worry about on that score, because Mitch told me how hard Kyle works and how he deserves a day off.'

'He's gone to explore Central Park.'

'On his own?'

'I wouldn't mind betting he and Scarlett arranged something.' Even though Nathan had made it pretty clear he didn't want them anywhere near each other.

'Young love, nothing like it.'

Her phone pinged again with a message from Paul, this time with a photograph of the Statue of Liberty. Amelia had expected him to be hounding her all day, checking up on her, but was pleasantly surprised he hadn't been tracking her every move. Maybe some time away from each other had enabled both of them to evolve and know what they each wanted. He was out sightseeing, having a great time he said, and couldn't wait to meet up at his hotel later. Not one moan about her working the market stall to help out a friend. Maybe as well as her seeing things from his point of view, he was seeing it from hers.

A customer beckoned his wife for the fourth time to finish choosing something at the knitting stall. He held a tree upright, it was huge, and his wife muttered something about getting a tree delivered next year when he made her take one end. Cleo and Amelia were busy laughing when the couple left, and when Amelia looked up she realised she'd been right with her theory about Kyle, because he was standing there with Scarlett.

'Does your dad know you're together?' She directed her question to Scarlett and by the look on her face he didn't.

'I do now,' came a voice on the street behind them.

Busted. Clearly Manhattan wasn't big enough for the kids to stay incognito for long.

Amelia fished in her pocket for some money, handed it to Kyle, and told him to go grab her and Nathan a hot chocolate each so they could talk.

Cleo had everything on the stall in hand for now and Amelia stepped out of the way of Christmas shoppers swarming the markets. 'I hope you've calmed down after last night.' She figured he must have done because he'd let Kyle and Scarlett disappear to do as she asked.

'Is that why you sent them for drinks? In case I'd come here to punch him?'

'Now I know you're winding me up; you wouldn't do that, no matter how angry you were.' He was too gentle to do it to anyone despite his bravado.

As he stood there looking at her, neither of them knowing what to say now, his breath came out in puffs of white, mixing with the fog that shrouded Manhattan's buildings and tampered with the idyllic skyline views.

'I don't want her to ruin her life,' he said, his eyes not leaving hers.

Her heart went out to him. He was doing his best as a father, trying to manage the teenage years the best he could. 'I know you don't.'

'It's not that I think Kyle will do that, at least not on purpose, it's just, given my past experience, it could happen. Mistakes happen.'

'Mistakes are part of life.'

'I've spent years trying to give Scarlett the world.'

'Maybe that's half the problem.' She smiled up at him. 'She doesn't need the world, she just needs you on her side.'

'Maybe.' He shook his head. 'But they've only just met... jumping into bed together. I can't get the picture out of my head.'

Time for some honesty. 'It wasn't Kyle who bought the condoms and it wasn't him who suggested they go upstairs at the inn. According to Kyle, who had no reason to lie about it, Scarlett was the one who had the condoms and wanted to take things further.' She put a hand on his arm when he winced. 'I'm not trying to upset you. I just think having all the facts is important. Kyle was the one who said he didn't want to.'

He had no time to react before Kyle and Scarlett came along with the hot chocolates. Amelia waited, held her breath to see whether the drink Kyle handed Nathan ended up being thrown all over him in another rage. But it didn't.

The awkward silence in the group was only broken when a man carrying a Christmas tree walked right through the middle of them.

'I'm going to grab a hot dog,' said Kyle. 'Want one?'

Amelia shook her head.

He looked at Scarlett, Scarlett looked at her dad, the silence deafening until Nathan had Scarlett hold his hot chocolate, pulled out his wallet and exchanged his drink for a few notes. 'You both go get yourselves some hot dogs. I'll see you back at the inn by five o'clock, don't be late.'

Scarlett took the escape route while she could and Kyle only glanced Amelia's way once in hesitation as he went with her.

'I guess I need to accept the fact she's growing up,' Nathan admitted when the kids left them to it. His gaze was fixed on the street Scarlet had disappeared along, the market stalls providing a glitzy fringe to the sidewalk.

'Give me one second.' Amelia had a word with Cleo, checked it was all right to leave for the day. 'Want to walk?' she offered Nathan, who looked as though he'd dropped fifty bucks and found a quarter. She knew it must be hard for him to loosen the reins with Scarlett.

'Sure.'

They bustled between shoppers until they reached the end of the markets where Mitch was busy at work at the Christmas tree stall, netting a tree for a customer. 'I'm sorry I stormed over to your apartment last night,' Nathan began as they crossed the street. 'I know I came down on Kyle too harshly. Again. But it's hard having a daughter; I don't know if I'm supposed to talk to her about boys, or, if I am, how I'm supposed to do it.'

'I'm not a parent but I suppose it must be like trying to find your way out of a strange building in the dark. You might turn the right

way and find daylight, you might take several wrong turns, stumble
over in the pitch black, but you get up again and carry on.'

His laughter rumbled on the foggy air enveloping Manhattan.
'Sometimes it really does feel like that. I worry about making a
move in case it's wrong, other times I leap on in without thinking.'

They wandered, chatting about girls versus boys, the perils, the
rewards, and when they came to one of the access points that would
take them up to the High Line, it was Nathan who suggested they
walk it.

It was busier than she'd thought it would be, plenty of tourists
waiting for Instagram- or Facebook-worthy shots of Manhattan
with its juxtaposition of new and old buildings, street views totally
different from this vantage point. He pulled her in close to him and
crouched down, pointing to a plant that looked bare until she
spotted perfectly round red berries in a cluster and a bird noshing
on them. 'Look at that.'

'A bit of colour,' she smiled. 'And festive too.' Suddenly aware
she could smell his shampoo or aftershave and see the faint stubble
on his jaw up so close, she stood and looked around them. 'Imagine
this place in the snow.' By now the sun was fast descending and it
was amazing to be up this high, take it all in.

It didn't take long for the moon to come out from its hiding
place and the whole city to take on another personality as the lights
of the city glowed near and far. 'Spectacular,' he said.

'I'm coming back next year,' she grinned. 'Cleo's getting
married.'

The city carried on about its business below. 'Will Paul come
with you?'

The elephant on the High Line with them had finally been
addressed. 'I've no idea.'

'When did he show up?'

'About twenty minutes before you did.'

'Bad timing on my part, sorry.'

Or good, depending on how you look at it.

They carried on walking, past an elderly couple sitting on a bench, weaving their way through a crowd chattering about the public park elevated above the streets of Manhattan and built on what was once a freight rail line, saved from demolition.

'Is he staying at the apartment with you and Kyle?' Nathan asked as once again they were able to walk side by side.

'He's in a hotel in Times Square. He wants me to go for dinner with him tonight.' He'd sent another couple of texts. He'd never been this communicative when they were together and she had a hard time reminding herself that the Paul she knew rarely took such an interest in the mundanity of life, tourist traps of a new city.

'Are you going?'

'I am.'

Nathan stopped, looked around, down at the city streets, absorbing the quietness from up here. 'If I worked in Manhattan, I'd use this place as an escape.'

'Depends where you worked. You might be way uptown or downtown.'

He shook his head. 'Must you always be right?'

'Yes.'

'That makes two of us. My brother was forever going on about it when I was little. I do my best to let others have their say now, but I am headstrong.'

'Don't apologise for it.'

'I need to be more laid back, or at least that's what Scarlett tells me.'

Back to the subject of teens, she suspected they'd both found their comfort zone. 'Kids can be quick to judge no matter what age they are. They think adults have zero idea about the world around them, especially if the adult is a parent.' She pulled her scarf a little tighter as the wind whipped around them when they passed on to a different section of the highline, the crowds at least moving. She couldn't imagine what this place was like come summer. When she'd been chatting with Dylan after Cleo's visit to the UK, he'd talked about his running and how he sometimes came up here but only if it was very early.

'I know I need to talk to Scarlett.'

'About the condoms?'

'About Kyle.' He smiled. Who'd have thought we'd come all this way to another country and face more teen turmoil than when we were at home?'

'I definitely didn't see any romance on the air.' She was glad it was dark and Nathan couldn't read the awkwardness on her face at the mention of romance, because it was her own feelings about the man beside her that she was thinking of the most right now.

'Me neither.'

She wondered, was he thinking the same? 'Kyle hasn't had the easiest time, happiness seemed out of reach, but seeing the way he is around Scarlett, well, it's changing him for the better. We really talked – about her, his dad, his mum, the scumbags he's been hanging around with. Who, by the way, he doesn't want to associate with, but Kyle being Kyle is too nice to tell them to bugger off.'

'What does he say about Scarlett?'

'He talks about her qualities, what she loves, her art, her talent. When he talks about her it really tells me that his feelings are genuine and go way beyond teenagers fooling around.'

They took the next opportunity to exit the High Line and headed to a café for warmth. And over coffees they left the teen conversation and any reference to Paul and the impending dinner date tonight and instead talked about the friendships that had brought them here.

'Do you knit a lot?' he wanted to know as they talked about how much she was enjoying helping out on Cleo's stall.

'I'm crap at it,' she admitted. 'I got the job with Cleo's aunt and uncle in their shop because my parents knew them. I worked hard. I learned a lot about the different sorts of wool, knitting needles, knitting patterns, and I bought plenty of things for myself, but I never really had it in me to practise. Cleo is keen for me to give one of her workshops a go out at her store in Inglenook Falls, but luckily distance prevents me from doing that.'

'She was telling me at the inn the other night that her store was once in Manhattan, and Dylan put her out of business. Did I understand that right?'

'You did. The store had been in Cleo's family for years until he sold the buildings.'

'And now she's marrying the guy?'

His raised eyebrows made her laugh. 'Sounds ridiculous, I know. But they're so in love and I'm really pleased Cleo is so settled. How do you know Myles?'

'We worked together in England, he's a good guy.'

'He seems it, and Darcy's lovely. Are you enjoying staying at the inn?'

'It's great, suits us perfectly, apart from finding my daughter in bed with a boy that is.'

When her phone rang Amelia expected it to be Paul and was about to set it to silent but it was Connie. 'Do you mind if I take this?' She wanted to talk to her sister about Kyle, tell her how much her letter and the decoration meant to him, how much he was looking forward to a trip away with her.

She moved from the table to a quiet corner of the café, away from the music speaker.

'Connie, say it again, I'm struggling to hear you,' she said into the device a second time, pressing it hard against one ear to make it easier.

But what Connie said next brought her whole world crashing down around her.

She finished the call. She made her way back to the table, stumbling into a waitress carrying a plate of eggs, toast, hash browns. Food splattered to the floor, the plate cracked as it hit.

Everything smashed to pieces.

16

AMELIA

'Amazing, isn't it?' Paul wrapped his arms around her from behind as they stood at the window of his penthouse suite in Times Square looking out over the entire city. Manhattan, spread out before them, full of opportunity, full of promise.

'It's wonderful.' But then she already knew that. She'd come here without him and in doing so had found the missing piece of herself that she hadn't known when she was with him. She had a confidence, something she lacked when they were together. And it was that confidence that told her all she needed to know.

He turned her to face him. 'Amelia, what's going on? I thought you'd be impressed.'

Here she was dressed up in a midnight-blue woollen dress she'd bagged from Cleo's stall for Christmas day, with polished leather boots she'd brought with her on holiday but hadn't worn nearly as much as the comfy thick-soled boots she favoured on slippery foot-paths. The view was indeed like something out of the movies, but right now she'd rather be back at the apartment with the peeling paint on the ceiling, its thin windows, street noises and Kyle mooching around. Up here in the quiet with New York muted down below them felt wrong.

'It's my sister.' She leaned her head on his chest for comfort. 'She's sick. She's got cancer.'

'Oh, Amelia, I'm so sorry.' He pulled her in tight, reiterating his sympathies.

She felt safe, protected from hurt even though she had all that to come. They all did. Connie had wanted to wait until they came home after Christmas, she hadn't wanted to spoil the holiday by sharing her news, but as she'd found a buyer for the house and things had moved unusually quickly, she'd had to make the call. Because she'd be up in Amelia's neck of the woods by the time they returned to England.

Amelia told Paul everything. He poured them each a large glass of wine as he listened; he cancelled the dinner reservation and said they'd order room service if they needed. He was there at her side in a way that surprised her as she told him about the shock of the phone call, her worries about her sister, who had undergone one round of chemo already with another looming soon. For someone who never let her rant about her family, he was here for her.

'Those times I thought she was hungover,' said Amelia. 'She wasn't, she must've been suffering, couldn't tell me. What sort of a person am I that my own sister can't confide something so important?'

'For once, I think she did the right thing. Look at what you do for her, Amelia.' He pulled her down next to him on the sofa. 'Your head must be all over the place.'

She let herself close her eyes. For the first time since that phone call her body relaxed.

'Does Kyle know?'

'I haven't told him yet. Connie would rather I waited until the end of the holiday.'

'You can't keep it from him.'

'She wants him to have a good time here. They've been talking more lately, she wants to have time away with him when we're home. He has a girlfriend, he's looking to the future more than he ever has before. And now...' Her voice wobbled and she bit down on her lip to steady herself and stop the tears. She didn't want to completely let go in front of Paul, she couldn't.

'Are you really happy to hide all this from him?'

She dabbed beneath her eyes with a tissue before her mascara and eyeliner did its worst. 'Not really, but what choice do I have?'

'If you think he needs to know sooner, tell him.

'It's not my call.'

Paul stood up and jolted her on the sofa as he did so. He went to the window and looked out into the darkness punctuated with city lights. She could see his reflection in the glass, his expression set.

'She's always done this to you,' he said without turning round.

'What? Get cancer?'

'No, put you in a position where you can't do what you think is right.'

'She has, but I also don't want to hurt Kyle more than necessary. This is going to be one hell of a shock.'

'She didn't have to ruin your holiday though.' He sounded angry.

'She's kept it from me for long enough and I'm gutted she did. I can't imagine the pain she's in, neither can you.'

'You're being taken advantage of again.'

'I know Connie would be there for me if I was sick.' She'd been there after Paul broke her heart; she'd sat up with her well into the night listening to her sob and wonder what she'd ever done wrong. 'I can't imagine how Kyle will take this, he's already lost his dad.'

He turned to her briefly before looking out of the window again. 'It's not fair, Amelia.'

'It's not the same this time. It's not taking advantage, it's about my sister trying to move forwards in any way she can and protect those she loves. This isn't the moment where I can put my foot down.'

'You never will.' The accusation flew her way in a voice she barely recognised.

'Of course I will, but even you must see the timing isn't right.'

'What's that supposed to mean... even I?'

'I know you've never had much time for her or Kyle.'

'Don't turn this back on me to be my fault.'

'I'm not.'

She joined him at the window and reached a hand out towards his arm but changed her mind at the last minute.

'What's the prognosis?' he asked eventually.

'I think it's too early to tell, but she's preparing for the worst. She's thinking about Kyle by coming to live nearer to me. It'll get him away from that crowd he's been hanging out with too, which can only be a good thing.'

'And it'll mean you're on hand to help.'

She pulled back. 'And to see her. She'll need people who love her. She has cancer, Paul, she might not even be alive much longer.' Her voice wobbled and it angered her that she couldn't keep it together.

'What about Edinburgh?'

Her silence told him how much she'd thought about that. Not at all. 'I haven't had a chance to think about that yet. You sprung it on me six months after you dumped me without explanation. Now who's taking advantage?'

The muscle in his jaw twitched. 'I know you, Amelia, remember? I know you'll always put your family first. Edinburgh won't get a look-in.' He distanced himself by walking over to the kitchen counter, the stainless-steel appliances insistent on gleaming despite the low lighting, the expensive coffee maker poised and ready for one of them to demand attention no matter the time of day or night.

'I haven't thought much past Connie's news. My head is all over the place.'

'But your head will settle back to where it's always been and you'll stick by Connie. I'm not suggesting you don't, I'm not that much of an arse, but it'd be nice if you put yourself, us, first for once.'

Her voice softened. 'You could put Edinburgh off for a while, until she's better, until we've had a chance to get to know one another again.'

'We were apart six months, not sixty years. And the job offer doesn't work like that.'

Her mind was turning over so fast she could barely keep up. 'Would you wait for me? Go up there, make a start and wait for me to join you?' She had no idea whether that was what she wanted, but she needed to know how he really felt, she wanted the truth.

He came over and wrapped his arms around her. He planted a kiss on her lips and tilted her chin towards him, looked deep into her eyes.

He held her again, this time for longer, and when he pulled away he looked sad, defeated when he said, 'I think we both know you'll never come.'

Tears pricked her eyes because he was right. And it wasn't only because Connie needed her now more than ever; it was because being apart from Paul had shown her that a life with him wasn't the right thing. He'd always wanted her to himself and whenever anyone else came into the picture, family or a troublesome kid at work, he hated it. She didn't think him a bad person for being that way, but he wasn't right for her. He wanted someone at his side, supporting him at work functions, moving across the country or farther whenever his career demanded it. He wanted the neat idea of a relationship with nothing outside the lines and Amelia knew she'd never be able to give him that. And she didn't want to either. She didn't want to morph into a lesser version of herself, not for him, not for anyone. And, now, she realised she hadn't really missed Paul in their time apart. She'd thought she had but what she'd really missed was companionship. Paul had become a habit, like an old comfortable shoe that had holes in it but you didn't mind, it fitted well enough. But the shoe had started to cause her pain, blisters in the relationship, and it was time to accept that it wasn't doing her any good.

'What will you do now?' she asked. 'It's Christmas, nobody should be alone. Come over, I'll cook.'

'I've got a friend in Brooklyn, I'll look him up. And if not, I'll be fine. You don't need to worry about me.' They gazed out to the moonlight beyond the window, the glow caressing the illuminated buildings of the city.

'Merry Christmas, Paul.' She picked up her bag, ready to leave.

'Merry Christmas, Amelia.'

And with a final kiss on his cheek, Amelia said her goodbyes and left the penthouse and Paul behind for good.

17

NATHAN

He wasn't sure what had happened earlier with Amelia. One minute they'd been chatting along happily, talking about what had brought them to New York, the next she'd taken a phone call and caused a big commotion by crashing into a waitress. He'd paid the bill, he'd walked her home to her apartment, struggling to keep up the pace. She didn't want to talk about whatever it was and when they got there she barely turned to say goodbye before she disappeared inside the brownstone.

Nathan had assumed the phone call must have come from the boyfriend, Paul, making his presence known, perhaps unhappy she was out with another man. Shame, he'd only met the guy for a few minutes at the apartment but even those moments had been enough to tell him he wasn't right for Amelia. Not in his eyes anyway. Then again, hadn't he been telling Kyle and Scarlett all along that they hardly knew one another well enough to be having deep feelings about a lasting relationship? Perhaps he was getting far too carried away in the holiday spirit. Blame it on New York? Maybe he would. It seemed a good excuse.

Scarlett came back to the suite at the Inglenook Inn well before five o'clock as he'd specified and he managed to ask her all the usual questions about what she'd seen, had she enjoyed herself, before he launched into the topic he needed to.

'We're not kids any more, Dad.' She jutted out her jaw in defiance.

He'd sat her down to talk about the birds and the bees or whatever he was supposed to call them. At moments like these he missed Dawn even more. She'd know what to do. Girls needed their mum at a time like this, but he'd do his best. 'I'm well aware.' He took a deep breath. 'Were they your condoms?'

'Dad!'

'Much as you don't want to talk to me, you're going to have to if I'm to trust you. I need a bit of honesty.'

His demands had the desired effect. 'I bought them, coming up here was my idea, not Kyle's.'

'So why did you let me blame him?'

'You were hardly in a mood to be reasoned with, if you remember. I yelled after you but you'd already manhandled him out of the inn.'

'He took the wrap for you.'

'He did it because he likes me and wants to see me again when we're back in England.'

Why had his heart just plummeted like a lift with broken ropes going from the top floor to the bottom with a crash? 'You live in totally different parts of the country.'

'We can make it work.'

He'd tell her she was being ridiculous if he hadn't been thinking along the same lines about Amelia. Although that was a dead end now Paul was back in the picture.

He tried to look at Scarlett's budding relationship in a different way. At least with Kyle he had a contact – Amelia – to keep this pair in line should anything go wrong. If Scarlett didn't carry things on with Kyle, she'd probably have another boyfriend soon enough. In an ideal world it wouldn't be until she was well over eighteen and the boy in question would have a squeaky clean past, he'd be studying as hard as she did, he'd be polite, and he wouldn't find them in bed together.

'We should go find somewhere to eat,' he suggested. He blamed his voracious appetite on the freezing temperatures in the city as well as all the walking.

'What sort of food?' She leapt at the peace offering being silently exchanged. 'We could have anything, anything's possible here in New York. We could ask Amelia and Kyle to eat with us, give you a chance to see what a kind person he is.'

'How about you reserve tonight for your dad?' It was the only way he could cope with the thought of Amelia on her date with Paul, snuggled up somewhere together, warm and cosy, perhaps in bed together already.

She put her arms around him and hugged him the same way she had when she was little. 'As long as we can have pizza.'

'I'm happy with that but only if we go to a decent restaurant, I'm not standing at a table like last time.'

'Deal.'

* * *

They found an Italian café on Canal Street that was casual enough for Scarlett so that it wasn't pretentious, upmarket enough for him so they at least got a seat. With a candle in the centre of the table to set the tone and impeccable waiter service, they were both happy.

Full from pizza, steak with rosemary-garlic sauce, and a decadent dessert of cream semifreddo with a chocolate crumb, Scarlett hooked her arm through his as they walked back to the inn.

'I really think if you got to know Kyle you might even like him,' she ventured.

'Who knows, maybe I will.'

'You're getting on well with Amelia.'

'We've been forced together thanks to you two.'

'It doesn't exactly look like you're hating it from where I'm standing.'

'I thought I was supposed to lecture you on your love life, not the other way around.'

'I want you to be happy.'

He looked at the girl beside him who'd blossomed into a proper young lady and he felt a pang of loss at how quickly time marched on, how many moments he longed to savour all over again. They talked about everything they'd managed to see in New York so far, how it had lived up to expectation and beyond. And when they passed an ornament shop in Soho, Scarlett dragged him inside and they ended up buying something else for their tree. She came out with two golden angels, one playing a violin, the other playing a harp, plus a centrepiece of a Santa kneeling down with a sack full of presents.

'If your luggage is over the limit at the airport I'll make you throw that in the bin,' he told her when she swung the bag back and forth, happy to have found something new.

'Don't be such a spoilsport. You'll love the memory on our first Christmas back in England.'

'I'm missing our Christmas movies this year.'

'Me too. But I'm loving being in the city where so many movies are set. Sometimes I have to pinch myself,' she grinned, and stopped out front of a clothes store not far from the inn. 'It's beautiful,' she said, admiring the sparkly dress in the window.

'Go try it on.'

'Really?'

'Why not?'

Twenty minutes later and they left the store with what he now knew was something called an A-line princess scoop-neck dress. Scarlett had looked stunning in it and never mind the price tag, when her eyes shone as much as the sequins on the bodice he'd got carried away and insisted on buying it for her as an extra Christmas gift.

'I'm going to wear it to the Christmas Eve party at the inn,' she said after they left the store. 'Did you pack anything smart?'

'I packed my best shirt, don't worry. Just like you packed a black dress, from what I remember.'

'A new dress called out to me, what can I say?'

'I hope Kyle appreciates it.' He knew Kyle and Amelia had been invited because Darcy had made a point of telling him and already he wondered what Amelia would be wearing, how she'd style her hair, whether she'd look his way. Whether she'd bring Paul.

The last thought stopped his daydreaming.

'Amelia will appreciate you in your smarter clothes,' smiled Scarlett. 'Girls at my school talk about how hot my dad is.'

'Really?'

'Yeah and it's gross.'

'Thanks!'

'Kyle told me Amelia's ex-boyfriend is in town. He doesn't sound like the type of guy who deserves her.'

'No? Why, what have you heard?'

'Not much. Kyle doesn't like him, says she can do better. And if there's a possibility she might bring someone, you need a date. Why don't I ask Darcy if she knows anyone?'

'I don't think so.' Maybe he'd just lie low, do the rounds and say hello and then escape until everyone buggered off home.

They stopped to take in another impressive window display, the magic of Christmas brought to them there on the street corner. The air around them hinted that the snow symbols on the weather forecast for next week might not be a figment of an enthusiastic weather station's imagination, and eventually they turned into the road that housed the Inglenook Inn, away from the busyness of the main streets, the chaos of December, Christmas Eve looming in front of them tomorrow.

He and Scarlett were laughing about his appalling singing voice when it came to Christmas carols, how she'd forbidden him from singing loudly at any school recital, when Nathan saw a familiar figure sitting on the stoop of the brownstone between the two pine trees wrapped in lights and marking the entrance to the Inglenook Inn.

'Kyle.' Scarlett's eyes lit up but faded the second they both got closer.

Was that a bottle of vodka in his hands?

'What's going on, mate?' Nathan would pull her back if Scarlett got much closer. 'Where did you get that from?'

'Found it.'

'Give it to me.' He held out his hand. The Christmas tree in the lounge of the inn twinkled at them from its position, a low glow from the fireplace still burning helped him see that the inn was quiet at this time. Lucky for Kyle.

'And what if I say no?'

'You'll probably get arrested sooner or later. You're under age.'

'You're over age.' Kyle began to laugh, a hollow sound, in an attempt to disguise a sadness that was written all over his face.

For once Nathan wasn't angry; he was confused, shocked. It was almost like looking into a mirror because this had been him once upon a time when he'd thought the world couldn't get much worse. 'Scarlett, go inside please.'

'Dad—'

'Now, please.' He expected Kyle to stop her from going past but he didn't and Scarlett shut the heavy wooden door behind her.

Nathan sat on the top of the stoop beside Kyle. 'Revolting stuff that, at least you could've picked something with a bit of taste.'

'Don't even like it. But it burns when it goes down.'

Nathan took the bottle from his hand and he didn't resist. 'Does Amelia know where you are?' He didn't answer. Nathan set the bottle down by the pine tree. His butt was freezing against the concrete. 'What's going on, mate?'

'It's my mum,' he said before Nathan tried the question again.

'What's she done?' She'd already shirked responsibility for her own child going by what Amelia had told him. What damage could she possibly do over thousands of miles?

'She's selling our house, she found a buyer already and has to move out. I heard her and Amelia talking on the phone.'

'When was this?'

'Right before I came here.'

'I thought Amelia was with Paul.' He was confused.

'Jackass wasn't around. Hopefully he's buggered off. He's not good enough for her you know.'

'Language.' Although there was a moment of joint appreciation of Paul's unsuitability for Amelia. 'What exactly did you overhear?'

'Like I said, the house has gone, Mum is trying to find somewhere to rent close by and I heard Amelia offer to let me stay with her for a bit. Which means Mum wants me out. She threatened it once you know, now she's going through with it.'

'Having to move out for a house sale is hardly the same as throwing you out.' But the rushing into it did seem odd. Why do it when Kyle was away and call to tell them? It didn't make sense.

'It's the first step.' He harrumphed. 'I thought we were getting somewhere, me and Mum. I thought... I thought she wanted to spend time with me.'

'Have you actually asked her what's happening?'

'I'm not talking to her. Auntie Amelia can do that, she can pick up my stuff and I won't even have to embarrass Mum by going near her. She won't ever have to see me again.'

'If I were you I wouldn't jump to conclusions.'

'You're a fine one to talk about making assumptions.'

Nathan didn't argue the point. He rubbed his hands together and blew into them for extra warmth before he hunched over more. He'd rather do this inside but he didn't want Scarlett involved when Kyle was in this state. 'I don't know much about you, Kyle, and you don't know much about me. But can you tell me why you came here tonight? Was it to see Scarlett?'

'It was hardly to come to you for sympathy.'

'No, but what's with the vodka? It's hardly a packet of condoms, but do you see why I might have a problem with you spending time with my daughter when you show up like this?' He grabbed Kyle's arm before he bolted and persuaded him to sit down again. 'Amelia told me about your dad.'

'None of anyone's business.'

'It isn't, but would you believe me if I told you I understand how you feel?'

'No.'

'I didn't lose my dad, but my brother – my best friend, my side-kick – he died, and it's almost like I was bookended by what happened. There was the Nathan before he lost Robbie and then there's the Nathan afterwards. Death changes people.'

'Fuck's sake,' Kyle muttered when a group of carollers gathered at the bottom step singing 'Deck the Halls'.

'Don't you move, I'll sort it.' Nathan, one eye still on Kyle, went down the stoop, paid them enough to move to the other side of the street and leave them to it.

Back beside Kyle, he took away the vodka that Kyle had picked up again and this time, tipped the contents into the pot for the pine tree. 'So you're not tempted.'

'You've probably killed the tree now.'

'I doubt it, and if I have I'll buy Darcy a new one.'

The strains of 'Good King Wenceslas' mingled with the mist high above the buildings and the carollers moved along the street gradually.

'I was sixteen when my brother died,' said Nathan. 'I kept up with my school work so my parents were none the wiser, but out of school I was a nightmare. I started drinking, got involved with petty crimes. I hung around with some horrible people. Your auntie Amelia seems to think I might understand a bit about what you're going through. I still have my dad so I don't completely get it but I know what it means to have your world fall apart.'

'I bet your parents never turned their backs on you.'

'They didn't, I shielded them from most of what was going on.'

'Mum knows everything I get up to, she's embarrassed about me. She's every right to be. But she never lets me talk about my dad, she changes the subject whenever I bring him up.'

'That must hurt.'

'It does.'

'People handle grief differently, do what they can to cope. I know I did.'

'I spoke to Mum the other day and she didn't say a word about the house. She was nice to me, I felt good about myself for once. Now she's got Auntie Amelia promising to look after me. Amelia was crying, too, which is understandable – I'm not her child and she's stuck with me.'

'What else did you hear?'

'Nothing, I'd heard enough. I left.'

'That's the problem with eavesdropping. You only hear part of the story.'

Kyle found a stray branch from the pine tree closest to him and picked its needles off one by one, dropping them onto the stoop. 'I got the gist.'

'Where did you get the vodka?'

'Found it at the apartment.'

'Does Amelia know where you are?' He shook his head. 'I'll check on Scarlett then walk you back.'

'I don't need a chaperone.'

'Don't argue. We'll grab you a coffee on the walk and get you sobered up a bit.'

'It was only a few swigs.'

He wasn't stupid, it was more than a few swigs by the way Kyle was acting. He could hold his sentences together but he had an edge of agitation fuelled by the alcohol and Amelia wouldn't be fooled.

Nathan took out his phone and pinged a text to his daughter. He'd be more comfortable getting this kid home now. 'Come on,' he said to Kyle.

He tried to get Kyle talking as they walked their way from the inn, past iconic buildings and sights filled with festive cheer, but the boy would only grunt or grace him with monosyllabic replies and so Nathan gave up.

They grabbed strong black coffees and drank as they walked, Nathan keeping his eye on Kyle in the crowds in case he tried to give him the slip, and soon enough they'd bypassed Madison Square Park and were outside the brownstone.

'I can take it from here,' Kyle insisted. 'You don't need to deliver me to the door again.'

'I'm not going to mention the vodka, but I want to make sure you're in the apartment, that Amelia isn't going nuts with worry.'

'What's it to you if she is?' He kicked the brick wall outside the brownstone. He smacked his fist up against it. And he turned to run off down the steps but Nathan was too quick for him and caught him by his jacket.

'Settle down,' he said more than once. 'Upstairs, now.'

Inside, as they followed the stairs up the first flight, Kyle sniffed. 'I respect her you know.'

Amelia? Scarlett? It didn't really matter, because they were already at Amelia's door and she came straight out when they knocked.

'Kyle, where have you been?' She pulled him into a reluctant hug. 'I was going out of my mind with worry.' She looked to Nathan. 'What happened this time?'

'Chill,' said Kyle. 'I went to see Scarlett, not that he let me get anywhere near.'

'Probably because you were drinking that bottle of vodka. Weren't you?' she demanded, relief replaced by frustration. 'I'm not stupid, and you even left the cupboard door open after you took it – kind of a giveaway.'

'Whatever.' He stomped into his bedroom and slammed the door.

She looked at Nathan. 'I don't have the energy for this tonight. I'll let him calm down.'

'What are you doing home? I thought tonight was the big date night?'

'It was.' She didn't elaborate. 'I appreciate you bringing him home for me. I'm not sure I could've coped with scouring the streets of New York the night before Christmas Eve.'

'He was waiting at the inn when we got back there.'

'I don't get it. He was fine this afternoon, wouldn't have answered back to either of us. Seemed intent on proving himself, in fact. And when I texted to say I'd left money for takeaway he replied telling me to have a good time.'

He followed her inside when she walked over to the sofa and

slumped down. It was then he noticed the blotchy cheeks and redness around her eyes. 'He overheard you on the phone. To Connie.'

She looked towards the small corridor down which were the bedrooms, where Kyle was now. Then she looked back at Nathan. 'What did he hear?'

'Enough.'

She walked over to the window and stood looking outside. The hum of traffic was soothing in a way, like those sounds that are noisy at first but soon become a comfort.

'Is it true? Is she throwing him out?'

She turned towards him. 'What makes him think that? She's moving and is having trouble finding somewhere else. I said I'd watch out for Kyle and he can stay with me until she's settled.'

'So she's not throwing him out?'

'Definitely not. But she is going to need me to help her, which is why she wants to be closer to where I live.'

'Don't you help out enough already?'

'Don't you start,' she muttered. 'Sorry,' she added quickly enough. 'I didn't mean to snap.'

'You're in a difficult situation, I'm sure. I don't get it though. Moving and letting you know on holiday that she'll need even more help seems a bit odd. I know she's family. But what about your life?'

'Stop going on about it,' she snapped.

He waited a moment before he said, 'That's my cue to leave.'

Her hand on his arm stopped him. 'I'm sorry, you're being nice and I'm being a total cow.'

'Well...'

She managed a smile but it soon faded. 'Connie is sick. She has cancer, that's why the change and the urgency. And it's not all of a sudden for her – she's been keeping it to herself for a while and now she's panicking about everything.'

Reality dawned on him. 'It was her on the phone in the café, wasn't it?'

'That's when she first told me. She's been trying to sell the house for some time and suddenly got a buyer who wanted to move fast. She's renting a smaller place right near me so I guess she's giving me time to get my head around everything before we get back to England. We've talked a lot and we both know the move is a good thing for Kyle. It'll get him away from those so-called mates of his, they'll both have support.'

'They'll both have you.'

'Yes.' Her voice came out small and he noticed a tear escape but she swiped it away before it could run down her cheek. 'She feels like she's failed Kyle over and over again and now she thinks she's failing him again by getting sick.'

'But it's not her fault, she must see that.'

'She doesn't. Never mind the illness, her head is a mess.'

'How did she keep the cancer hidden from Kyle?'

'I've no idea. Probably the same way she kept it hidden from me. By pretending everything was fine, or claiming to have tummy bugs, the flu, whatever it took to shield us from the reality.'

'I don't know what to say, Amelia.' He wanted to put his arms around her and tell her she'd be okay, but how could he? 'So, Kyle really did hear it wrong.'

'Connie has been thinking about him in all of this, which is why she hid her illness and why this holiday was good. It took him away from it all and she could take care of herself a bit, knowing he was in good hands. She has a friend with her, which I'm glad about or I'd be going out of my mind with worry that she had nobody there right now. She's still planning on going away with Kyle to Wales when we're back, before she has to undergo more chemo, and she's excited about it.' She smiled then. 'I could tell how pleased she was to hear how happy Kyle's been since he met Scarlett.'

'It sounds as though things are changing. In some ways not for the better, in others...'

'Let's hope so. But what if she dies?' A blanket of fear fell across her face. 'What if Kyle loses another parent? What if I lose my sister?'

He had no words to say otherwise, no words of comfort, no platitudes that would quell her fear. Cancer was a bastard that took whoever it wanted, whenever it liked. The disease had no reasoning. It had its own schedule that they'd be forced to follow.

'How could I not notice my own sister had cancer?' Her voice demonstrated the pain she felt, the turmoil she had yet to come. But now, instead of looking at him, her face drained of all colour and she was looking past his shoulder.

When he turned, Kyle was standing there.

'Mum's sick?' was all he said.

And in that moment Kyle was stripped of his teenage years, left a vulnerable little boy who had to face far more than losing his home. He could lose his mum.

18

AMELIA

Over the years in her job, Amelia had seen kids she worked with progress from children into teens and adults and she knew it didn't always happen on a reliable timeline. For some, they grew up when they moved through their education; with others, it happened the second they got a job and had to stand on their own two feet. They were all different, and managing the transition was fraught with angst for them and everyone around them.

For Kyle, his movement from a wayward teen to one with maturity and an outlook unlike ever before happened last night, the second he heard his mum was sick. Amelia expected him to flip out, upend the furniture, and wreck the place, or find more alcohol, maybe break into a car and steal it. But he'd done none of those things. Instead, he'd hugged her tight and she'd held on to him, looking at Nathan standing there not knowing what to do.

When Kyle finally let her go he picked up his phone to call his mum, no matter the time difference. And Amelia and Nathan had stood by the Christmas tree, in contemplative silence, until he came back from his bedroom a long while later. That was Kyle's moment. The moment they could all see the irresponsibility ebb away and the hint of the man he would become emerge on the horizon. He'd begun talking about pulling his weight, being there for his mum with her hospital appointments, getting a job. Nathan pitched in and emailed a friend with a cleaning business on the outskirts of London and lined up work for Kyle in less than an hour. And the boy stepped up by accepting it on the spot, no questions asked.

This morning Scarlett and Nathan had turned up at the apartment bright and early, leaving Amelia and Kyle no time to wallow. They'd handed them coffees and ushered them out of the door and into an awaiting cab that took them up to Central Park and the Wollman Rink. Scarlett and Kyle had shown off their superior skills while Nathan did his best to show Amelia he could do this. A welcome zip of excitement zigzagged up her body when his hand reached for hers. It was only for balance, but the feeling she got told her she was right to end things with Paul.

She hadn't mentioned Paul to Nathan, and Nathan hadn't asked. Since last night all the focus had been on Connie and Kyle, and Christmas Eve in New York City. And they'd all been keeping themselves so busy with festive activities that Amelia kept her personal relationship details to herself for now as she reluctantly left them all to it while she did one final stint at the Garland Street winter markets.

'Christmas Eve.' Cleo was waiting at the front of the chalet when she arrived. 'There's nothing like it. Come on, snow, show us what Christmas is all about,' she demanded, looking up at the sky.

'The sky can't hear you, you know,' Amelia giggled.

'You seem happy.'

'I've been ice-skating. It was amazing.'

'With Paul?'

'Not exactly.' This time Amelia did share her personal details and filled Cleo in on everything that had been going on, with Paul, with Connie, with Kyle. And between them they served customers and unloaded the last of the stock onto the display tables.

'It been an eventful holiday for you,' Cleo concluded once she knew everything.

'It definitely has, but I'm still smiling, still having a great time.'

'Are you and Kyle still coming to the Christmas Eve party at the inn?'

'I'm not sure I can face it. Celebrating while Connie is sick doesn't feel right and I doubt Kyle will be interested either.'

'What's Connie up to tonight?'

'She's with her friend Jill. They've planned to watch a movie and Jill is cooking up a surprise dinner. The woman is the best cook in the world, my mouth is watering thinking of the cinnamon buns she made last time I saw her.'

'Sounds fun.' Cleo bent down to pick up the pair of gloves she'd knocked to the floor and repositioned them on the shelf. 'I bet she wouldn't want you and Kyle to mooch around the apartment and miss out on Christmas Eve fun, especially here in New York City. That's why she didn't want to tell him the truth all along isn't it?'

'I suppose you're right.'

'Of course I am.' She shifted her focus to another customer before she came back to Amelia's side and asked, 'Is that Nathan over there, across the street?' She nodded to where a man had his back to them. He was talking to a woman, a redhead who was laughing at whatever it was he had to say. 'It is him, look.' Cleo waved.

But as soon as Amelia realised it really was Nathan, she hoped he didn't hear Cleo and prayed he wouldn't come over either.

'You didn't answer my question by the way.' Cleo followed her back inside the chalet. 'Who did you go ice-skating with?'

'Kyle.'

'*Just* Kyle?'

'Hey there.' It was Nathan's voice behind her. No hiding now. She wasn't sure whether he'd rescued her from Cleo's scrutiny or introduced a whole new slant of jealousy after she'd seen him with a woman. Maybe it was someone asking directions. Perhaps he just explained it in such an amusing way that the other woman was totally captivated.

'Nathan, hey.' She feigned surprise.

'Did you talk to your sister?'

She pulled a face before she remembered she'd told him she was going to call Connie on her way over here to the markets. 'I did. She's doing okay. She's even been talking to Kyle about careers and him joining the fire service.'

'Wow, that's progress.'

'It really is. Anyway, I'd better get back to it.' Customers were milling and Cleo was trying to take payment from one and advise another.

'Will we see you tonight at the Christmas Eve party?'

'Wouldn't miss it for the world.'

'Will Paul be coming along?'

She was about to tell him the truth, keen to gauge his reaction, when the same woman she'd seen him with came up to him and enveloped him in a hug.

'Who's that?' Cleo whispered in her ear as she was popping a sea-blue sweater into a brown paper bag for a customer. 'She's stunning.'

With a shock of red curls, she really was. 'I've no idea. And stop looking at me funny,' she whispered back. The woman was still cuddling up to Nathan.

'You're jealous,' Cleo whispered.

'Am not.'

'Are so,' Cleo giggled.

She opened her mouth to deny it again but Cleo would see

right through her. Whoever the woman was, Nathan looked pretty pleased to see her. He hadn't mentioned anyone this morning at the Wollman Rink, when they'd skated around together, as he'd held on to her, as she found herself wanting more of his company. Then again, she hadn't mentioned Paul either.

Kyle and Scarlett turned up next, cheeks rosy from the cold, smiles on their faces despite everything that had been going on. They were spending all day together. Mitch had understood when Cleo called and explained Kyle might need to stay away from the market today given what was going on in his personal life, and according to Mitch today would be very quiet anyway given most people already had a tree, so he'd manage just fine.

Kyle was rifling through the table at the front. 'I want to take Mum home an extra present.'

Cleo asked her colouring, recommended a few items, and it gave Amelia the chance to talk to Scarlett. 'How is he?'

'Dad?' She seemed hopeful this was about Nathan.

Amelia smiled. 'No, I mean Kyle.'

'Oh, sorry. He's good. He was a bit upset this morning when we left the rink but he keeps saying his mum will beat this.'

'It's a good attitude. And I'm glad he's got you.'

She blushed under the scrutiny of a parent-figure.

'Is your dad's friend coming to the party tonight?' She asked Scarlett the question as she adjusted the scarves on the table closest to her, although they were already neatly arranged and hadn't had a chance to be mussed.

'Friend?'

'The woman with the red hair.'

'Ah,' she smiled, 'You must mean Valerie. I've no idea, why?'

'Just wondering, that's all.' She pounced on a glove that had fallen to the floor to hide her awkwardness at asking such a juvenile question. She couldn't help it though. Was she going to be one of the only people there tonight who didn't have a date?

She waved Kyle and Scarlett off, Scarlett still smiling and watching her, probably likely to report Amelia's interest in her dad back to Nathan himself. Talk about awkward.

'What are you wearing to the party tonight?' Cleo asked.

Thank goodness Cleo hadn't heard her quizzing Scarlett about her dad. Amelia pulled her scarf a little tighter as the wind whipped around the chalet. 'I've got a woollen dress I can wear, which is warm. Although I have brought a party dress with me, and heels, just in case.' She looked up at the skies, felt the icy nip on her face. 'The pavements were really slippery this morning, I'm not sure heels are the best idea.'

'So get a cab from the apartment.'

'I doubt I'll get one, it's Christmas Eve.'

'Order one.'

'I guess I could try.'

'That's the spirit. So come on, tell me about this dress.'

* * *

Amelia had taken Cleo's advice and ordered a cab. And now here she was, sitting in the back seat wearing an ebony, vintage, swing dress that hugged her around the bust and her rib cage, flared flatteringly across her hips. She had on gold rhinestone open-backed strappy heels she'd worn only once and which made her feel confident. She'd been looking forward to tonight's party before, but now, as they made their way slowly through the traffic across town to the Inglenook Inn, she felt a sense of excitement that took her by surprise. Out in New York City, dressed up, going to a party, single and happy.

She wasn't quite so happy when she walked through the door

and Nathan was already there, the same redhead at his side, laughing away.

Nobody had spotted her as she stood conspicuously in the hallway of the brownstone, but the second she stepped out of the shadows minus the coat that Rupert, who was acting as chef plus helper tonight, hung on the hook, all heads turned, including Nathan's.

Cleo was first at her side. 'I'm so glad you came. You look amazing.'

'So do you.' She hugged her friend before plucking a glass of champagne from the tray Darcy whizzed around to her side with, ever the attentive hostess.

'Where's Kyle?' Cleo wondered.

'He's finding his own way here. He and Scarlett are making the most of the rest of the holiday, I think.'

'Don't blame them.'

'They'll be here soon.' Nathan came to join the conversation, his girlfriend over by the Christmas tree chatting with Rupert, who was circulating with a platter of canapés now. 'You look beautiful.'

She gulped. 'Thank you. You don't look too bad yourself.' She tried not to look at the skin on his neck where the top button of his white shirt stayed undone, or glide her eyes down his body taking in this man in the sharp suit, one hand in a pocket, the other holding his bottle of beer as they chatted. And she definitely did her best not to think of the feeling she'd got when he'd grabbed her hand at the ice rink. They'd both been wearing gloves but it made no difference; the spark was still there.

'Where's the boyfriend?'

She was about to tell him when she became aware of Holly snapping away with her camera. 'Sorry,' she grinned from behind the lens, dropping the equipment so they could see her face. 'I like to get natural shots of everyone when they least expect. Doesn't work so well when you see me.' She moved on now they knew she was there.

'Scarlett and I came to an agreement,' Nathan told her, not persisting with his question about her love life. 'I thought you might want to know.'

'Of course. What kind of agreement.'

'I'm going to read up on art courses for her, go and visit some universities together and we'll take it from there. I'm going to remain open to suggestions.' He made the announcement much like a master of ceremonies telling everyone that this was what was happening.

'I'm glad to hear you're looking at it from her point of view too,' she said.

'We're going to work together while she makes some decisions,' he smiled. 'You know, Scarlett and I were worried you and Kyle would hide away after the news about Connie. That's why we showed up so early at your apartment this morning and dragged you ice-skating.'

'It was the right thing to do.' Seeing him this morning had been the best Christmas gift she could hope for and she'd relished every second of their time together. She wondered, had he? 'Connie would've been annoyed if I hadn't come tonight.'

'She's not the only one.' But his comment ended there because Mitch joined them, shook Nathan's hand, kissed Amelia on the cheek before telling her how impressed he'd been with Kyle and his hard work at the markets.

'He's been an asset to my business. Can I hire him next year?' Mitch asked.

'I'll let him know you're interested. But I think he might be embarking on a new career pretty soon. He wants to join the fire brigade,' she announced proudly. And Mitch was all ears, wanting to hear more. He seemed a man who made friends for life, regardless of their age, their background.

Nathan was commandeered by the redhead, who was extolling the virtues of Rupert's latest canapé on offer – golden-crumbed arancini bites.

Myles grabbed Amelia's attention next. 'Thank you for looking after the apartment, saved us having to check on it. I always worry about frozen pipes, water leaks, it's been good having someone around.'

'I can't thank you enough for letting us stay there. Honestly, not being cooped up together somewhere dingy and very expensive was a real help, and we've felt like proper New Yorkers. Are you still planning to sell up?'

'In the New Year. I need to paint it first.'

'When will you ever fit that in with your work schedule?'

Darcy appeared at his side. 'Maybe we should make the announcement now,' she grinned at Myles.

'What are you two hiding?' Cleo, astute as ever, had overheard and wanted to know more.

'I'm curious too.' Holly, Mitch's girlfriend, had her arms resting on her other half's shoulder and leaned in to him.

'Here goes.' Darcy looked nervous, not an emotion Amelia associated with the together, well-groomed hotelier.

Darcy moved to stand beside the desk in the communal lounge, the fire flickering gently in the grate with stockings lined up along the mantel and a garland strung across the top, the tree dominating the window and shining onto the street. And with Myles's mischievous encouragement she kicked off her heels and let him hold her hand to help her climb up onto a chair.

'Last time that happened,' said Dylan, 'it was me climbing onto a chair at the Little Knitting Box to propose to Cleo.'

'They're already married,' said Holly. 'Wonder what's going on.'

Darcy clinked a knife against her champagne glass and almost lost her footing but Myles held her steady.

'That was close,' Darcy laughed. 'Right, now I have everyone's attention, it seems like a very good time to make this announcement. As some of you know, Sofia intended to sell this wonderful inn, and I'm not sure how many of you know that Myles and I have been doing our best this past year to get our finances in order so we might be in a position to buy it.' She quelled any enthusiasm. 'Sofia has since decided she can't bear to part with this place, and I for one am glad, because I think we'll all agree, it's gorgeous.'

'Hear, hear!' someone hollered.

'I was worried someone would buy this place and make so many changes it would lose its character, but that won't happen now.' More cheers, but Darcy hadn't finished. 'I was disappointed that I wouldn't get my hands on it, but financially it was never going to be for us without a lot of stress and sacrifice.' She reached a hand out and Myles took hold of it. 'Myles and I were both in agreement on that. But, we do have another announcement.'

'Out with it,' Holly begged. 'I'm dying to know!'

'Myles and I have bought another inn, one that needs a bit of TLC.' They were both smiling and Darcy held her glass aloft. 'You're looking at the new owners of the Chestnut Lodge, in Inglenook Falls.'

The crowd of people in the communal lounge erupted with whoops of joy and congratulations, there were hugs all round, questions fired their way, and all the magic of another Christmas Eve party at the Inglenook Inn.

Cleo rushed to Darcy's side. 'This is brilliant news. You'll be near me, I can't believe it.'

Holly was next. 'The owners never said a word about you being the buyer.'

Myles brought Amelia up to speed. Holly knew the owners

already and had been staying at the Chestnut Lodge around the time she'd fallen into Mitch's life.

'I wanted to wait until it was all definite before I said anything to anyone,' Darcy confided. 'I wanted all the paperwork out of the way and then I decided tonight would be the perfect time for the announcement. It's a nice way to start Christmas, dreaming of our plans.' She had hold of Myles's hand and pulled him to her side. 'And this one is finally getting out of the rat race. Finances are all lined up, we'll be partners.'

'Are you sure you're ready?' Dylan teased Myles.

'Ask me again in a few months' time.'

'You fully deserve it,' said Cleo. 'I assume this is why Myles has been working such long hours again?' she asked Darcy. 'You had me worried for a while there.'

'I apologise. And hey, we should be fully renovated by spring so spread the word.' Darcy was beaming. The decision was so right for them.

Amelia and Nathan, finding themselves back together again by the Christmas tree, hung back from the crowd. 'There you go, accommodation sorted for you next year,' he said.

'Sounds like it.'

The redhead came over and planted a smacker on Nathan's cheek, staking her claim with the red lipstick mark she left behind. She extended a hand in Amelia's direction. 'I'm Valerie, lovely to meet you.'

'Good to meet you too.'

But before the conversation could go any further, Mitch ushered Amelia and Nathan to one side. 'It's Scarlett and Kyle.'

'What about them?' Amelia had a bad feeling now.

'They're at the markets. I had Kyle double-check I'd locked my chalet, but he just messaged me. There's some kind of trouble down there.'

'What kind of trouble?' Nathan put his beer bottle down. 'Is Scarlett okay?'

'I don't know, but you'd better go, both of you. And quick.'

Neither Amelia nor Nathan needed any persuasion. Amelia grabbed her coat, Darcy found a pair of trainers and gave them to her to replace the heels, and she kept up with Nathan as they hurtled towards the Garland Street winter markets, which resembled a ghost town now that they were closed and people had moved to where the festivities still continued.

'Where are they?' Her breath came out cold, the icy wind lifted her dress and she pushed it down again as they walked on.

'I've no idea, there doesn't seem to be anyone around.' Mitch had sounded so dramatic back at the inn, but Garland Street was quieter than she'd ever seen it.

They kept on going, moonlight guiding them on the way past all the other chalets, now closed up for Christmas. On all the nights they could get into trouble, did it really have to be Christmas Eve? And when everything had been going so well too.

They reached the chalet but there was still no sign of them and already the snow had started to fall. It would be magical if Amelia wasn't worrying herself sick right now. 'Where the hell are they?' She looked around them. Nathan was hovering by the door to the chalet, which no longer had trees surrounding it although the scent of pine still drifted in the air along with feathery flakes that landed on her coat and the bare parts of her legs.

Kyle stepped out from the shadows and made them both jump. 'Kyle, what's going on?' she demanded. He didn't look as though he was hurt or bleeding, and Scarlett was next to come out from hiding.

'Scarlett?' Nathan directed his questions to his daughter.

'Go inside,' she told Nathan and Amelia.

'What have you done?' Nathan asked but Scarlett merely rolled her eyes and repeated her request.

'What's going on?' Amelia asked as they went inside the chalet. 'What's all this?'

Both of them took in the fairy lights strung all around the interior, the table with the bottle of champagne in the bucket, two glasses, the double beanbag she'd seen back at the apartment in Kyle's bedroom now here with a baby-soft chocolate blanket draped over it.

'You both need to talk,' Scarlett clarified as Kyle turned off the fan heater that had toasted up the interior good and proper.

And with that they shut the doors and all Nathan and Amelia could hear was them both giggling outside.

'It's a conspiracy,' said Nathan, the hint of a grin appearing.

'I think you're right. Apparently we need to talk,' she said, repeating what Scarlett had said.

'Are they trying to set us up?' Nathan took in the romantic atmosphere the teenagers had managed to create. 'Maybe Paul would appreciate it more, although from what you've said, posh hotels are more his thing.'

'Paul's gone. I haven't seen him since the night at his hotel when I told him it was over.'

'Right.'

Was that all he had to say? 'Just so we're clear, nothing happened between us at the apartment the night you showed up. And this time, I was the one who ended it, told him to go.'

'You did?'

'Turns out six months and a few thousand miles was what it took for me to realise we were all wrong together.' Awkward, she reached out and toyed with the stem of one of the champagne glasses. 'We should go. Valerie will wonder where you are.' She became aware of him stepping closer.

'She's probably too busy with Harper to notice.'

'Harper, one of the guests?' She remembered being introduced to a bubbly woman with a sharp pixie cut at the inn shortly after Darcy's announcement.

'I work with Valerie in England, we're good friends, nothing more.'

She left the glass alone. 'What, so you and she aren't...'

He'd come so close she had to look up to see his face. 'Harper is Valerie's girlfriend. Valerie is gay.' She felt his soft breath against her skin. 'She and I spend a lot of time talking about our kids, the trials of being a parent in the teenage years. Scarlet adores Valerie, I think she wanted us to get together until she realised that Valerie was already spoken for. And Valerie let me in on a secret tonight.'

'What kind of secret?'

'Scarlett and Kyle had both picked up on something between you and I, and being meddlesome teens thought they'd do something about it.'

She hesitated, caught out in the moment. 'So this was all planned?'

He shrugged, amused, eyes glittering with mischief. 'Scarlett asked Valerie to flirt outrageously with me at the markets and again tonight. She asked Valerie to gauge your reaction, text her whether she thought you were interested in me.'

'And then they put all this into action. With Mitch's help too.'

'It seems that way, doesn't it?' He laughed and shook his head. 'I was wondering what was going on. Valerie kept touching me, kissed me on the cheek enough times and left her lipstick there.'

'I noticed.'

'I would've asked her what she was playing at but we were accosted to come here.' His hands reached up to either side of her face as he moved his closer. 'Do you think we should be furious with Kyle, Scarlett, and Valerie for conspiring to do this?'

'That depends.'

'On what?'

'On whether we both feel the same way.'

'And what way is that?'

'You're not making this easy.'

'Where's the fun in that?'

But now it wasn't time for talking. He bent his head closer to her, moving slowly, making the moment go on forever, until his lips finally met hers. And it was everything she'd hoped it would be. Tender, oozing with passion, and like it was meant to be.

'You need to promise me something, Amelia,' he said when they came up for air. 'Promise me you'll stop putting everyone else before yourself.'

'I can't.'

'How did I know you were going to say that?' Laughing, his lips hovered dangerously close to hers again.

'Promise me you'll be my date to Cleo's wedding next year. Come as my plus one. There's nothing worse than turning up at those sorts of events on your own.'

'It's a deal. But you need to do something for me, he grinned. 'Lose those trainers the second we get back to the inn. You look like you've got clown feet. How did you ever run in a pair so big?'

'Kyle needed me, I knew I had to be there, I just ran.'

His eyes never leaving hers, he told her, 'You're amazing, you know that? Promise me you'll never change.'

She smiled, looking up into dark eyes, a hint of stubble on his jaw, as the moonlight managed to sneak in between the tiny crack of the doors to the wooden chalet at the winter markets. 'Kiss me again, for longer, it's already getting cold in here again.'

And when he kissed her this time she melted into him, the dizzying feeling of falling in love in Manhattan. Their own holiday romance, their own happy ever after.

EPILOGUE

On Christmas Eve, Nathan and Amelia had eventually gone back to the Inglenook Inn, where the champagne was flowing and the party was still in full swing. They danced together and kissed when they thought nobody was looking, at least until Kyle did his impression of Nathan and dragged them apart. Thankfully Nathan saw the funny side.

The snow that started on Christmas Eve had carried on until every inch of pavement and street was covered, making for a magical Christmas Day dinner at the Inglenook Inn. And now, on Boxing Day, here they all were in Inglenook Falls to take a look at the Chestnut Lodge. Darcy and Myles led the way from the station towards their new guesthouse, Holly and Mitch had been waiting at the top of the track that led down to the Christmas tree farm and Cleo and Dylan had just arrived to meet their friends.

'Inglenook Falls is kind of special,' said Amelia as she stood next to Cleo. 'It's got the small-town charm I never knew existed any more.'

'It really has.'

'Would you think about getting married here?'

Cleo began to smile. 'I've already put in a request to book a venue.'

'That's amazing, where?'

Cleo tapped the side of her nose. 'Not telling, at least not yet, not until it's one hundred per cent confirmed.'

'Spoilsport.'

Holly agreed. 'I'm desperate to know too, but I've already been hounding her and she won't give in.'

With the snow giving Inglenook Falls that magical feel, they gathered in the small parking lot out front. Despite its proximity to Main Street, close to a little library and an Italian restaurant, the guesthouse was well hidden and would make a wonderful escape.

Nathan kissed Amelia before joining the other men to talk building plans as they walked to the side of the lodge, inspecting it from all angles as though they were structural experts.

'Are you going to keep everything mostly the same?' Cleo wondered. 'The porch is delightful, really wonderful in the summer months.'

'It is,' Holly agreed. 'I've sat up there drinking homemade lemonade with the previous owners. You can see enough of Main Street to feel part of it all, but it's still so quiet and a great place to relax. Not that you two know how to do that,' she added, looking at Darcy now.

Darcy smiled. 'I'm hoping that even though we're as busy as ever, it'll be busy together rather than running our lives on separate tracks. Does that make sense?'

Cleo put an arm around her friend. 'Perfect sense, and I'm so happy for you both.'

'What about the name?' Amelia asked. 'The Chestnut Lodge is quaint, I like it.'

'Actually, we have a new idea for the name,' Darcy admitted.

'Tell us!' Cleo did a shuffle on the spot to keep warm and

rubbed her hands together as the snow began to fall again, dusting the porch rail in front of them and the roof of the soft-grey, colonial home with its matching grey sign depicting its name hanging from a white post on chunky silver chains that groaned in the breeze.

'What do you think to… the Inglenook Lodge?'

'Love it,' said Holly.

'Perfect, given it's in Inglenook Falls,' Cleo agreed.

'From the Inglenook Inn to the Inglenook Lodge,' Amelia smiled. 'You'll make it wonderful, I'm sure.'

'I have so many ideas,' Darcy beamed. 'I can't wait to get going.'

'I'm desperate to see it,' Cleo urged.

'Then shall we go inside?' Darcy had the keys in her hand and anyone could see she was aching to step within the walls of her new home and business.

'Lead the way,' Holly encouraged, following after her along with Cleo and Mitch, who'd reappeared to join them and was already recommending having a wood store built at the end of the porch.

Amelia was about to step up to the entrance to see how beautiful this place was inside when Nathan wrapped his arms around her from behind and nuzzled her neck. 'Not so fast.'

She turned, nestling into his chest. 'You finished talking structure with the men?'

'I've left Myles and Dylan talking websites.' He pulled her onto the porch as the snow began to fall more heavily.

'I wonder how Kyle and Scarlett are doing.'

'Making plans when I left.'

'Plans for what?'

'To see each other in a few weeks' time.'

'And you're okay with that?'

'She's growing up. I have to let her.'

'You're a good man.'

'I know,' he grinned. He'd managed to find a way beneath her scarf and the kisses he'd planted on her neck were making her wish they were somewhere a little more private. He'd done the same in the chalet on Christmas Eve, he knew her weak spot, and they'd barely left one another's side since.

He was still kissing her neck, making his way slowly towards her mouth, when Cleo opened up the sash window and called out, 'Get a room!'

Laughing, Amelia told her, 'We will... Darcy...' she called in through the open window, 'book us in for next Christmas would you?'

'Done!' she called back from inside the Inglenook Lodge.

'It's a date,' said Nathan, and this time, ignoring any comments from anyone else, he pulled her in for a kiss that warmed her all the way through.

ACKNOWLEDGMENTS

Firstly, thank you to everyone who has picked up this book and read the story. I've loved writing the *New York Ever After* series and adding book five to the collection allowed me to introduce new characters as well as meet up with a few favourites in a setting that I adore. I hope you enjoyed it too!

Thank you so much to Katharine Walkden for her brilliant editing skills at the beginning and to the fabulous team at Boldwood Books for continuing the process on to ensure this story is well and truly polished before it reaches my readers. Again, thank you to the Boldwood team for another stunning book cover.

Thank you to The Write Romantics, a group of ten writers who support each other in what could be a very lonely job. I'd also like to thank the online community of other writers, friends, and readers, as well as the book blogging community who are so generous with their time. All of you make such a difference to authors.

And last but certainly in no means least, thank you to my husband and children who are with me every step of the way when I'm writing my books. I couldn't do this job I love without their ongoing support and encouragement.

Helen x

MORE FROM HELEN ROLFE

We hope you enjoyed reading *Christmas Promises at the Garland Street Markets*. If you did, please leave a review.

If you'd like to gift a copy, this book is also available as an ebook, digital audio download and audiobook CD.

Sign up to Helen Rolfe's mailing list for news, competitions and updates on future books.

https://bit.ly/HelenRolfeNews

You can now order the next book in the New York Ever After series, *Moonlight and Mistletoe at the Christmas Wedding.*

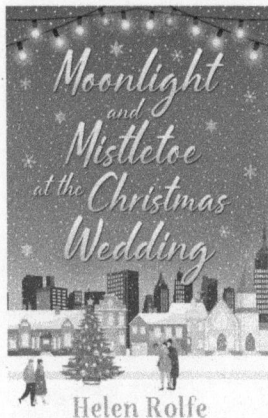

ABOUT THE AUTHOR

Helen Rolfe is the author of many bestselling contemporary women's fiction titles, set in different locations from the Cotswolds to New York. Most recently published by Orion, she is bringing sixteen titles to Boldwood - a mixture of new series and well- established backlist. She lives in Hertfordshire with her husband and children.

Follow Helen on social media:

twitter.com/hjrolfe

facebook.com/helenjrolfewriter

instagram.com/helen_j_rolfe

Boldwood

Boldwood Books is an award-winning fiction publishing company seeking out the best stories from around the world.

Find out more at www.boldwoodbooks.com

Join our reader community for brilliant books, competitions and offers!

Follow us

@BoldwoodBooks

@BookandTonic

Sign up to our weekly deals newsletter

Milton Keynes UK
Ingram Content Group UK Ltd.
UKHW041321171124
2901UKWH00049B/518

9 781804 156476